JFA Presents: Yemoja's Tears
An Anthology of Water, Bodies and Bodies of Water

Volume 36/ Number 1
Whole Number 122

I0666032

JFA

JFA Presents: Yemoja's Tears
An Anthology of Water, Bodies and Bodies of Water

Volume 36/ Number 1
Whole Number 122

FAVIAN PRESS

[Table of Contents]

THE CREATIVE AND SCHOLARLY CONTRIBUTIONS in this anthology immerse the reader in water awareness. Authors have contributed their thoughts and dreams about water: its availability and scarcity, its precariousness and its resilience, its generous ability to heal and its fragile inability to wash away inhumanity or greed. Immersion in this anthology inspires each of us to see ourselves, both individually in our aloneness and collectively as a water activist community, as the solutions we can be to solve the multiplicity of problems stemming from clean water scarcity, worldwide.

From the time that Joshua Keghnen Ichor and Oghenechovwe Donald Ekpeki approached the Editors-in-Chief of the *Journal of the Fantastic in the Arts* with a proposal for an anthology project to raise awareness and funds for water safety engineering throughout vulnerable communities in Nigeria and the African Continent, months were spent exploring potential charitable hosts for this innovative enterprise. But, as short stories, memoirs, essays, and poetry were donated to this anthology project, and while the fame of and interest in the GeoTek Monitor is widespread and growing, our fundraising goals were generally considered too small-scale for the hosting we pursued. We took the time to get expert and legal advice on how best to direct funds raised to provide communities with water while maintaining transparency. That did take more time than we initially expected, but we felt it was important not to risk legal missteps or misperceptions in the handling of charitable funds, if they could be foreseen and avoided.

While the *Journal of the Fantastic in the Arts* is sponsoring this collection's publication, *Yemoja's Tears* is not subject to the standard reprint obligations of the *Journal*. All donated writings will be made available in perpetuity in *Yemoja's Tears* in print, electronic, and audio format, as they become available. Rights to the contents donated to the anthology revert to their author six months after publication in *Yemoja's Tears*. Sales of the anthology will continue to fund researched charitable clean water projects as long as the anthology is available through the publisher.

Thank you to all these talented writers for your contributions to *Yemoja's Tears*, and thank you to those who purchase it for spreading hope and, with it, the opportunity to heal and thrive, with clean water.

--Novella Brooks de Vita, Acquisitions Editor-in-Chief, *Journal of the Fantastic in the Arts*

When Novella asked me if I would consider taking part in this project, I never could have dreamed what I was signing on for. Some of my fondest memories of the summer of 2024 involve sitting in my mother's backyard with my laptop, sometimes so riveted by what I was reading that I forgot to edit, and had to go back and start over.

This anthology includes, among other things, informative factual pieces, breathtaking snapshots of other worlds, breathtaking snapshots of *this* world, keen analysis, stirring poetry, gritty space opera, haunting mystery, chilling futures, histories both idyllic and enraging, and incisive political commentary. It is, by turns, hopeful, fearful, elegiac, otherworldly, quite rightly furious, moving, and galvanizing.

It has been a magnificent honour to be part of the process of getting *Yemoja's Tears* ready for publication, and I hope you enjoy it as much as I have. Authors—thank you for writing. Readers—thank you for reading!

--Cat Ashton, Production Editor-in-Chief, *Journal of the Fantastic in the Arts*

Introduction

[Introduction: A Water Scarcity Awareness and Alleviation Anthology]
[Alexis Brooks de Vita]

JOSHUA KEGHNEN ICHOR is a young Nigerian scientist, engineer and inventor with degrees in Hydrogeology and Environmental Science. With a background in the study of earth sciences and a strong concern for sustainable water management and environmental conservation, Ichor has invented the GeoTek Monitor, an innovation that promises to revolutionize clean water access throughout the African continent. The GeoTek Monitor provides data on water availability, quality, and usage in real time, helping communities and organizations to make informed and accurately calculated decisions about water management in the face of challenges to health and water sustainability.

Ichor's advocacy for environmental stewardship has led to his collaboration with international research institutions and agencies concerned with water and climate resilience. His work has been awarded the Young Climate Prize, Swarovski Creative Prize, and the USADF Digital Innovation Award. Ichor is a visiting Fellow at CERN and the United States University of Africa, Nairobi, and a 776 Fellow sponsored by Alexis Ohanian through the 776 Climate Fund. Together with multi-awarded author, editor, and publisher Oghenechovwe Donald Ekpeki, these two young changemakers came up with the concept of *Yemoja's Tears*, an anthology to both raise water scarcity awareness and to give in exchange for contributions to aid communities throughout Nigeria, the African continent, and other water-endangered areas of the world. We have researched charitable organizations that have a proven history of providing clean water to the world's most vulnerable global communities in crisis, and have decided to begin by donating initial funds to these three: WaterAid, Water for People, and Baitulmaal, Inc.

Yemoja's Tears: An Anthology of Water, Bodies and Bodies of Water was conceived and adopted as the first JFA Presents title by the Editors-in-Chief of the *Journal of the Fantastic in the Arts*. During the two years since its inception, invited authors from several continents have contributed their original water-centric works of poetry, memoirs, short stories, and essays that together immerse the reader in awareness of the threat to clean water access that is an increasingly severe danger, globally.

This anthology is rich with thought-provoking material, most of it having been years in the conceptualizing and finding of the right home. Just as Jenekacy's front cover acrylic painting of Yemoja undersea, titled *Ji*, offers a vision of Afrofuturistic apotheosis, reflected by the corresponding gritty hard work in the montage of Isaac Nesla's photos of Ichor calling for revolution while GeoTek digs for clean water south of the Sahel, so this entire anthology is a collection of aspirations, ideals, and questions reflecting light above their subsurface realities, dreads, and warnings.

Oghenechovwe Donald Ekpeki's "Source" opens the anthology with hope amid images of desert and ocean, followed by the relentless interplay of shattering rock and surging sea in Mame Bougouma Diene's "Doomed to the Storm," wherein a crying child reminds me of a prayer that opens with "humanity is bowed down with trouble, sorrow and grief, no one escapes; the world is wet with tears," melding fabled past and legendary future in a drought-devastated world where one small being's cannibalistic thirst for tears brings about a deluge. Alex Jennings's "Stone Bridge and Laughter" brings longing through water-carried memories of mother to the point of pathos, heightened by Candice Thornton's "GodIsLove: Signified Sankofarrations, Personified Deities, and Mythatypical Patterns in *The Joys of Motherhood* and *Freshwater*," analyzing the anguish of loss of the mother in the waterborne birthing of self. This equation of water with lifegiving erupts through layers of mud, myth, generation, and regeneration exquisitely simplified in Joyce Chng's "Emerging." Annette Meserve's "A Pocketful of Precious" walks with a sun-scoured wanderer carrying a handful of beautiful dreams before Eileen Gunn asks the reader "Whose Water Is It, Anyway?" in flashbacks and conversations about water access, water sharing, and the combined impositions and responsibilities of the concept of rights to lifesaving water.

Solomon Uhiara demonstrates in "Bayelsa, Water for All" that water can in fact be made universally available in communities supported by their governments to achieve water equality; but this hope is challenged in F. Brett Cox's reflective "Miriam After the Flood," wherein a recently stable community is forced to dig itself out of the debris and detritus that remain when there are no bulwarks against the results of drastic climate change. Global regulation is needed, argues Wuraola Kayode's "The Revenge of Yemoja," a police procedural detecting the supernatural consequences of climate abuse, a problem simultaneously explored half a world away in Gillian Polack's "Water Guzzlers and Time Wasters."

"Quizani and the Eagle," presented in both the original Spanish by Mexican poet laureate Alfonso Arteaga Rodríguez and the translation by his son, Alfonso Arteaga Martínez, follows a boy on a vision quest with the eagle who is teaching him how to mature and thrive in his threatened world, just as the heroine of James Morrow's "The Ship of Sisyphus" plummets through layers of hierarchical privilege that the right to water consumption implies. A. E. Fonsworth's "Ocean Scourge" likewise plunges through Earth-covering water that has been forced for far too long to absorb, cleanse and recycle the consequences of acquisitive inhumanity while Uchechukwu Nwaka's "Inmates of Ikenga Point" sweeps readers into a breathless attempt to escape death in an abandoned prison in outer space. Will water follow the trail of humanity's failures to nurture greed's outcasts, its conquered, and its reviled survivors? Mingle Moore, Jr.'s sobering "Fanon and Soyinka on Traditional African Ecoharmony, Colonial Greed, and the Mystic Functionality of Water" reminds the reader that the earthly counter-balancing of fire with water has always been inevitable.

Virgília Ferrão's "The Turning Part" questions reality and the effects of time on memory, progress, and ultimate loss, queries that Regina M. Hansen's "Laundry" probes at a poignantly personal level. Albert Uriah Turner, Jr.'s "le mot, la mort" examines at the intersections of academia and art the traces a poet leaves to his readers, while MultiMind's "Stalwart" smiles upon a clever inventor who challenges her society's local politics in the face of water shortage. Water erodes the edges of memory reshaping itself in James H. Ford, Jr.'s memoir, "Finding Water to Fish with Friends and Family: *Daybreak*." Mary A. Turzillo's "Water Is Life, Water Is Death, There Is No Truth or Joy Without Water" riptides into the presence of the Queen of the Sea, decrying water abuses, pollutions, privations, and inexcusable scarcities.

Desireé Y. Amboree's "Love, Temptation and the Downfall of a Water Rig in Kai Ashante Wilson's 'The Devil in America'" comes ashore in the aftermath of the war that ended U.S. chattel enslavement, where a little girl battles to protect her loved ones from supernatural malice. What may be the most dystopic of this anthology's works, Ceschino's "The Weird Sisters of Onapatu

Bog," wades into a cave's eerily lit, devouring maw, where doomed heroes are forced to ponder, if water ruination and systemic pollution have not been reversed, what adaptations has Nature made?

Can the Earth, the oceans, and their denizens be healed? Have those who still have agency and opportunity sufficiently learned the lessons of ruination and embraced the sacrifices necessary for the Earth's salvation? Culminating with Lakunle Whesu's "Water for Tears" as a counterpoint to Diene's crying child, and Vuyokazi Ngemntu's "A Dry Death" mirroring Ekpeki's "Source," these are the questions and challenges that all the contributions to this anthology cumulatively ask and strive to help the global community of climate change survivors contemplate.

◆

End

Source

[Source]
[Oghenechovwe Donald Ekpeki]

BUOYED ON by the waters of my soul
How can I feel so strong?
When I am so weak?
Could it be my weakness
lends me strength,
And the desert
Is the source of the sea

Storm in my mind
Hurricane thoughts
Pleasant thoughts swept away
Sanity floats.
Sadness and loneliness
Shattered wreckage
and floating debris fill my world

I grasp the slender branch of knowledge
The far-reaching rope of inspiration
Wound around my neck
Inspiration birthed by asphyxiation
Supped on ambrosia and sipped from the fountain
I discern all
I drown in the waters of my soul

The grand puzzle of life connects
I gather broken pieces
flotsam and jetsam from murky waters
Recreate my mind from swirling chaos
Rebuild the damned, doomed
dam flooding broken streets and cluttered canals
And I must sink

Woes of life in my ardour
Let them loose, waters of the river Lethe
Storms brew
Clouds clash
Rains reign
Floods flash
And the ground is an ocean of loss

Tidal pain
sweep me away
Pebbles of water
pelt me
My heart smashed
against cliffs
My absorbent soul must take it all

Until storms are exhausted
And I find the calm blue
the underdark
the center
eye of the spent storm
I am buoyed on
In settled waters of my soul

I feel strong
when weak
Weakness
lends me strength
For the desert
Is the source
of the sea

♦

End

Doomed to the Storm

[Doomed to the Storm]
[Mame Bougouma Diene]

I. The Son

BEFORE THERE WAS A SEA, people drank their own tears.

Before there was a sea, there was a child, a selfish child, a thirsty child who drank everyone's tears.

But the selfish boy hankered yet, and drank his own tears while the others thirsted.

So they placed him at the bottom of a deep valley, and left. And he cried, and he cried. He cried and drank, and cried so much that he couldn't drink it all.

He cried until his toes were wet.

He cried until his knees were wet.

He cried up to his chest, he cried up to his throat, and still he sat, waiting for his people to return.

His tears reached over his head, and yet he cried, and his tears filled the valley, and then the world.

And his people thirsted no more.

◆

The tip of a cruise ship sank soundlessly into the eternal darkness, plunging down a deep crevasse to places no human eyes had seen.

Peculiar creatures reflected in its windows, basking in their own phosphorescence, slimy things, clawed and crawly things, who knew no love, no anger, and no hatred, whose malevolence was only survival and something millennial, something else.

The pressure of hundreds of gravities bore down on the metal hull, its glass windows vibrating and popping, sending small shards of colored glass into the depths, collected at random by cave-dwelling octopuses who had never read about interior design, but knew about beauty.

Human remains floated out through the gaps, up the chimneys, and through holes in the hull, in a slow-moving ballet of decapitated mermaids, guiding the vessel into the abyss to the echo of whale song.

The tip of the ship slammed into the bedrock and sand of the bottom. The shockwave would have levelled a city on the surface, but on the bottom, there was sand, a mountain's worth of sand and rock, spreading through the water, obliterating the curious things who wandered too close, removing a million years of instinct, of the fragile, delicate dance of unwritten, unspoken, blind and mute history of the seas. A piano shot out through one of the windows, carried over the underwater maelstrom for miles, and landed before a little boy, a skinny, fragile boy rolled up on a rock, weeping in his sleep in the loneliness of the depths.

◆

His will was strong, but he had been alone for so long.

Behind his trembling eyelids, the nightmare repeated itself again, a chaconne variation on the theme of death.

He had never wanted death. He had only wanted to drink. To drink and be happy. He did not want these dreams. He wanted his people.

He cried himself to sleep when the loneliness was too crushing, and slept to visions he could not understand. Amaranthine expanses of tears under the stars. Smoking, screaming metal giants riding the wavy waters under a full, but smaller moon than he remembered, and glowing towers by the shores, full of the life and love he longed for. Then the wind would rise, waves would grow, the metal giants would tip over and sink, water would wash away shores, and waves as big as the mountains of his arid youth would slam into the towers, taking out the lights, taking out the lives, taking out the love.

Was it the world that he had known, or was it a world he dreamt into existence and destroyed with every sleeping cycle? Was it the world he had created?

But he was no God, he was merely a child. A very, very old child.

◆

He opened his eyes to a large marble box in a circle of bones, half-buried in the sand before his rock.

The marble box's lid lay flipped over; looking like an open mouth of black and white teeth, the meddling of ebony and ivory reminded him of the patterns of the Orca. He remembered the Orca from when they were still small, ambitious creatures, hunting in packs of hundreds, losing most of their members in their coordinated assaults, occasionally migrating his way bearing trophies, giant carcasses they had ripped to shreds and cleaned to the bone.

He would bang the bones together, creating infinite ripples in his silent world, commemorating their dead for them.

Then the tiny Orca had gone, until later, much, much later they had returned, in smaller numbers but as immense beasts, and he had ridden them, had seen them battle sharks, take down whales ten times their size.

But this wasn't an Orca, or anything he had seen before.

This was...

18

He landed a finger on one of the keys, and the ground trembled violently. He pulled back with a gasp.

He had felt something, a brontide vibration of deep bass, not quite a sound, and not a note, but something that shot up his arm and calmed his heart.

It connected him to the world of his dreams, but it was flawed, it was broken somehow.

♦

It snowed over the cherry blossoms.

Tiny flakes neared the ground, landing on buildings, passing by the dimly lit windows of children's bedrooms, while they peeked behind their curtains at the first winter snow. In the next room, their mother cleaned out the sink, or their parents argued, pulling down the blinds against the wind and their neighbors.

The foremost flake drifted down the night streets, narrowly dodging passersby, floating along the bullet train, and pushed down by a sudden gust of wind towards Hachiko Square, crosswalks covered in shoppers, screens of commercials and music videos drowning out the light of the Christmas tree.

It touched the ground and melted.

A small fissure spread along the concrete between the crosswalks, the ground rumbled, there was a pause, something cracked, and people screamed.

♦

"An 8.6 magnitude earthquake has just struck the Kanto region. Casualties in Tokyo are estimated at seven hundred thousand and rising. Rescue missions are currently underway.

"Coastal and surrounding areas are on high alert for aftershocks. The army is underway to implement evacuation

19

procedures. You will hear a banging on your door; do not panic, and do not attempt to leave on your own.

"Emergency units will be open all night for all residents. Please use them for emergencies only; many of our neighbors may be in more need of them than ourselves.

"Our thoughts are with the deceased, and our prayers with the survivors."

◆

He drummed the keys in a mute frenzy, but for all he tried, he could not remember music.

His people had not known it; each tear was a song, but only the dying sang, their parched throats releasing their soul in a dissonant, and melodically discordant, moment.

Then they were gone.

Around him everything trembled, the keys, his fingers, his heart, his world.

And still the vibration eluded him.

But he had all the time in the world to get it right.

Worlds of time.

◆

Small bubbles floated to the surface, and the tiniest of waves grew.

The Batroun beach was crowded for a Ramadan Sunday, but this was Lebanon, not Saudi Arabia, and the jet skiers found yet another way to impress the crowd resting and drinking on the stone shores.

One of the jet skiers leaped into the air, performing a somersault, and landed harder on the surface, finding the wave closer than he had expected, but from the beach, no one could

20

tell. Everybody clapped, except a small Syrian refugee, a pack of Chiclets in one hand, pulling uselessly on someone's arm with another, looking firmly at the sea, or rather at the creeping wave, and saying: Schouf.

No one listens to a grubby refugee among millions, and they cheered the jet skiers on.

He pointed to the waters and tugged harder. "Schouf..."

A jet skier hit the wave and never rose again, and then another, and then another.

The little boy dropped his chewing gum, let go of the arm and tried to run up the steps away from the beach, the wave growing into a wall behind him.

The wave took out the skiers, it took out the swimmers, the onlookers, the bar and the fleeing boy, smashing them all against the cliff.

♦

The lights went out on Piccadilly Circus.

She dragged her son away as well she could against the tremors. He could not haul his own weight, but she could get him out of the streets, and to an open square, surely she could.

A glimmer of moonlight broke through the taller buildings, and she smiled, but then plaster started flaking, objects smashed into cars, and she looked up to a three-story slab from a concrete tower bearing down on her and her son, and the lights went out.

♦

The most successful raid in his young life.

He had killed four Dinka of his own, stolen two cows and brought back three of their women. Somewhere north they were fighting over what to call this country. It mattered not to him. He was of the Nuer people, and that was all that would ever matter.

He should have earned something from his ancestors for his deed; then why had the ground shaken on his way back? Why was there a crack spreading through his village? Where were his cattle? Where were his parents? Where were his relatives?

The Dinka must have cursed him, he thought, so he slit their women's throats, drank the blood from their cows, and slept.

He was still alone when he woke up, surrounded by the corpses of his success, and still alone.

And the ground shook some more.

◆

It took off before the first boulders loosened from the mountain.

The snowy peaks disappeared as it rose, circling higher up until the boulders looked like pebbles to it and it settled its ten-foot wingspan in a glide, floating gently on the gales.

Beneath it, the boulder-sized pebbles crashed down on the small mountain resort it had breezed through at night, hunting rodents and rabbit while the bipeds slept, exhausted from days of sliding down the slopes. The rocks rolled over wooden houses, the humble material saying nothing of the wealth and luxury they held inside, but giving way all the same.

It couldn't hear their screams; the rumble was too loud, there were too many boulders, but how couldn't they have sensed the shift in the elements, the subtle signs that the world was about to cave in?

It saw others of its kind floating lazily in the distance, their calm drifting hiding their panic. They flew high again, and they would never be hunted again, not now that the bipeds everywhere faced their doom, but in the shattered grounds

22

beneath, in the oozing cracks of magma, where would they land? Where would they nest?

♦

And higher yet, above the layers of clouds, above the ring of self-involved technology orbiting the small world, no one could witness the planet shaking slightly in its rotations.

The eastern hemisphere shifted into darkness as the terminator made its way west. The giant land masses defining the globe trembling visibly even in the hundred-thousand kilometer distance, shedding bits of stone the size of countries like tears, gradually breaking apart, and taking on new shapes under a growing grey cloud, that little by little made the day side look like night.

No one was there to witness the eastern hemisphere reemerging into day only a few hours later, and no one could have. There was no more day, no more night, only a planet shrouded in the fog of its own collapse.

♦

And under the waters, at the bottom of the deepest pit, where fault lines met and things changed, a young boy hammered away on his piano.

All around him, the ground shook, the deep-sea walls he had grown to know as home fell apart and dissolved; mammoth sized stones drifted over and around him continuously, threatening him until they fell to his passion.

He played for as long as he had been sitting and crying, then played as long as he had sat there and waited, and played for longer than he had been at the bottom, and longer yet, oblivious to the calamity, uncaring of the changes, if only he could get the vibration right.

The Orca had bid their last farewell. He couldn't tell how long ago, but they would return, they had before...

He played until the world shifted, changed, and changed again.

He played until the rumble subsided, until the boulders stopped raining through the oceans and landed at his feet. He played until he saw something break through the murky waters, something new, not quite an Orca, not quite the Orca of old, an even smaller creature, glowing purple and green, soon joined by tens of others, hundreds of others, tens of thousands of others, circling him in a halo of new life.

His mind reached to them. No, not quite the Orca, not as intense, but creatures with a potential, with a vision.

He let himself sit on his rock, the tiredness of eons on his skinny shoulders, his arms and fingers strained and tense with the effort of playing, prey to an unfamiliar feeling: his eyes were dry, his heart was calm, and for the first time in all the lives of all the worlds, he did not weep.

So he slept.

♦

Beneath his eyelids flashed visions of a world he had never seen.

He saw the tiny fish grow bigger and stronger, he saw tiny bacteria multiply and evolve, he saw a clawed hand landing on a beach, and then another, helping pull a flabby but determined creature into its first taste of an atmosphere, and slept deeper and longer yet.

Things grew and changed. He saw a desert bloom until it was drowned, only to be a desert again. He saw mountains rise and fall, and yet he slept deeper, until he sensed a presence.

And there he saw something that scared him; a species of remarkable wit, of unimaginable hatred.

Huge and segmented, blue-green bodies with dozens of legs, antennas, large mandibles, and huge brains flowing from their heads, and down their backs in a carapace of neurons and nerves.

A hive mind sitting in a primordial valley, waiting for their queen to urge them on into the world, away from the underground tunnels where they had dwelled for a million years.

He felt fear, fear that almost woke him up, almost sent him back to his toy, to unleash creation yet again, but then, he saw something else, something warm.

On a distant continent, he saw them. Tall, strong, covered in blue brown fur, with sharp teeth, clawed hands, powerful forearms, and familiar faces.

He saw them leap from the ground to the trees. He saw them gather. Saw them build fires they didn't need just for the sake of companionship.

He saw them hunt. He saw them trade. He saw them fight, yet come together for safety. He saw them build and saw them laugh. He saw them war and saw them love.

One day they would meet the other creatures, and they would clash. There was only room for one. There would be a great war, the first war, perhaps the only war, but there was still time, and space between them. There was room to grow.

Those were not *his* people. His people would never return, he knew that now, but they were *a* people, a people he could guide now that he knew peace, a people he could love from his rock at the bottom of the sea, where he would play for them.

He would watch them multiply, he would egg them on, he would watch them fight and watch them die, and watch them win.

They weren't his people, but they were a people.

♦

Before there was a sea, people drank their own tears.

Before there was a sea, there was a selfish child who starved his people for their tears.

But the child grew, the child found love in loneliness, he knew pain and sacrifice.

After there was a sea, there was a child, a child whose heart consumed everything until it all began again.

At the bottom of the sea there is a child, a child whose tears are the storm, whose pain is the earthquake.

But that child cries no more; that child suffers no longer.

II. The Father

Before there was a sea, people drank their own tears...

◆

Looking over the canyon that faded with the world's curve, Ra'Ymen dreamed that it was filled with tears of joy at the birth of his newborn, his son. He had to be a he. Ka'Ila wanted him to be a she, of course she would, but Ra'Ymen felt it in his bones.

The canyon would fill to the brim, every canyon in the world, from its deep valleys thousands of meters below, dripping off dusty orange crests, and pouring tears falling in cascades from the highest summits of the land, and spinning dangerously around stone spires. There would be streams, he could see it where the dust raced across the arid lands, there would be tears flowing over hills, and down into bottomless holes where they would get lost streaming underground and bursting out on the other side of the world, and things would grow, everywhere.

They would cry tears of joy and they would never be thirsty again.

They still had a ways to go, down the cliff and across the stepping-stone plateau to the cave walls of Ka'Iden, the sangoma. Ka'Ila couldn't carry much longer; she looked strong, standing in her green loincloth, black hair flowing with the wind, tan skin blending with the dusty landscape, and her spear rising behind her back, but she needed to be with the midwife and deliver him his boy.

♦

"Focus on the sun. Do you see it well?"

"Yes." Ka'Ila answered the sangoma, breathing deep, her eyes intent on the entrance of the cave.

"Where is it?"

"There." Her face contorted with the first contraction, "Setting between the twin spires."

"Good. Very good. Now let me guide you."

Looking at his wife from the edge of the cavern, naked on her hands and knees, Ra'Ymen remembered her determination climbing down the cliff, her belly broad, each hook cutting into the stone precisely, bouncing down the uneven surface without a gasp but a teasing warning to watch his step.

The sangoma had started singing: a tenor melancholy that struck a chord back to his childhood, and sent a tear running down his cheek. He pulled out his leather flask and caught the small drop with the muzzle. The gourd was almost half full; Ka'Ila would need it after delivering her child.

They'd stored the little water they could from the thirty days of rain the world received and gobbled up every year in order to pay the witch, and tend to Ka'Ila and the child. It was strange, the singing at birth; his people only had a song for death, and only the dying sang. The cave was stranger yet: strings of bones hung from the ceiling dyed in red; skulls larger than any beast

27

he'd ever seen ornamented shelves covered in small candle; and a thin half pipe of carved out bones hung over a bed of small green plants, connected to a heavy leather bag filled with tears, or the water she collected in tribute, or both.

He didn't really want her that near to Ka'Ila. The old woman had the air of the older folks' stories, the kind where eyes were gouged and melted over flame: thin and gnarly-skinned, thick dusty twisted braids, and the few marauding teeth that made it worse than none, but what could he do? She had delivered the children of many of the tribes for hundreds of miles. There were people who lived so near the bottom of the canyons they never saw the sun, who climbed up to have her deliver their babies. He heard she was a hundred and six and lived off a single tear a day.

Ka'Ila's moan broke through his daydreaming. *At a time like this*. But he had to wait until the wise woman called for him.

"Focus on the sun. Hold in your tears. Push. Good, very good."

Her belly hung heavily under her. He couldn't see the sangoma kneeling behind his wife, but her soothing words made it to him under the pulpy sounds of childbirth.

"Its head is here; it's a beautiful head and a rich crown of hair."

A beautiful head, a boy's head, yes? Ka'Ila's face twisted with the strain, but there was a smile there. *You're beautiful my love, and so close.*

Something dropped with a loud plop, followed by a burst and a splash, and his wife collapsed forward, panting, her head on her forearms.

A wail broke the air. He broke inside. It was still the women's time; they would know first, as they should. He had to wait longer, only a little, but so much longer.

The sangoma moved over to Ka'Ila, holding the wailing creature wrapped in a cloth. It screamed like a demon, like the whooshing winds lashing from deep crevasses, echoing gusts with voices that drove the lost mad.

He heard Ka'Ila laugh, then cry, then both at once.

Ka'Iden turned a rare smile to him, waited, and waved him over.

He ran to his wife. She looked exhausted; the skin stretched on her cheekbones looked about to tear off her face, but her smile sent a flush into her cheeks and her purple eyes glowed. He turned around slowly.

It was a beautiful head, a beautiful face, and a rich crown of dark hair. The sangoma opened the cloth. He dropped to his knees. A boy.

He began to cry. It ran down his chin and poured on the baby's slimy face. He shouldn't waste so many tears but the baby lapped them up already, barely minutes after his birth. He drank all of his father's tears and smiled; Ra'Ymen knew he couldn't smile that young but he had his mother's eyes and they glowed the same.

"What do you want to do with the tail?" the woman asked him.

His mother's eyes. When the tribe saw him they would weep as he had and they would never be thirsty again.

"The tail?" the sangoma insisted.

The cord stuck out of his son's stomach like a sickly snake, contorted and twisted and ugly. Some considered a long stomach tail a sign of strength especially in boys, but to him it looked like his son had two *tchouchous*, and he wouldn't have that.

"No." he said, shaking his head vigorously "Cut it off at the base."

"As you wish," she said, tying a string at the tail's base, cutting it off to his son's yelp, before dipping her fingers in the dripping fluid and lining his son's lips with it. "This is good for him; he will grow stronger."

He knelt by Ka'Ila and held her head in his hands and winked at her.

"I told you."

She smiled wanly, on the cusp of sleep.

"You can stay for two days rest," the midwife said formally. "You will bring the following items when you next return..."

◆

"He cries a lot," Ra'Oren, the head of the council, told Ra'Ymen around the fire along with the rest of the elders. Presenting his son wasn't going well. No one had been made to abandon a child for generations, a hundred rains at least, but the Elder's deep-set eyes were unusually dark over the flames, and held only reprimand for Ra'Ymen.

"Yes," he said full of pride and building anger. "But he drinks them all. He isn't wasteful."

"Yes, but he cries a lot."

He hadn't expected the cold welcome, the stern and disapproving looks. They had walked into the valley slowly to accommodate Ka'Ila's healing body, holding their child high over his head, the boy weeping such that Ra'Ymen had to attach a small satchel under him, where his tears collected. Crying so hard that the tribe had known about him miles before their coming, his screams resounding through the seven hills surrounding the tribe's grounds.

They had approached, dipped their fingers in the satchel, and sucked them dry, and then walked away shaking their heads. He had offered more tears than it was customary for young parents to share. And still.

Perhaps the echoing screams had scared them, perhaps someone had read the bones and announced some ill coming, perhaps they thought he and Ka'Ila boastful pranksters. Perhaps they were all jealous of his son who would change the world.

"He will grow, it will stop, children are always such, aren't they?" Ra'Ymen insisted.

"He might; he might weep himself dead first," the Elder said with a look of mild disgust, as if he were about to *spit*. "He cries too much. The others will not like it. Do something about it."

◆

"They don't want him, love. They don't want our boy," Ra'Ymen told his wife, his child's need screams, full of need, waking them up at night.

"It's fine. You know children; he's got your father's temper and my mother's strength. He's shedding them to come into his own. We'll be fine. Now, let me sleep; it's your turn to tend to him."

"I know, but you didn't see them; they are serious, too serious." He hesitated and plodded on. "They won't let us name him. He will have to leave if they don't, climb down the cliffs..."

"Tsk. Don't be silly," Ka'Ila answered, her voice already drifting back to sleep. "That doesn't...happen anymore, and it's not until he's... six rains old... now go... he's hungry."

◆

Their small hut stood on the outskirts of the village, spread over the hundred-mile valley connecting the seven brown hills that secluded it from the rest of the region. Other tribes attacked sometimes, but the hills were treacherous, the footing unsure, and the land prone to avalanches of gritty soil.

You could see small flames glowing in the distance with distorted shadows spreading across the valley at night, and the wind blew away from their hut, carrying the baby's calls into the drafts dashing and bouncing fiercely through the hills, scaring any would-be attackers with a warning: Here lives death, and it's thirsty.

My boy, bringing the flood, Ra'Ymen thought, lifting himself out of bed. Ka'Ila, uncaring in her sleep, pulled the dusty sheets over herself and turned over.

Something dropped, and his son's wails stopped, replaced by wheezing bubbles, and then nothing.

He rushed into the next room. His son lay flat down on his face, tiny body immobile in a puddle of tears twice his size, so thick the ground was slow to drink it, his tiny hands and feet spread around him in a cross, his rich crown of black rising over his drowning head...

He threw himself at his son's body. He cried too much, he *had* cried too much, cried himself to death...

His son screamed louder than when he was born the moment he lifted him out of the puddle, his hands and arms reaching for the tears, his tongue licking them off his dripping face, and he screamed and fought for more.

Ra'Ymen looked at him, terrified, and lowered him slowly back into the puddle. The baby giggled, and plunged his head into his tears, slurping them up faster than the ground ever had while his father trembled, and when he was done, when there wasn't a tear left on the floor, he cried more.

♦

"You look thin, Ra'Ymen, and you, Ka'Ila," Elder Ra'Oren told them. "Are you well?"

It was easy to feel well in the rays of the setting sun bathing the valley in fractal bursts. Your eyes believed in things that weren't there: trees, a demon or a kindly spirit, if only for a brief second. It was only a few days after the rain, and there was still moisture in the air, and colors that broke the brown monotony of life.

But they weren't. They weren't well at all.

Ka'Ila nodded at the Elder, looking at the other parents bringing their children for their initiation before they were given a name and accepted into the tribe.

His son tugged at his hand. His crown of hair had grown long, just as he had, gaining on his father day after day, questioning, inquisitive about any small thing, anxious to explore the hills and the world beyond on his own, and eager to be with the other children his age. Ra'Ymen had been just the same, but of course not exactly.

"Yes!" He answered as enthusiastically as he could muster. Most parents looked sad at leaving their children, but he wasn't, and he couldn't imagine Ka'Ila was either.

His son didn't cry as much anymore, and not in front of his friends and their parents, at any cost, but they had to bribe him with their tears. He always needed more tears; he drank all his own then most of theirs, every day, increasingly as he grew bigger. They were exhausted all the time. Ka'Ila had never fully recovered from delivering him, and Ra'Ymen hadn't thrown a spear straight in months. They were short on rations and the boy was always thirsty.

Ra'Ymen had tried to train the boy, and he had promised he would earn his name.

His enthusiasm did nothing to belie their gaunt and drained faces, and the Elder insisted: "Are you sure? We've been worried about you, Ra'Ymen; the last hunt did not go well. The cave beast almost killed you..." He turned to Ka'Ila. "We will take care of the boy until his naming; you would do well to rest."

Ka'Ila smiled. "Oh, he's a handful. You'll find out soon enough."

Ra'Oren raised an eyebrow and looked at her, then the boy.

"I see he has finally shed his ancestors and cried himself dry. Very good. I can imagine how difficult it must have been, given how he started. You've done well."

He had no idea.

◆

"What's the trouble about?" Ra'Ymen asked a villager he thought was named Ra'Aten, on his way back from collecting some of the water rationed from the rains.

His son had only been gone for a week, but he was feeling stronger already, and so was Ka'Ila. The flush in her cheeks was back and they were both strong enough to enjoy each other again, without a thirsty wail interrupting their passion.

Several elders were leaving a hut, headed for the heart of the valley with one of the initiates' mothers. Her eyes were wet. Perhaps her child needed a few years before it was ready.

They had spent the first few days on edge, expecting an elder to rattle the bones on their hut at any moment, dragging their son by the hair, leaving a trail of moist earth behind him, and a crowd of rage on his heels. But one night had passed and then a second and then they'd fallen asleep and were in love again.

"Haven't you heard?" Ra'Aten replied. "Her daughter died. Cried herself to death in her sleep; couldn't find a tear around her though, strange..."

◆

"What have you done, boy?"

Three more children had died in a week, their eyes glass, every ounce of moisture gone from their bodies.

Sitting on the floor next to the boy, Ka'Ila ran her hand lovingly through his hair and whispered into his ear. Ra'Ymen

34

couldn't hear what she said, but he knew her well; she would weep every tear in her body for her child. None of this was right. He had wanted him to be special, had had him delivered by the sangoma at great risk. This was what they had, what Ka'Ila had suffered for. Their boy, their special boy.

The boy hadn't said a word, just smiled and cried and drank, and then he stopped and tugged at his mother's arm.

"I missed you," he said; his small fist wrapped around her forearm. "I'm thirsty."

♦

"She's dead, my love."

"Already? But it can't have been a week?"

"Less. Five days. He drinks them faster every time."

"What are we gonna do?"

"I'll mutilate the body," Ka'Ila answered. "You'll leave it in the hills. If anyone finds it, they'll think it was a raid. They did before. We'll feed him ourselves for a few days and find someone else. We'll be fine."

♦

"We have gathered you to patrol the hills," Elder Ra'Oren told the assembled men of hunting age. "Your wives must keep an eye out for the village while you're gone."

The two thousand men gathered by the Elders eyed each other suspiciously. Two Elders responsible for the children had marched away from the tribe and had fallen thousands of meters from a cliff in remorse, and all the recent victims were elderly and defenseless.

Ra'Ymen eyed them with the same anger.

"However," Ra'Oren went on, "the bodies were carved and

dried of tears, but we don't believe they died of their wounds; there was too little blood. They were drained first, just as the children were, and since we don't know what happened to the children—yet—we will be investigating every house soon."

◆

"Please Elder Ra'Oren, have a cup of tears."

The Elder nodded at Ka'Ila and accepted the small cup. "Thank you. We know these are hard times for you. We do not wish to delay anyone's naming any more than we have to, but we cannot take more chances, you understand."

"Of course, Elder," Ra'Ymen answered, while running his hand playfully through his son's hair. "We're grateful to have him back, and safe, that's what matters now, but it hasn't been easy for him."

Ra'Oren looked into his son's eyes, but found only what he and Ka'Ila always saw: a mischief that lingered on the verge of perpetual sadness, and an innocent absence of awareness.

"Yes, I can see it, he's hurting. Most of the other children are as well. We don't think the children were responsible, rest assured, not with adults disappearing too; none of the children are strong enough."

The council suspected a villager, or several. After weeks of scouting the hills, they had run into only four raiding parties from other tribes, all of them killed, and yet two more people had vanished. Ka'Ila had done well.

"You look tired again, Ka'Ila. All of this isn't easy on you either."

One of those two was still alive, if barely. He was hidden inside the latrine, not strong enough to whimper. Ra'Ymen had gagged him for good measure, but he was passed out most of the time, unaware of his son draining the life out of his eyes.

36

Ra'Ymen had thought the investigation would be weak-willed. It was the first time the tribe had to deal with a mystery of this kind, and no one wanted to investigate people they had known their whole lives, whom they'd raised. Those who did would lay blame on people they disliked, making things harder on the Elders.

"You've been asked before of course, but…" A groan came through the small window from the latrine. It could have been the wind; it was common enough for it to howl this near the hills; it could have been anything, but it halted Elder Ra'Oren in his question.

"Come to think of it," he said, sipping from the cup, looking firmly away from the window and down at the ground. "I recall your son being extremely needy as a child. Uniquely. How did you manage to sever him?"

Something snapped inside Ra'Ymen, but he kept his calm and smiled at his wife. They had prepared for this, knew to remain calm if the questions were strange. He laughed it off. "Ha ha! Well it wasn't easy, but it might run in the family. I was a tricky one too, and I came out all right."

The Elder's responding laugh didn't sound contrived, but Ra'Ymen saw Ka'Ila's brow darken. She thought he had heard; she knew he had heard. Ra'Ymen leaped at the opportunity; they had discussed this too.

"Elder," he said his voice conspiratorial, "can we speak freely?"

The old man's eyes lit up. "Yes, of course."

"Can you come back tonight? After nightfall. Alone. Please don't tell anyone. There have been strange things at night, very strange things and…" He feigned concern, looking at the window and door in turn. "No one must see you. If someone did and anything happened…I…I fear for my family, Elder."

Ra'Oren frowned, and his left eye narrowed as he looked at

him, then at his boy and his wife, and nodded.

"Yes. Yes, Ra'Ymen." He nodded and rose, handing the small cup to Ka'Ila with a tight smile. "I'll return tonight when it's dark, and you can tell me what it is that scares you so much."

He pushed the beads and bones away and stepped out of the hut, glancing at their child one last time before walking away.

"He knows," Ka'Ila said, just the sound of his steps, headed towards the nearest hut, faded out of earshot. "He thinks he does, but not for very long."

◆

"He won't be long now," Ra'Ymen told his wife. "We let him in, I stab him through the stomach, and we make for the hills. We'll head back to the sangoma's cave; if she's trouble, we deal with it. Once we're there we can use the plateau and cliffs to our advantage. We can live on what she's stored for months, maybe till the next rains, even."

Ka'Ila seemed to hesitate for the first time in weeks, looking at her son. He was kneeling on the floor, bent over their last victim, and sucking the little moisture that remained out of the old man's eyes, oblivious to what he had brought upon himself, his parents and the tribe.

The idea of killing people bothered her. Not feeding them to their son but truly killing them. Perhaps she'd convinced herself it wasn't the same thing, perhaps even a small mercy for the elderly. After all, the elders are to become ancestors; what better way than through feeding a broken child?

Ra'Ymen had his doubts too. The boy would drink more as he grew bigger; he would never stop drinking, he would drink them eventually, and then he would drink the world...

"Ra'Ymen, Ka'Ila?" Elder Ra'Oren's voice called, ringing low in the darkness outside the bone curtain.

He nodded at his wife, who moved closer to the door, standing halfway between him and their son, the window a few feet behind her just in case they had to flee. He picked up his short spear, held it behind his leg, and stepped towards the entrance.

He breathed in and his hand caught the bones.

"Elder Ra'Oren, we thought you wouldn't come." He pulled the bones away to let him in and caught a glimpse of torches outlining the Elder. "Run!" he turned and yelled at his wife as two men tackled him at the knees. His chin hit the ground while someone climbed in through the window and caught his wife's arm, twisted it and pushed her to her knees.

"Let her go, you..."

A foot landed in his face just as his son began to cry; he saw lights and then nothing.

◆

"We do not kill. And that monster is yet a child."

"And what? All monsters were children once. What will happen if he feeds and grows stronger and returns? We kill outsiders all the time; we have no reason to..."

"But he is *not* an outsider. He is one of our own. I see Ra'Ymen's father in him. I had known Ra'Arem since I was a boy. This demon is one of our own; maybe we brought this upon ourselves...can someone stop his crying!"

Ra'Ymen forced his eyes open, each eyelash weighing as much as a boulder. It seemed to him a generation had passed before he managed to keep them open, and yet another before his vision lost its blur. He must have been as old as the sangoma by then or more, but the voices kept him going. The voices, and the heavy breathing and the smell of his wife next to him, but it was the wailing of his unnamed son that broke through the haze.

Their boy needed him. Someone wanted to kill him, their special boy...

The cords cut into his arms and chest. No matter. They cut deeper and started bleeding. He paused for breath and turned his head. Ka'Ila's eyes were wide open. She was tied to a stone pillar a few feet above the ground in the center of the valley, just as he was, but she wasn't struggling; or maybe she had, and realized how useless it was. Instead she stared intently at their son, sitting by the fire in the middle of the circle of Elders, sitting in a puddle of his own tears, his eyes on his mother's, those same eyes staring at each other, and the boy cried and screamed and drank his pain, and cried more.

"What have I done wrong, Mommy? Why are they angry with me?"

Ka'Ila's eyes started flowing.

"Someone, wrap some cloth around the boy's mouth," Ra'Ymen heard Elder Ra'Oren say, though he couldn't see him. "They're awake, and this is a time for judgment, not sentiment."

He turned to them, his deep-set eyes heavy, his face twisted in pain, his reluctance evident.

"I have known you since you were children, both of you," he said, a tremor lacing his voice. "Your father used to bully me as a child, Ra'Ymen, until we became friends. You, Ka'Ila, did you know your mother and I were lovers once? It was a long time ago. What have you done to us? What have you done to yourselves?"

Their son wept over his mouth-gag, looking at him and his mother imploringly. The tribe couldn't kill his son, they couldn't kill their boy...

Through the veil of red madness that covered his eyes, Ra'Ymen heard Ka'Ila beg, "Do whatever you will to us. But don't harm him. He doesn't know, he doesn't understand."

"We know," the Elder said. "We know..." He hesitated briefly and plunged on. "He will be taken away. Far away, and left to his own devices..."

Ka'Ila's mouth opened, but the Elder cut her short.

"If you argue he will die." He watched their mouths shut and their faces tighten. "Good; I will not let the memory of your parents keep me from feeding you all to a cave beast, do you understand?"

Ra'Ymen nodded and saw Ka'Ila do the same.

"As for you, you will be brought out here, every day from sunrise to sunset, and you will give your tears freely to whoever wishes it until you have withered and died." He turned to the other Elders. "Now take the boy; we will leave with him with the rising sun. You will never see him again."

Ka'Ila began to scream as the Elders lifted their boy onto an old shoulder and walked away with him, his purple eyes glowing against the moon with the constant stream of his love. They faded into the shadow of the hills at night, the last purple ember gone. He heard his wife screaming well into the night, until she fell asleep, and he kept shouting their pain until morning.

♦

They knew by the echoing wails that their boy was making his way through the hills and away from the valley forever.

The village brought the pair out for a whole week, and yet the Elders still didn't return. They brought them out again, and by the end of the second week they saw torches in the hills, and the Elders returning. Ra'Ymen and Ka'Ila held their dry eyes open for as long as they could against hope, but their child wasn't with them. And two days later the wind picked up.

It beat the valley mercilessly for weeks, tearing through their skins and lungs every day as the villagers took them out and tied them to the stone pillars; and it carried the voice of a crying

41

child.

The tribe went crazy; some suggested killing them, some suggested a spell or a curse, but after a few weeks the wind abated, and the crying stopped. And after a few months the ground began to shake, the earth to crack, and boulders fell from the hills and buried houses.

Beyond the hills a rumble grew, the sound of an incredible force tearing through the region around them, and when all the villagers had fled the outskirts and gathered at the center of the valley next to them, a torrent of tears broke through one of the hills. It turned into a deep river that swept through the east of the valley, running along the cracks and crevasses of the land, then carried on to the other side and flowed and flowed forever.

Our boy. Our special boy.

♦

The years passed; his hair grew longer and white, as did Ka'Ila's. They grew frailer and old.

They didn't need their tears anymore. The hills were green and brown with trees, small rivulets ran in the most unsuspected of caves, and new creatures lived in the branches, filling the days with song. Yet the villagers still brought them out, day after day in memory, whether it rained or shone. Children would run past them laughing, and if they asked, Ka'Ila and he would shed a tear for them.

Their boy had never returned, their special boy, but they saw him every day, in everything they saw.

And sometimes, on stormy nights, they thought they heard him cry.

♦

End

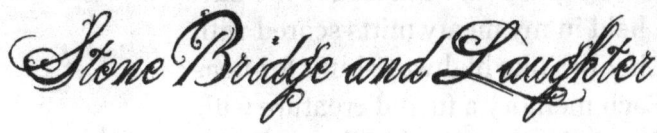
Stone Bridge and Laughter

[Stone Bridge and Laughter
(for Elizabeth)]
[Alex Jennings]

Omnia Gallia est devisa in tres partes...
--Julius Caesar

I

How can you be gone?
Trees branch a spiral staircase and up
Onto the landing outside the kitchen
Elder voices, wrinkled hands, apple
Sauce simmering on the stove I stand
Unseen, enfolded by memory like
Wet wings on a butterfly See their crazed
Print glistening in the dim I will unfurl
And fly to meet you

I ask too much, I know, but in this in-
Between time, I feel as if I'm losing
My grip On what, who knows? What

Have I grasped, what fragile life have
I held in my meaty mitts scored with
Lifelines like highways built for fleas?
Each memory a furred creature with
Jeweled eyes and rabbit haunches
Birthed from convulsing throat

Lately my dreams feel incomplete A concert
For a band I don't care for but the music is
Not as I remember, instead, there
Is an absence of sound, of spirit, of com-
munication Is that you? Is this how you
Reach for me? What of the dream where
I returned to Paramaribo to live in a Tunisian
Villa where the owner, wanted for murder,
Hid secretly on the grounds? Or was that
Mexico—you never went to Mexico

I thought of you today as I wrote about
Our trip across the Surinam River into
French Guyana The sky fell and
Rain like nails drenched us all in seconds
Wheelchair folded like a paper crane in
The back of our canoe, and your face up-
Turned in the stormy light to the battering
Drops and that smile that smile, O

II

How can you be gone? How can you be
Gone from me? I have So much yet to ask
Your passport sits on my bedroom book case,
The one by the bathroom door Sometimes I

44

Look at it handle it when I feel I'm losing
Your face, or the sound of your voice, and
I hear that bellowing call from downstairs
Where your voice bent at the top but your
Eyes are nowhere on me

My life, my identity have not kept you
from me--Nothing has:

There are dreams I can't recall further
Realms than I can call to mind, and there,
At the deepest—the *almost* deepest center
Of my labyrinthine memory, where the serpent's
head meets the tail, we stand together on an
Ancient stone bridge neither of us knew in
Life It kneels like a squire before his queen
Ready for the Accolade and we speak in
Hushed tones broken by sudden barks

My memory of you is not aged, not leather-
Skinned or always-tired or enfeebled after your
Stroke when for a week I watched your breath
In the hotel room certain you would leave me then
That you would rush past me out the door not even
Bothering to close it after you, and I'd be left alone
In your absence to feel the hole where you'd been
In the middle of the air and I wouldn't know what
To do, whom to call—alone, alone abandoned—
But you stayed Your eyes rolled and you clasped
My hand in yours, your wrinkled skin so
Soft, and we said nothing of that room again So

III

In the end, you were a space shuttle preparing
To launch, unmooring your bright and feathered
Spirit from the scaffold of your body, your frailty
I couldn't believe I wouldn't You were ill, but
As every other time, you would shrug it off, say
It's only liquid sunshine and charge on over rutted
Jungle roads into the little French colony with
Its candy-colored houses and impossibly old men
In straw hats with skin so brown it was less complexion
Than a geologic stratigraphy, scoured by wind and time

When I sat to write this verse, you were a blank-
Ness, absent to me, silent, but as I worked the stony
Words, your image resolved into view: Youthful
Once more, looking out across water and laughing
Laughing for me in your white dress and crimson cape

Like a paper boat, this vision floated downstream
To me I lifted it into my waiting hungry heart
Like language, like Story and the Word

One more gift from you

◆

End

PUBLISHED IN 1979, *The Joys of Motherhood* is a multi-perspective novel that contextualizes the complexities of motherhood, the impact of European colonization and patriarchal hegemony in Nigeria, and the cultural shifts that catalyze intergenerational discord between parents and their children. As demonstrated throughout Diaspora women's literature such as *Beloved, Kindred* and *Their Eyes Were Watching God,* Emecheta's novel relies on mythic elements and mythatypical characterizations to signify cultural values and cosmological ideas while simultaneously critiquing the intergenerational implications of cisheteropatriarchal hegemony.

The Joys of Motherhood depicts multiple non-linear mythic journeys, comprised of mythatypical figures and patterns (characters and settings) that convey the cyclic and multidimensional nature of womanhood. Additionally, through the protagonist's interpersonal relationships, Emecheta creates binary oppositions of tradition vs. modernity and love vs. duty to contextualize how agency, identity, and value are differently informed and affected by colonial cisheteropatriachy. The novel opens with a twenty-five-year-old woman (2+5=7, the number for the ocean goddess Yemoja), Nnu Ego, backing out of a room and bolting through the streets of Lagos—including the Oyingbo market, which is significant to both the lake goddess Uhamiri and the river goddess Oya—headed towards Carter Bridge. The unidentified narrator explains that Nnu Ego sought to "meet her *chi*, her personal god" to "ask her why she had punished her so" (Emecheta 4). Nnu Ego's dynamic characterization signifies the presence of multiple African deities, including Oya, who represents transformation, rebirth, and justice; Yemoja, the mother of all Orishas; and Uhamiri, also known as Mami-wata or Ogbuide, an "amalgamation of many different African water goddesses" (Adadevoh 35). In a few introductory pages, Emecheta lays the framework for Nnu Ego's multidimensional mythic journey.

In *Moorings and Metaphors*, Karla F.C. Holloway explains that "there is a textual place where language and voice are reconstructed" by Black women writers "as categories of cultural and gendered essence" and that the writings of these women "have inversive, recursive and sometimes even subversive structures" (Brooks de Vita 4). Holloway continues: "it is through the ancient spirituality of this literature that the unity of soul and gender is [...] recovered and celebrated" through the "metaphor of the goddess/ancestor" (4). Brooks de Vita further asserts that it is "through identification of a protagonist with a perceived ancestor and in the conflation of the deceased ancestor with spiritual forces or female deities that the work transcends a narrow or individualistic space and enters a realm that Holloway terms 'spiritual'" (4). This is clearly illustrated through Emecheta's chapter titles ("The Mother," "The Mother's

Mother," "The Canonised Mother") and the subsequent characterizations of the protagonist Nnu Ego, her mother Ona, and Nnu Ego's children.

Another important aspect of Emecheta's novel is the ritual of naming, as each name signifies an attribute, cultural origin, or value that comments on the binary oppositions of tradition versus modernity. Nnu Ego's name was bestowed by her father because upon seeing her, he declared that "this child is priceless, more than twenty bags of cowries. I think that should really be her name, because she is a beauty and she is mine. Yes, 'Nnu Ego': twenty bags of cowries" (26). Nnu Ego's name is ironic, particularly because in the traditional Igbo nation, girls held less value than boys. Although Nnu Ego is named by her father, as was customary, her father's choice represents how men assign value to women based on subjective qualities such as beauty and the ability to contribute to men's legacies. Additionally, as Nnu Ego ages and struggles with infertility and poverty, her social value decreases. This is particularly illustrated when she travels to Lagos and is immersed in a colonial capitalistic community, where money is required to sustain one's life. She eventually bears seven children, having endured nine pregnancies, because Nnu Ego's value in her community is predicated upon her ability to give birth.

Emecheta uses the protagonist, her ancestress/ancestor, and her *chi* (personal god) to develop "interactive relations among protagonist, ancestor, and deity, [which] Holloway concludes, animates African American and West African women's literatures concurrently on three levels of time, experience, and existence: the individual [...] the historical, and the mythical" (Brooks de Vita 4). The characters, although human, signify ancestral and deified qualities, which further develop the novel's plot and resolution. Ultimately, Emecheta's mythatypical figures and patterns and binary oppositions brilliantly contextualize the intergenerational implications of colonial cisheteropatriachal hegemony as they relate to agency, identity, and value.

Freshwater by Awkwaeke Emezi is a bildungsroman about a gender expansive African person called the Ada. Published in 2018, the novel details the chaotic interior thoughts of the Ada and gods whom she is embodied by. Through the Ada's and the gods's journey, Emezi immerses readers in a dynamic story about mental illness, sexual trauma, gender identity, migration, and spirituality. Early in the novel, an unidentified narrator asserts, "I have lived many lives inside this body. I have lived many lives before they put me in this body. I will live many lives when they take me out of it" (14).

Although the Ada is one person, she is claimed by the god Ala and embodied by ogbanje, or godlings. The gods explain that "we did not come alone. With a force like ours, we dragged other things along [...] this compound object [...] the oath of the world. It is a promise [...] that says we will come back, that we will not stay in this world" (25). While some chapters are written from the Ada's perspective, others are written from the perspective of Ala, the god she is claimed by, and the ogbanje, Asughara and St. Vincent, who also embody her. Through the Ada's characterization, semiotic settings, and ritual of naming, Emezi contextualizes African and European ontologies.

In *Myth, Literature, and the African World*, Soyinka speaks at great length about ritual archetypes, and describes "a chthonic realm, a storehouse for creative and destructive essences" (2). In *Freshwater*, the Ada's birth and physical body serve as literal and metaphorical sites of creation and destruction. When the gods describe the *iyi-uwa*, or the oath of the world, they explain that "when spirits like us are put inside flesh, this oath becomes a real object, one that functions as a bridge. It is usually buried or hidden"; while Western epistemologies often regard these as separate manifestations of consciousness, in *The Spirit and the*

Word, Montgomery explains how images in the text serve as "evidence of the African concept of opposites and the notion of balance" (41).

Through the Ada's characterization, Emezi depicts how complementary oppositions manifest, in part, to orchestrate divine order and to fulfill one's purpose. The Ada's most volatile ogbanje, Asughara, represents destruction and retribution; she is tempered by the Ada's other gods who are more gentle and less demanding in their use of the Ada's body. In the beginning of the novel, the gods explain:

> That morning (the day we died and were born), [Saachi's] labor started [...] Meanwhile,
> we were wrenched, dragged through the gates, across a river, and through the back door
> of [Saachi's] womb, thrust into the rippling water and the small sleeping body floating
> within. (Emezi 15-16)

Through the gods' narration, readers are introduced to several aspects of African ontologies, where life and death are complementary occurrences. Ngangah explains:

> [T]he four core aspects of the Igbo belief system consist of *Okike* (creation), *Alusi* (Deities), *Mmuo* (Diverse spirits), and *Uwa* (the visible physical world) [...] since supernatural and natural forces are interlinked in Igbo cultural belief system, these four aspects are necessarily interconnected. (4).

A few pages later, the gods, while analyzing the significance of the Ada's true name, explain that, "All water is connected. All freshwater comes out of the mouth of a python" (Emezi 20). These are some of the earliest examples of Emezi's extended metaphor and semiotic language, in that *Freshwater* incorporates mythatypical patterns of Igbo spiritual tradition.

The Ada, who is claimed by Ala, is the deity of earth, morality, fertility, and creativity in the Igbo belief system, Odinani. In an article titled "Odinani: A Discourse in Philosophy of Culture," Ngangah explains that "'*Odinani*' means 'inherent in the land,'" and that "Ani or ala (land) is the place where the monotheistic God, Chukwu [...] created and domiciled humans, animals, spirits and the elements" (Ngangah 2). Although the Ada is named by her "human father" Saul, and described as "the child Saul asked for, the prayer's flesh," the gods explain that "it is better not to even say her first name" because "in its truest form" it means "the egg of a python" (Emezi 21). They further reveal that "before a christ-induced amnesia struck the humans, it was well known that the python was sacred" as "the source of the stream, the flesh form of the god Ala, who is the earth herself, the judge and mother, the giver of law" (Emezi 21).

In *Mythatypes: Signatures and Signs of African/Diaspora and Black Goddesses*, Brooks de Vita writes that "naming oneself and being named by others is a crucial act of claiming self and community" (15). Although readers are initially not made privy to the Ada's first name, Emezi signifies the mythatypical characteristics of the god Ala, the Ada's *chi,* and the circumstances surrounding the Ada's given name. The gods explain that Saul "allowed her name and it was later, when we were awake, that we knew that and understood at last why he'd been chosen. Many things start with a name" (Emezi 19).

The Ada's name and relationship with Ala and the ogbanje contextualize the relationship between life and death, the connection between physical and spiritual realms, and the symbiotic relationship of gods and humans. This is further demonstrated when the gods recount the Ada naming them, saying, "our forms were young and indistinct, but this naming was a second birth, it sorted us into something she could see" (Emezi 48-49). They assert that "she named me this name,

Asughara, complete with that gritty slide of the throat halfway through" and establish, "When you name something, it comes into existence" (Emezi 72). Through the Ada and ogbanje's naming, Emezi signifies certain values within African ontologies, and their respective relationships.

Ultimately, *Freshwater* is a bildungsroman that incorporates semiotic setting and signifying language to develop a complex protagonist who simultaneously navigates physical and spiritual realms despite being embodied by chaotic deities. The gods explain that "there are limitations in the flesh that intrinsically make no sense, constraints of this world that are diametrically opposed to the freedoms" because "[t]his world was meant to bend" (Emezi 23). The Ada does their best to bend and serve the deities within them; however, the gods resist, proclaiming, "we were hungry inside her, raging against this useless mortality, as if we could rage right back to the world we came from. We raged at the displacement of a new country" (Emezi 54). Through the Ada's and ogbanje's actions and interior thoughts, Emezi illustrates differences between African and Western ontologies, the implications of being displaced from one's ancestral home, and the manifestations of misalignment and trauma.

[Works Cited]

Adadevoh, Anthonia. *Personified Goddesses: An Archetypal Pattern of Female Protagonists in the Works of Two Black Women Writers.* July 2013. Clark Atlanta University. https://radar.auctr.edu/islandora/object/cau.td:2013_adadevoh_anthonia. Accessed March 18, 2023

Brooks De Vita, Alexis. *Mythatypes: Signatures and Signs of African/Diaspora and Black Goddesses.* Greenwood Press: Westport, CT, 2000. Print

Emecheta, Buchi. *The Joys of Motherhood.* Heineman International: Oxford. 1979.

Emezi, Akwaeke. *Freshwater.* New York: Grove Press, 2018.

Ngangah, Innocent. "Odinani: A Discourse in Philosophy of Culture." Available at SSRN: https://ssrn.com/abstract=3590960 or http://dx.doi.org/10.2139/ssrn.3590960. Accessed March 18, 2023

Soyinka, Wole. *Myth, Literature, and the African World.* New York: Cambridge University Press, 1967.

♦

End

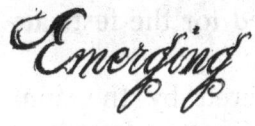
Emerging

[Emerging]
[Joyce Chng]

THE FIGURE EMERGES FROM THE WATER, like some primordial dryad. It wears a suit made of dried reeds, blending into the sea of lotuses, seamless and green. This late in the season, the lotuses are beginning to wilt, their large pink petals curled up boat-like on the pad.

It is now harvest and the figure's basket is filled with the mud-caked roots thick as a woman's wrist. Soon, they will have to wait for the seed pods that form after the falling of the petals. Some of the seeds they will leave behind.

And hence, the cycle will begin once more. The water, the lake, the lotuses, the roots, the seeds and the huge circular pads.

The figure raises their face to the setting sun, now glorious in the golden hour. The lotus lake is tinted gold, flaming beautiful for a while. As beautiful as the offerings they leave afloat during festival, later to be washed away, washed anew and recycled by the water.

For tonight's prayers, they have reverently cut three lotus buds, still folded tight. Late-bloomers, but part of the cycle, part of the living breathing eco-system. The lotuses rise from the mud, the life-giving mud, and the ever-clean water. The entire village depends on the lake. The water is used for the festivals and rituals.

Nearby the filters do their work, powered by the sun, protected by the village's children.

"From the water emerges forth life," the figure whispers to themselves, a personal prayer. They will be back tomorrow, at the lotus lake. Going in and emerging once more. Just like the lotus.

♦

End

A Pocketful of Precious

[A Pocketful of Precious]
[Annette Meserve]

AS ALWAYS, I WALK THE DUNES, the shifting ground in tiny ripples underfoot as if I travel the bottom of a great sea, my way sculpted by wave after wave, shaped by an unimaginable liquid volume. But this is not a sea and my path has, instead, been made by the hot scouring air; relentless, pointlessly moving tiny grains, authoring miniscule rim and furrow and then rim again; mounds and mounds growing into hills and then into great mountains; a monotonous horizon of sand to get lost in, to be aimless in, to enter and perhaps never again escape.

Though constantly changing, it is a place with which I am well acquainted. My days and months and years—maybe lifetimes—have been spent wandering, searching for meager bits to eat, for the rare drink of water. It is a place where each step takes gargantuan effort, forward momentum absorbed by the shifting depth, every footstep an exercise in near-futility.

In this parched inferno of a place, respite is to be found only in the wide sky above: the breathtaking beauty of its sunsets, the release of its vast dark nights and infinite starfield.

I must travel, though, in the crushing heat of mid-day and, at times, I find myself on the ridge of one dune or other. Even in the bright of high noon, I can momentarily ignore the buffeting, pelting wind to pause and sit surveying the vista of this desert. In these times, my fingers move within the recesses of my worn and soiled cloak, finding the precious bits hidden there, lovingly polishing the small objects collected, curated throughout a precarious life. And in these times, I've looked beyond this place, to the very edge of the shifting grounds, to another world.

The world beyond here is a place of growing things and *of water!* It is where the thunderstorms go, after skidding across my sky, after having blocked the brutal sun for only the briefest of times, taunting me with their grey heaviness but never releasing even a droplet. It is only upon this other world that they shower their life-giving rains. Sat there on the sandy elevations, I have seen the great columns in the distance, the seeming pillars between sky and earth that form and move, torrential downpours bursting forth upon the green living-ness of that other world, watering abundance, swelling rivers, nurturing gardens.

And once the rains have exhausted themselves, the golden sun of evening reaches in under the clouds. I have seen the pavilions, hues intensified by the wet, festive slices of primary greens and reds and blues and yellows, deeper and more vivid in the oblique light; the pointed circular rooftops' unapologetic colors dripping and running through the landscape.

I have seen, in the glow of that evening sunlight, the gleam of brass fittings, the brightly painted animals held by them, animals moving up and down, up and down, up and down and around and around. I have seen joyous figures riding these creatures, whooping and laughing as they grasp the poles that emerge from the animals' backs, poles that anchor the enameled creatures to the polished wooden deck boards, keeping them on track as the carousels spin. I have heard the music, streams of playful notes made thin by the waves of heat through which they've wafted to reach my ears.

On these occasions, I've brought out the tiny gemstones, glistening pottery shards, and time-smoothed wood chips that live in my pockets, have laid my small treasures out on the sand, arranging them this way and that, ordering their colors to match those of the oasis, holding them up in the setting sun's rays, superimposing them over the glorious far-away scene to see if any might fit in that world.

There is pavilion after pavilion there, some large enough to accommodate a hundred riders or more, their mechanisms covered with mirrors and jewels and glittering lights. Others among them are small, simple metal rounds with modest pole structures placed around their edges, poles not to hold gloriously decorated animals but, instead, to be held on to, for a rider to brace themselves against the centrifugal force of the spinning. And it was on one of those smaller merry-go-rounds, if one can believe it, that I found myself one day, a day not so long ago, the day before this one in which I walk once again on the sand of the dunes.

It was a day that started no different from the rest, I with my feet pointed in the direction of that other world, as they'd been since first I'd sat watching from afar. But, on that day, as I'd trudged, the terrain had grown shallow, my footsteps easier, and I moved forward faster than ever I had. I'd come to a path, clearly marked, through a break in the dunes. Almost euphoric with the feel of solid ground beneath my feet, I followed and soon the sand's rippling gave way to gravel and then to small, rounded stones at the edge of a stream, *running water!* Only an inch or two deep, it was easily crossed but still miraculous in the splashing of my dusty sandals, in the running over my sun-cracked toes, in the feel of slippery, pebbled river bottom.

I knelt in the middle, the crust of years melting away from the knees of my cloak, and drank. The long draught was sun-warmed but still a deliciously alien coolness sliding down my throat, flooding my bones with a hope I'd not dared before.

As I stepped up the far bank, my shoes squished tiny rivulets upon the carpet of mossy green, and there were infinitesimal droplets in the air too; a mist, *a mist!* hung all around, wetting my face and beading the strands of my hair.

I traveled through the airborne water's billowing, coming then to one of the smaller discs that I'd watched so many times, spinning, its deck mounted low to the ground. It had a pattern of rusty ridges upon its surface and waist-high, rounded arches at intervals marking its circumference. As I approached, a small screeching emerged from the thing's unseen mechanisms, a rhythmic metal-on-metal sound. Some part of the thing was out of round, wobbling upon the other parts and it was a bit grating to the nerves yet somehow not unpleasant, as if triggering some long-ago familiarity from a memory I had never lived.

The sound provided a small comfort as I stood in front of the merry-go-round's stern operator, a well-muscled man whose job it was to grasp the arched handles, each in turn, and give a mighty tug to keep up the spinning. A price was asked, and I eagerly drew out the collection from my pocket. Never before had my treasures been seen by another set of eyes and I was certain, with my cupped hands held reverently outstretched, that this man would view them with my same delight. However, his gnarled finger poked indifferently at stone and shard, finally selecting one of the lesser pieces, an earth-colored rock, striated and smooth.

He held the piece up to the diffuse sun that was making its way through the mist, a light oddly friendly in its gentle warmth, wholly lacking the skin-flaying heat of the sun on the dunes. The softness shone through my stone in a way I'd never seen, lighting it from the inside, making it glow almost with an awareness of its own, as an eye from some ethereal tiger-beast peeking into our reality on a whim.

Seeming pleased with the eye, the operator stopped the merry-go-round and, holding fast to one of the rounded arches, pressed my stone into the metal. With a slight hissing and a slip of steam, my bit of precious was imbedded, a skilled craftsman setting it there. He then grasped the arch and, flexing his mighty arm, set the disc to spinning again. He turned and nodded at me, indicating that this was the time. I was allowed to take my turn, but I would have to find the courage to mount.

So, I ran alongside, watching, the arches passing by in a blur, until I simply had to jump. And jump I did, holding my breath and, I think, even closing my eyes! I reached out, grasping for and finding the smooth coolly rounded metal, lifted off my feet by the momentum and clanking down upon the rusted deck.

And then oh! the movement! The wind! Not like the gales that blew on the dunes, day after day, ever and always coming, me the stationary object interrupting the flow. No, now I *was* the motion and the particles of air, the refreshing water droplets, were the objects that I, with my mere presence, set to moving, making a wind of my own! *I was the flow!* I felt the freedom as effortless movement, on my face, in my hair, setting my cloak to waving, everything else falling away, all the worries, injustices, discomforts, too slow to keep up.

In the turning, I glimpsed the colors of the pavilions further up the grassy field, then the drabness of the dunes, then the bright colors, then the browns and beiges, one quickly following the other until they blurred together, the earthy complementing and underscoring the festive, the festive enhancing the earthy, a peace and a calmness in their mixing.

But as quickly as I'd been allowed on, I was flung off, as if even the person that I was was too slow, too weighed down to spin at that speed, too world-weary or too tainted to revolve at such a high rotation. I was thrown, the momentum of the ride carrying me fully back across the stream, the moisture in the air dissipating palpably as I flew. Finally, after what seemed like an age, I landed hard, rolling and bumping to a stop at the foot of the dunes. Seconds later my tiger's eye landed beside me with a small *thunk* and a tiny cloud of sandy dust.

I walk, again now, through this place, through the hot and the dry, unable to keep from looking back at that other world, at the small merry-go-round and the larger carousels beyond and I wonder what it was, what unknown custom had I offended. My fingers find the bits that still rest deep inside my cloak—feeling their smoothnesses, their brightnesses, their preciousnesses— knowing that, given the chance, each would find a place in that world, could be pressed into the walls of the larger rides to add their particular qualities to the glittering. And I long to step past the little merry-go-round that spat me out, to mount a prancing horse, a growling lion, or even a snarling tiger and hold fast to his gleaming pole, to move up and down, up and down, up and down and around and around while the cool clean rain patters all around the pavilion.

But here, on this side of the stream, my skin dries in the desert wind, sand rubs between my sandaled toes, my precious bits clatter together in my pocket and, as I trudge along, sifting them through my fingers, I am afraid.

♦

End

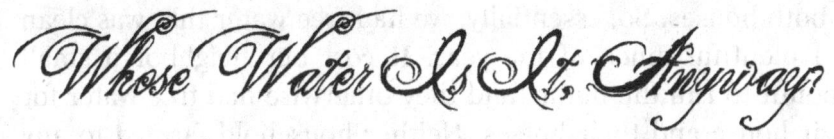

Whose Water Is It, Anyway?

[Whose Water Is It, Anyway?]

[Eileen Gunn]

I GREW UP IN THE 1950S in the United States, mostly in semi-rural small-town Massachusetts. We lived in a 160-year-old house and for water we depended on shallow wells dug many generations earlier in a field up behind the house. In late summer, the wells ran low and some years they went completely dry. The prelude to that, as I recall, was muddy orange water, not useful for drinking, cooking, or washing clothes, and, as I found out, for bathing: I came out of the bath orange, as you might expect. If the wells went dry, in early- or mid-August, there was no water at all. By September, with the arrival of the hurricane season, the water table refreshed, and we had water—maybe too much of it.

Having the wells dry up was an inconvenience, but it was not life-threatening. The township had deeper sources of water, and in drought conditions they made some of it available to those of us who did not have what we called "town water." We had a car to go get it, and I, as an eleven-year-old, did not have to spend hours every day fetching water for my family.

We were not worried that our water would make us sick, even though the well was only about twenty feet deep. It was uphill from local houses and septic systems, and the main risk was from horses stabled nearby, whose owner also depended on our wells and had the water tested from time to time. He also paid for and maintained an electric pump that moved the water to both houses. So, essentially, we had free water that was clean and plentiful much of the year. It cost our neighbor a small amount to run the pump, and they otherwise had free water for their house and their horses. Neither household farmed to any extent, and we were careful about our water usage in the summer. As far as I know, there was never a problem between us in any matter.

During the 1960s, Massachusetts went through an extensive drought, and our township laid pipes and extended water service to our part of town. There were times when the town water supply itself was at risk, and strict conservation rules were enforced. Most people obeyed the rules, and the town never completely ran out of water.

I now live on the opposite side of the country, in Seattle, a city with a relatively good supply of clean and tasty water, sourced directly from mountain lakes. The water department tests for chemical and biological contamination, and we users have no serious concerns there. But the availability of our water depends on the amount of snow the central Cascade mountains get every winter and on how quickly that snow melts in the spring and summer. If the snow melts too fast, it will flow furiously down our rivers, flood the lowlands, empty into Puget Sound, and be gone by August. During droughts, just as in Massachusetts, we have to conserve water usage and limit the amount of water that is used to bathe and water yards and gardens.

While I was working on this essay, a friend of mine from Zimbabwe came to visit Seattle. My friend is a farmer and beekeeper living in a country where access to safe drinking water (or even to farming water) is unreliable, in both the city and the rural areas. I asked him to tell me about the water situation there.

There is little residential water in Harare, he said, except among the wealthy, who can afford private wells. There are a million and a half people there. Most of them must go to communal wells or boreholes to draw water, and water from those sources is not safe to drink. The water infrastructure is pipes laid down seventy-five years ago, for a population one tenth of what it is now, and the treatment plants have neither capacity nor chemicals. The city water is drawn from a lake polluted by sewage and industrial waste, and when it comes out of the pipes, if it does, it is undrinkable and smells bad, because the city government cannot afford to purify it.

In the countryside, where there is no water infrastructure at all, people might dig ponds to access water, but livestock and other animals access the ponds as well, and the water is not safe to drink without treatment. Wells drilled into the aquifer, where the water is clean and safe to drink, are not common. My friend had a deep well drilled to water his farm. "I paid extra for them to drill a really deep hole, because the water table is receding," he said. "I wanted my neighbor and his family to have safe water too, so I had a pipe run out to his place to give him free direct access, and I asked him to use that water just for drinking and cooking. He agreed, but then I could tell he was using it for other things. I talked to him about it, and he said, 'Water belongs to everyone.'" My friend shook his head sadly. "I told him, 'Yes, I agree, the water belongs to everyone, but it was very expensive to have that well installed, and if the water table drops below the depth to which I drilled, none of us will have access to the water.' He would not agree to conserve. I could not trust him, so I had the pipe turned off. But I want them to have clean drinking water: his daughter has a young baby. So, they are still welcome to the water from my well: they are free to come and get it at my pipe, and they do."

My friend's conflict is a microcosm of what is happening

globally: clean water is hard to get, and it's problematic to share. During a drought, when the water table is dropping, it's difficult to trust others, and sometimes they are not actually worthy of trust—large agricultural and industrial operations even more so than other human beings. And yet it's hard for people of good will to deny water to their neighbors, and that is as it should be. Like air, water is essential: it should belong to everyone. (Readers of Oghenechovwe Donald Ekpeki's work will here be reminded of his short story "O_2 Arena," in which people must pay to breathe clean air.)

When I was a child, my family had the well and our neighbor had the pump, but neither of us owned the actual water, which came and went as it pleased. We were fortunate in several respects: that the water was reliably clean, that we trusted one another to use it sensibly, and that other resources were available when the well went dry. Drought was not a life-threatening situation: our town government provided some relief.

In most of the world, including in the United States, conflicts about water are not just between neighbors. Agriculture and industry, which are often transnational business entities, use huge amounts of water, and they are not necessarily good neighbors: runoff and waste from their enterprises pollute the clean waters around them. In the United States, there is a history of scarcity in the southwest and of unpotable water in cities such as Flint, Michigan and Jackson, Mississippi.

The seasonal water insecurity that I remember from my youth is trivial compared to what is happening in Africa and the Middle East. The problems globally are larger than local governments can handle, and, because of technology, climate change, and population growth, much more complex than they were fifty or a hundred years ago. And yet, people like my Zimbabwean friend can try to resolve conflicts in ways that do

not deny clean water to others. They agree that water, like air,
belongs to everyone.

♦

End

[Bayelsa, Water for All]
[Solomon Uhiara]

"I AM WATER. My children are the billions of droplets that descend from the skies unto my glassy eyes. I was made to provide succor for the children of God, the offspring of men. I am water. I am seventy percent of nature. I am life."

♦

Bayelsa is a state located in the South-South region of Nigeria, enriched with crude oil, natural gas, and fertile land for cultivation of agricultural produce.

It is ironical that several water bodies snake within and around the area, and some even channel into the great Atlantic, yet getting clean drinking water is like hitting a jackpot. The waters encircling the state are polluted by hydrocarbon discharge, chemicals swept into these water bodies by rain and annual floods, and overflows from oil spill sites. The harsh reality is that to acquire potable water in Bayelsa comes at a high cost; so, the important question is, how do the inhabitants access clean drinking water? Your guess is as good as mine. They purchase great volumes of water from water companies, whose products are sold in transparent sachets, disposable plastic bottles, cans, gallon containers, and even tankers.

There are several potential sources of potable water in Bayelsa, but there are challenges associated with their use:

(1) SURFACE WATER SOURCES

This incorporates water bodies such as streams, lakes, the seas, and oceans. But, of course, not all these water sources are drinkable. In past times, the streams in Bayelsa had countless visitors who depended on the water being colorless, odorless, tasteless, and preserved in its uncontaminated natural state. However, nature is not stagnant. There must be movement, and the changes can be positive or negative. We can only anticipate and yearn for the positive. But as postulated and proven over and over again, some of the challenges that cause shifts and imbalance in water bodies are propelled by artificial—manmade—dynamics. Every action has an equal and opposite reaction; in this case, enormous ripple effects accrue.

A challenge affecting the potability of surface water sources is that most water bodies have natural contamination, which makes it non-palatable for human consumption: contaminations such as salt, alkalis, and dusts. Oil and gas equipment failure along pipelines, and crude storage facilities with close proximity to rivers and streams, are additional reasons why potable surface water is scarce in most of Bayelsa's eight local governments (LGAs). When these natural chemicals continuously infiltrate surface water bodies, the natural compositions of those bodies are altered, poisoned: uncharted nature against charted nature, the bridge being humanity's inventions.

(2) UNDERGROUND WATER SOURCES

Due to the ripple effects of oil and gas mining activities and aquifer structures in Bayelsa, contaminants have now settled into the earth. But because there is a natural filtration process, contaminants are less present in aquifers. According to several surveys and analyses by researchers in the state and capital, the aquifers are naturally placed at shallow levels. This has resulted in their steadily being compromised, due to the settling of organic and inorganic infiltrations. Thus, if potable water is to be sourced from these aquifers, intensive treatment methods have to be deployed. This process is not rocket science, but the presence of chemicals such as iron, manganese, nickel, and zinc, as well as alkalis and acids that drive water's PH values beyond World Health Organization standards, pose challenges when sourcing potable water from underground. Are we saying clean water cannot be drawn from underground sources? No. But aquifers should be drilled to a depth of at least 50 to 80 meters, in order to reduce contamination by iron and other impurities to the barest minimum.

(3) RAINWATER

Precipitation rates in Bayelsa are the highest recorded in Nigeria. The tropical state has annual precipitation of 241.52 millimeters in approximately 296.16 days. But all this precipitation cannot be consumed directly; it must be collected, stored, and intensively treated in order to prevent adverse effects to the human system over time, particularly for those with depressed immune systems. These are the challenges. The universe is connected by visible and invisible threads magically, scientifically and naturally. What goes up must come down. If contaminated ground water and the toxic gases exposed during gas flaring evaporate, condense, and mix in atmospheric chemical reactions in the clouds, the impurities in the resulting precipitation have not been entirely lost. Residues of these reactions linger amongst the restructured clouds and return to the surface of the earth as contaminated rainfall, even though the contaminants are reduced in varying degrees. Gas flaring in the state and the Niger Delta region poses a great threat to the potability of precipitation. There are quite a number of flow station operations (sites that measure and control the oil and gas passing through pipelines), illegal crude oil fractional distillation sites, and instances of bush burning, all of which creates particulate matter that goes up and saturates the clouds. This alters the atmosphere and cloud structures. The resulting precipitation is full of accumulated nitric acid—what we know as acid rain. Obviously, the inhabitants do not drink it (Ezenwaji 102).

These potential sources of potable water, and the challenges associated with them, are well spread across Bayelsa's LGAs. There may be some variations from region to region, but they all share similar conditions and associated problems, and the impact is the same.

EFFORTS OF THE STATE GOVERNMENT

On January 16, 2017, Bayelsa's state government partnered with representatives of the European Union, UNICEF, and the World Bank—international organizations notable for spearheading humanitarian intervention programs—on a substantial project to aid the funding of production of potable water in over 200

71

communities in the state. In 2018, the state government, in a bid to expand these projects into more communities, including the town of Ovum, partnered with the European Union representatives, who presented a drilling machine to the Bayelsa government.

REASONS WHY THESE EFFORTS ARE LAGGING

(1) One of the silent reasons behind the lagging efforts of government-created water boards is the inconsistent power supply. The machines and equipment need to be in constant operation, but in Bayelsa, almost all the existing water board sectors have failed to function adequately because they do not have uninterrupted electrical power. Without power, the pumps cannot function; water cannot be distributed; residents cannot have water directly in their homes. Ensure that power is steady, and half of the water issue is solved.

(2) As of the time of writing this piece, there are road construction projects ongoing in several parts of the state. These roads cut across communities, disrupting previously laid piping connections. Gigantic heavy-duty construction machines have hence cut off the flow of potable water.

(3) To achieve the dream of a sustainable drinking water production scheme for the inhabitants of Bayelsa state, the area needs adequate funding, but astronomic inflation makes it virtually impossible to estimate what such a water provision system will cost, despite its value to the homes and communities of Bayelsa.

SOLUTION TO SCARCITY OF WATER IN BAYELSA

In-depth, on-ground analysis has to be conducted, and all vital areas aligned and updated. All the loopholes must be closed, and the voids filled, to present a grand design of a massive working system that can comfortably generate pure potable water for the people at a regulated, affordable cost.

The establishment of a working and sustainable water board begins with the design process. The focus will be underground water sources: not the shallow aquifers, but the down-deep aquifers, where contaminants are at their lowest levels, and where potable water flourishes in abundance, waiting to be tapped. Penetrating these deep aquifers demands the use of very effective drilling machines. These machines are not cheap, but it is important to fast track the implementation of water production for the people. For the eight LGAs in Bayelsa, one or two aquifers can be drilled based on their varying populations, in central accessible locations, where distribution will not be an impossible feat.

The next phase will be installation of hybrid pumps which can pull the potable water from the deep aquifers to the surface, at the required pressure and speed. This will depend on appropriate calculations, both before and during the project.

And of course, pumps will work only with a power supply. Depending solely on the power from the national electrical grid would set back the progress of the operation. To maintain continuous potable water production, the governments of the eight LGAs will use gas turbines to produce power to drive the water pumps. For this, gas must be available. Since Bayelsa state has an abundant supply of natural gas, gas cylinders can be conveyed to all the LGAs where the turbine pumps will be in operation. The transportation from the source to the supply points can be done using trucks. This method will be low-cost and effective.

Storage facilities are another link in the system's chain. Once the potable water has been drawn from the wells that penetrate the aquifers, a storage structure is needed. The United Nations and World Health Organization have specific standards for storage structure construction, and it is advisable that such modern and innovative standards be met, based on the current populations and projected population increases in the region. Overhead tanks of concrete and metal should be constructed in close proximity to the pumping machines, so their contents can be easily distributed. For an additional level of safety, a treatment unit can also be attached to the water storage facility. In order to further screen the water against alien contaminants that may find their way into the storage facility, water input and output can be measured, regulated, and treated if the need arises.

The UN standard of water consumption per average person is 50 litres to 100 litres every day ("Global Issues: Water"). This fact should be closely considered when constructing a reinforced overhead water tank.

Bayelsa's total population is estimated to be between 2.7 million and 2.8 million people. The populations of each LGA are estimated as follows:

Yenagoa: 524, 400
Southern Ijaw: 479,000
Ekeremor: 401,300
Sagbama: 278,200
Brass: 274,100
Ogbia: 267,400
Nembe: 195,000
Kolokuma/Opukuma: 118,000

THE WATER DEMAND FOR EACH LGA

To assess the water demand and determine the required supply for each local government area, a water demand calculator can be deployed. The formula for calculating water demand is as follows:

ADD = LPC D x P+ 10%
where
ADD = Average Daily Water Demand
LPCD = Liters Per Capita Per Day
P = Population Size (Syrek)

To find the average daily water demand of one of the local government areas, we plug in the estimated population of the LGA and the water consumption of an average Bayelsan per day and we will get the following results.

1. LGA: Brass
Brass ADD = LPCD x P + (10% of the population)
LPCD = 50 liters
P =274,100 (Brinkhoff, "Brass ")
Brass ADD = 50 x 274,100 + (10% of 274,100)
=50 x 274,100 + 27,410
=13,705,000 + 27,410
Brass ADD = 13,732,410 liters of potable water per day

2. LGA: Yenagoa
Yenagoa ADD = LPCD x P + (10% of the population)
LPCD = 50 liters
P = 524,400 (Brinkhoff, "Yenagoa ")
Yenagoa ADD = 50 x 524,400 + (10% of 524,400)
= 50 x 524,400 + (52,400)
= 26,220,000 + 52,400
Yenagoa ADD = 26,272,400 liters of potable water per day

To find the average daily water demand of each LGA, the same formula can be used, plugging in the different population values.

For each LGA to have enough potable water to serve every person's domestic use, reinforced storage tanks that can carry the calculated average daily water demand should be located in strategic areas.

SOME WATER DISTRIBUTION MODES /SIMULATION

In Yenagoa LGA, for example, it will be advisable to plant two high-capacity storage systems. Why?

Yenagoa has the highest population compared to the other LGAs, and its calculated average water demand is 26,272,400 liters per day. With the decentralization of aquifers and storage systems of equal capacities positioned at central locations, regulated flows can be evenly distributed to other communities within the LGA.

The same formation can be replicated in Ogbia LGA, with its high population. Two strategic locations can house the water projects. Ogbia Town and Otuaka can serve as central locations for drilling of aquifers and construction of storage and piping facilities that will branch out towards neighboring contours. Potable water can be piped from Ogbia Town to the communities of Obibio Island, Akalabaga, Ekpenkia, Ibobo, Agudama, Ibobio, Okodugu, Ekpeinbim and Akulabin. The second central location at Otuaka can convey water, via underground pipes, to Ewoi, Anyama, Alagba, Agbura, Elebele, Imiringi, Opkolo, Oteglia,and Otuesega.

Those communities that can be accessed by roads will have pipes run along the roadway, some meters away from the tarmac, to avoid future encroachment into the lines. Other pipes will reach communities by running over the surfaces of bodies of water.

A further consideration is that bodies of water are used for transportation of persons and goods. Pipes that run above the water should have detachable junctions, so that they can be uncoupled and recoupled at stipulated times of the day and night, allowing these water bodies to seamless convey goods, travellers, and potable water.

With this same approach, water distribution can be replicated in the state's other seven LGAs, so more potable water can be accessed by the rich, the poor, and the middle class.

AN EXAMPLE OF A WATER UNIT

To keep the water unit fully operational, personnel have to be on ground, at all stations. This will ensure the longevity of equipment and the functionality of the systems and processes, and create employment for qualified persons. A water unit might employ the following personnel:

1. A Supervisor will oversee and manage the activities of the entire water station.

2. A Technician will monitor equipment efficiency, service pumps, gas turbines and other mechanical and electrical equipment that keeps the station operational. The technician's job includes maintenance and machine repairs.

3. A Water Treatment Officer investigates and monitors the storage facility and inlet valves for any form of external contamination, sets up filtration sequences, and treats the water if the need arises.

HOW CAN FUNDING FOR THESE PROJECTS BE GENERATED?

This is where humanitarian organizations come in: the US Agency for International Development, the Economic Community of West African States, the African Union, the World Bank, the United Nations, the World Health Organization, religious organizations, and volunteer groups can help sponsor Bayelsa-Water for All.

To ensure that the project is sustainable and efficient, privatization of every aspect of the project—placing it in the hands of the private and corporate organizations, volunteers, and companies that are well-grounded in water production processes—may be a game-changer. This new Bayelsa water system should be corruption-free, to avoid any diversion of funds, incompetence, or use of inferior materials. The proposed water project should stand the test of time, and not collect dust.

With so many capable hands joined together to promote, fund and execute this very necessary water project, it is poised to transform the lives of the citizens of Bayelsa.

[Works Cited and Consulted]

Brinkhoff, Thomas. "Yenagoa." *City Population*,
    https://citypopulation.de/en/nigeria/admin/bayelsa/NGA006008
    __yenagoa/. Last updated August 23, 2022.
Brinkhoff, Thomas. "Brass." *City Population*,
    https://www.citypopulation.de/en/nigeria/admin/bayelsa/NGA00
    6001__brass/. Last updated August 23, 2022.
Davies, Kalango Stanley. Interview. Conducted by Solomon Uhiara,
    Bayelsa, 2023.
Ezenwaji, E.E. et al. "Effects of Gas Flaring on Rainwater Quality in
    Bayelsa State, Eastern Niger-Delta Region, Nigeria." *Journal of
    Toxicology and Environmental Health Sciences* vol. 5, no. 6. 2013,
    pp. 97-105
"Global Issues: Water." *United Nations*,
    https://www.un.org/en/global-issues/water. Accessed August 28,

2024.

Syrek, Agnieszka. "Water Demand Calculator." *Omnicalculator*, https://www.omnicalculator.com/ecology/water-demand#water-demand-formula. Last updated July 30, 2024.

◊

End

Miriam After the Flood

[Miriam After the Flood]
[F. Brett Cox]

ON THE SECOND DAY after the second hundred-year flood in twelve years, while going through a sodden pile of scrap, Miriam found an empty picture frame. The pile was from one of Montpelier's not-quite-antique-but-something-more-than-thrift stores, whose inventory had included a wooden crate of empty picture frames, placed between the end table stacked with period postcards and the washboard draped with jewelry. Like most of the stores downtown, and all of them here on Langdon Street, it now lay wrecked and stinking beneath the July sun that had shown up two days too late. Miriam was there with everyone else to do her part, to pitch in, Vermont Strong, etc. She didn't dare tell anyone how it had been almost impossible to get out of bed this morning, knowing what lay outside beneath her thank-God second story window, knowing what was expected of her.

But the frame was merely damp instead of soaked. Its dark wood glistened in the sunlight. It was whole. Miriam laid it aside, used her bare arm to mop her brow—stopping well before her already disgusting gloves touched her head—and went back to work.

The two people working beside her were chatting amiably; the woman on the other side of them was whistling a happy tune. The anger surged—what were they all so goddamned cheerful about?—but Miriam paused and took some structured breaths. In, count to four; hold, count to seven; out, count to eight; repeat four times. Let them chat. Let her whistle. Whatever gets you through the day, and the night, and the day after that.

"Would you like some water?"

Miriam looked up. A young man stood over her. The backpack he shouldered was bulging with water bottles, and he offered her one. She thought she recognized him, vaguely. Maybe wait staff at Sarducci's? Live even briefly in the nation's smallest state capitol, and pretty soon you recognized everyone, vaguely. Despite its perch directly on the river, Sarducci's had remained largely unscathed, thanks to its elevation and its fortress of a basement. So this guy could devote his energies to more at-large support. Miriam took the proffered water bottle, thanked him, and downed half of it in three swallows. She chose not to dwell on the cognitive dissonance of anything to do with water, or with passing out yet more plastic to ruin some more of the already ruined world.

Except that accumulating plastic was a different issue from climate change. Or was it? There was so much that was so wrong she couldn't keep it all straight. The corporate media were always corporately careful to point out that climate change itself was not directly causing more storms, but was, probably, contributing to their increased severity. Whatever. All Miriam knew was that the flooding that came with tropical storm Irene twelve years ago (and a "tropical" storm in Vermont? Really?) had chewed up much of the state and spit it back out. Seven dead and a billion dollars. No reported casualties yet, and the Wrightsville Dam had held so far. But the day after you could paddle a kayak down Main Street, and some people had done just that, and here she was mucking out a stranger's store. There was just nowhere for the water to go.

She took another swallow, set the bottle carefully beside her, and promised herself she wouldn't just leave it there with the rest of the scrap. At least that fool had quit whistling.

Around noon a few diligent types kept on working, but most of the people along the street stopped as if there had been a factory whistle. Some produced energy bars, others settled for whatever was in the bottles hooked to their belts, but there was general movement around the corner to Main Street, where there had been a food truck earlier in the morning. She followed the crowd and saw that the truck was still there. People were already starting to line up. She joined them.

She was almost relieved to see how many people looked like she felt: stunned and lost and beyond processing what had happened. But there were still some who were acting inexplicably social, chatting away, even laughing. The sound and the feel of them was suddenly familiar, and for a moment she could have been back in Alabama, tailgating before the big game. Then she made the mistake of breathing through her nose, and the damp rot of the flooded town brought her back to right where she was, and what she heard was not point spreads and bowl prospects, but where-were-you-when-the-flood-hit, and any laughter came with a shake of the head and a shrug of the shoulders: what're you going to do?

"Hey Miri!"

Her ex-neighbor Lakesha, moving away from the food truck window, holding something wrapped and something else in a paper cup. She had lived downstairs until two months ago when she had told her boyfriend to put up or shut up. He responded by asking Lakesha to live with him, and she had moved to his place on a hill outside Northfield. Miriam didn't believe in prescience, but she acknowledged the reality of luck.

Lakesha waved her toward a spot on the still-damp sidewalk. Miriam got to the truck window, picked up her wrapped and cupped lunch from the grandmotherly volunteer behind the counter—somebody was paying for it, but not Miriam; she hoped it was all of their taxes—and joined her.

Immediately: Where-were-you-when-the-flood-hit? Northfield, ten miles to the south, had sustained minimal damage, and Lakesha and her boyfriend (whose name Miriam simply could
not remember, so much so that she wondered if she had ever known it) had been safe on their hill. All the more reason, Lakesha explained, why she felt obligated to come back and help.

"But what about you?" Lakesha asked between bites of what looked like a leftover breakfast burrito. "Good thing you were upstairs, but it must have been rough."

What about her? Paralyzed by the window looking down on the street, watching the rain pour down and the water rise, and rise, and rise some more, lapping over the cars like waves on a beach. Strategically placing her single flashlight on the kitchen table after the power went out but sitting in darkness, hoarding the battery because she didn't have any candles. Sounds in the hallway. Sticking her head tentatively out the door. The guy who had moved into Lakesha's apartment, soaked to the waist: "The basement's gone." A few useless hours of sleep, then daylight, sort of, beneath a ceiling of clouds. Two people paddling down Main Street through the water that now covered the cars. At that moment the world had ended and she had no vision of its ever starting again.

Miriam swallowed a bite of her own burrito and washed it down with the flat soda in the cup. "It could have been worse."

"By the way, what's with the frame?"

Miriam looked down and realized that she had carried the empty picture frame with her on her lunch break. She had no memory of doing that. "It was in the pile I was going through from Marcel's. It just caught my eye."

"Looter," Lakesha said, and they both laughed.

Miriam was glad for Lakesha's company. They had met on the job, working for a nonprofit that no longer existed but had lasted long enough to give Miriam her long-sought ticket out of Alabama. They had immediately bonded over their shared southern expat status—Lakesha from Atlanta, Miriam from Daphne, Alabama, a small town outside Mobile that was still bigger than Montpelier—and their shared amazement at the degree to which the whiteness of Vermont was not just the snow. At least Lakesha could go to Burlington and find a few other Black people. To be from Miriam's part of Alabama was to have a reasonable chance of Creek ancestry, which in her case meant her maternal grandmother and paternal grandfather. But Indigenous people were almost nowhere to be found up here, the state's self-congratulatory embrace of the Abenaki notwithstanding. Lakesha had once had an English professor whose approach to *Moby Dick* was to intone "the whiteness of the whale" at least once per class, so pretty soon all they had to do to break themselves up was to say "the whiteness of the state," and for at least a moment they could forget that what they were laughing about wasn't funny.

When Lakesha moved to Northfield, Miriam did what she usually did when she lost something, which was to deny that she'd ever had it in the first place. That had been working up to now, but seeing her again, sitting here talking with her about unimportant things, it stopped working, and she had to put one more item in the loss column.

They finished their lunch and swore they'd be in touch and even managed another laugh as they made a big deal of their mutual sincerity—no y'all-come-see-us-sometime southern duplicity for them. They confirmed their phone numbers and hugged. Through the sweat and the greasy residue of mucking out the town, Lakesha still smelled good.

Five hours later—her arms a ton apiece, her knees beyond

salvage, every muscle aching, her thirst unquenchable despite a return visit from Sarducci's good Samaritan—the pile of debris seemed barely smaller than it had been that morning. Miriam told herself her weariness impaired her perception, and she chose to believe she had made substantial progress. Others were starting to drift away, home to another very dark night—but they probably had plenty of candles.

The two blocks back to Miriam's apartment seemed much longer, and the empty frame she carried unnaturally heavy. She trudged up the stairs to her apartment—would there ever be elevators again?—and collapsed on the mini-sofa that was, with her bed, about as much large furniture as her studio apartment would tolerate. She was convinced she would never move again and was surprised when she finally did get up and her phone told her she had been home less than an hour.

There was no telling when the water would be back on, so she went for the wipes that had mercifully been on her shopping list the day before it started raining. She wouldn't want to put up too long with the mixed odor of flood rot and lanolin that resulted, but it was tolerable for now. The water would come back on eventually. Wouldn't it?

She was still pretty full from the burrito, or whatever it was, so chips and a room-temperature beer was enough for dinner. Good thing, because that's all she had. She indulged herself with the thought that she was connected to history. Hadn't the popularity of beer been linked to the lack of potable water? Let's go with that.

Miriam returned to the sofa and looked out the window. She had leaned the picture frame against the bookcase she was determined to keep always full but never overflowing. She stared at the frame, trying, and for now failing, to understand why she had picked it out of that pile, kept it at hand all day, and hauled it back to her apartment. She didn't need it. She didn't have any pictures to put in it. She'd never much cared what, if anything, hung on her walls, an indifference that baffled every roommate she'd ever had. Why this thing, here, now?

As she stared at the frame, something else nagged at her. Then she remembered. Shit. The water bottles. She had gone through at least two while she was working, and she had sworn she'd carry them away, but she hadn't. She'd just left the fucking things right there. Just added to the pile.

The force of her wail, and the volume of her tears, startled her as much as anything else that had happened in the past forty-eight hours. It was only a couple of water bottles. Not even big ones. Nothing to shed tears over. The flood had cost people their businesses, their homes. There was already talk of exploring long-term plans for relocating the entire town rather than have something like this happen again. Crying over a small mistake? What was wrong with her?

My life has been nothing but a series of small mistakes.

No. We're not going there.

Miriam wiped her eyes and blew her nose and did her structured breathing. Four, seven, eight. Four times. She did it twice.

The sun was beginning to set. Normally the eastern view out her window treated her to late afternoon light that was sharp and soft all at once, but the clouds still cast everything in monochrome. There were beginning to be some breaks in the cloud cover, but the sky behind them looked blank.

Miriam went to the junk box that had wound up living underneath her bed and came back with a roll of twine. She tied it around one corner of the frame, looped it through the hook above the window that sometimes held a small planter but right now did not, tied it to the other corner, and hung the frame in the window.

Her aunt May, her mother's oldest sister, had been the one

member of that side of the family that had made any kind of a deal about their heritage. Aunt May gave the usual range of gifts every Christmas, but Miriam's gift was always accompanied by a dreamcatcher, the netted wooden hoop that was supposed to either keep the spirits at bay or invite them in, Miriam had never been sure which. A different design every year. The hoops had always been pretty, and Miriam loved her aunt, so she dutifully hung them.

Aunt May died just before Miriam moved to Vermont, and the dreamcatchers wound up in a box that stayed in Alabama. She wondered where that box was as she looked through the frame at the street below and the town beyond it.

She stared, and tried to regulate her breathing again, but that would require thought, and she didn't want to think. She stared through the frame and tried to see something that was not there, anything beyond the soggy ruins of where she was right now.

Miriam might have stared until full dark, but suddenly the street lights came on, and a moment later the smoke alarm in her apartment beeped, and there was light in her bathroom and by her bed. The window was closed but she could hear people cheering and applauding in the street below.

She walked over to her kitchen sink and turned on the tap. It shuddered and burped like it was going to throw up, and then a thick brown liquid oozed out. Eventually what poured out was recognizable as water.

She took a picture of the empty frame hanging in her window and sent it to Lakesha with the question, *What do YOU see?*

Miriam decided she would try to hold on to how she felt right now and file it away for future use. That came in handy three months later when the next storm came, this time with wind gusts that sent flying the sandwich-board ads outside the restaurants that had just reopened, and whipped the water that lapped at her ankles as she walked down the street.

◆

End

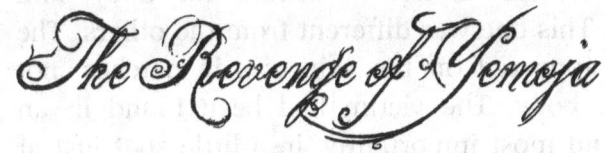

[The Revenge of Yemoja]

[Wuraola Kayode]

BOLA STORMED UP THE STAIRS through the swarm of police that had gathered to keep the press out. Apart from the press, many others had already heard the news and were terming it the revenge of Yemoja. The goddess of the seas coming on dry land to murder five, now six people? It couldn't be possible.

She pushed past the last of the police tape to meet the gruesome sight in the living room of the apartment. She was expecting the same thing as with the other five bodies they had found: a blackened body laid out peacefully as if in jest. This time though, the body wasn't fully blackened, and it was not laid out in a peaceful position.

A man, a plainclothes detective like herself, strode towards her. He grinned as he spoke. "He was found just like this, face forward, hand gripping the phone and blood under his hands. Everyone left the scene just as we found it, Detective."

"Wipe that smile off your face, Toni; there is another dead body and we're no closer to solving this case."

Toni snorted. "I thought you knew me better by now. Take a closer look at the body."

Bola knelt slowly, careful not to disturb the body, and inspected the neck. This one was different from the others. The black that usually appeared on the skin was in patches, not covering the entire body. The victim had been found in an agitated position, and most importantly, in a little spot just at the neck, the skin was elevated.

Bola turned, "He was injected!"

Toni nodded, his smile getting wider. "Exactly! This is definitely now the work of a human and not a goddess. Someone came here to attack him, not dry his skin with supernatural powers. Something went wrong this time, as the deed was not completed successfully."

"Do we have any idea of what was injected?" Bola's mind was racing. Finally, they had a break in the case.

"We need to send the body in for an autopsy. The victim is John Ogunro; he is unmarried and lives alone. We haven't found any information on a next of kin just yet; so, we can proceed with an autopsy, unlike the other cases."

Bola's gaze swept over the body once again. Not only was the body in an agitated position, but the position was also unnatural for a man of his size. She sat suddenly on the floor.

Toni enjoyed watching her get to work. They had been partners for six years, and while they hadn't gotten along in the first year, a near-death experience ending with his saving Bola's life by almost losing his, had endeared Toni to her. No matter how prickly she was outwardly, she cared for him, and she had shown it in the years they had worked together.

Bola was smart, motivated and liked well enough. Big-brained, she was moving fast through the ranks as a rising detective, and Toni loved working on cases with her. A 60% solved case rate was amazing on the force, and it was only some time before she cracked this case as well.

"Take a look at his knees," she directed. Toni obliged. "He is a large man. If he was falling down, I doubt he would land so heavily on his knees unless he wanted to fracture them. Perhaps his legs gave way?" Toni said nothing. Most of Bola's questions were rhetorical unless she looked up as she spoke. "Let's have the lab screen for toxins but also for natural components in the body that appear higher than normal."

She stood quickly and walked around the apartment, her eyes darting over each piece of furniture. She bent low and looked under the tables, stretched high and trailed her gloved hands on the desks. "Any fingerprints?" Toni shook his head. "Any other blood found in the apartment other than the blood on his hands?"

Toni's eyes widened. "You don't think...he nicked his assailant?"

Bola was nodding. "He didn't go down without a fight. Get the lab to carefully swab and check if the blood is a match in the database. Maybe we'll be lucky and something will pop up." Toni relayed the information to the lab techs.

This was the most they had gotten so far at any of the crime scenes. The first victim was Miss Fola Akinwunmi, member of the school board for district ten in Boni province. The second victim was a Mr. Gomino Saud, an accountant. His wife had refused an autopsy. The third was Mrs. Solabunmi Richard, a politician found dead by her husband, who had also refused an autopsy. The fourth and fifth were Mrs. Kiki Lanu and Mr. Robert, found together at a hotel, clearly married and not to each other, but still found wrapped together. Their spouses had wanted the situation hushed up. Mrs. Kiki was a prominent lawyer, and Mr. Robert was a school principal within district 10 Boni province. Nothing tied all the victims together, apart from the way they died. The families wanted everything private, and the court refused to grant any warrants because the police had no leads. The case had been hopeless just moments ago, but Mr.

John had fought back, and now hope was on their side.

Toni was back. "You have an idea. I can hear the wheels of your head grinding and turning. Say it and don't go running off without me."

Bola laughed. "I'm with you, partner; we're solving this together. I found it curious that despite the severe state of dehydration of the bodies we found, they were never contorted in pain. No one can stay still when they're in pain, unless they can't move. With that mark on the skin, that proves that something was indeed injected. No nicks were found on the other bodies because they were too blackened for us to distinguish ante-mortem injuries, or perhaps because they had ingested the substance that paralyzed them. Mr. John is huge. Perhaps the substance didn't work as fast as the assailant hoped, and they panicked and tried injecting it. Mr. John was still capable of crawling and attacked the assailant with his nails, clawing violently. In order to escape, the assailant tosses the second burning substance on him and flees. Mr. John realizes he is about to die and calls for help before succumbing to his injuries."

Toni burst out laughing. "You're amazing Bola, did you know?"

Bola swept her eyes downward. "We need to question the witnesses."

Crime scenes were always filled with a variety of people. Those who wanted to talk and had some knowledge of the facts, those who knew nothing at all, and those who knew a lot but were annoyed by the disruption to their day. The latter wanted to talk but they needed some form of encouragement.

All the residents of John Ogunro's complex had been gathered together but placed separately to prevent their talking to each other. There were about fifty people, and it was necessary to speak with all of them before the day ended, while all the information was fresh.

She squared her shoulders, "So Mrs..." She glanced at the sheet of paper where all the names were written. "...Ogundide, what can you tell me about Mr. John Ogunro?"

All the testimonials were the same. Mr. John Ogunro worked in the tax sector. He kept to himself. He was not well liked, he had a nasty temper, he often came home drunk and made a lot of noise. His neighbors kept away from him, and no one was suggesting anything special or interesting until Bola spoke to Miss Tinuade Wale.

Miss Tinuade had small lips that she pressed to make them even smaller. Her eyebrows pinched together, and she sat extremely still.

"John? There's nothing much to say. He was an insufferable man." Her lips drew tighter together.

"Did you spend a lot of time with him?"

Miss Tinuade sniffed. "Hardly that much time if you think about it." It was obvious that she wanted to talk; she just wanted some coaxing.

Bola said, "If you have nothing to say...perhaps we should call in another resident?"

Displeasure spread across her face. "We didn't spend much time together anymore. We had been seeing each other for a year, and then one day, he ended the relationship. Claimed he had left me behind; he was on another level and he needed a much wealthier woman." She huffed and rolled her eyes. "I wouldn't have believed his nonsense if I hadn't seen it with my own eyes. I was crying over the breakup and wallowing in terrible news; it was that time all those schoolchildren died. I remember because of how terrible I felt hearing such news at such a devastating time for me. Then, I hear a loud noise, and it's John driving in with a new car! Next thing I know, he is having parties and hanging out with the likes of millionaire Akoko! It was the worst period of my life. But looking at how things turned out now, all's well that ends well."

Bola wasn't so sure she liked Miss Tinuade anymore, but she had been useful. "Right; well, thanks for all your help, Miss Tinuade."

No other interviews brought up any important information. The next course of action was clear. She talked it through with Toni. "A government tax accountant spending time with Mr. Akoko, the millionaire? That's not something you see every day. We need to speak with him."

Mr. Akoko, Jr. had made his money from manufacturing. Growing up in District 10, he had a close connection to the people and he had been responsible for a lot of goodwill, sponsorships and scholarships. Many people looked up to him, and he made himself very available. It wasn't too hard to set up a meeting with him.

He welcomed Bola and Toni into his office. He was tall, even taller than John Ogunro. He had a booming voice, and his teeth were unnervingly white as he smiled. They stood out against his skin unnaturally. Bola shivered into the seat he offered her.

"Well, it is not every day I can welcome two of District 10's finest officers into my office. What can I do for you?"

Bola sat back and let Toni take the lead. He dealt better with people who saw themselves as important. He knew how to stroke an ego appropriately.

"Well, Mr. Akoko, do you know Mr. John Ogunro?"

Mr Akoko's expression didn't waver. "Of course. Nice chap. Big and burly, too. What's the problem?"

Toni paused and took a breath. Bola resisted the urge to roll her eyes. "We're sorry to inform you, but he was found dead in his apartment the day before yesterday morning."

This time, Mr. Akoko's face fell. His voice was barely a whisper, "How was he killed?"

Without missing a beat, Toni said, "We didn't say he was killed sir. Just that he was found dead."

Mr. Akoko wrung his arms. "Well, why else would the police be in my office? Not to tell me he died peacefully, of course."

Toni ignored the quip. "We are looking into his associates. We heard a report that you were friendly with him and often attended some loud parties?"

Mr. Akoko chuckled softly, but his heart wasn't in it. It was a weak chuckle. "Well, it was just once or twice. I enjoy a good party."

Bola stood to scan the room. This was their technique, and it usually worked. People panicked thinking about any incriminating items they left in their personal spaces, and ended up spilling too much to Toni.

Mr. Akoko's office was huge, so Bola took her time walking through it. She had once admired Mr. Akoko. Then she joined the police force and learned that human beings were terrible, and could be even more terrible when they had a lot of money. The scales had fallen from her eyes, and she had grown disillusioned with the lot. What she did know now was that Mr. Akoko was entwined with the case, and she would figure out how.

Her gaze caught a picture, and she grabbed it immediately. It was of a young Mr. Akoko with his teammates on the basketball court. Bola's lips parted as she stared at the man beside Mr. Akoko. It was a young John Ogunro.

Without wasting a moment, she called out, "Did you attend secondary school with Mr. John Ogunro?"

Caught off guard, Mr. Akoko was speechless.

He leaped and stretched to snatch the photo, but Bola stepped back in time. "Careful now. I'm stronger than I look, and you don't want to get arrested for assaulting a detective."

Mr. Akoko held out his hands in surrender. "I went to school with John, but we weren't very close. We reconnected not too long ago. That's it."

Bola didn't buy it. "If I'm not mistaken, this is a young Mr. Gomino as well. Did you attend school with all the victims?" This time, Mr. Akoko didn't answer.

"Mr Akoko, you had previous relationships with at least two of the victims and you've just lied to our faces about it. Tell me, did you have any recent disagreements with Mr John Ogunro? Can you account for your whereabouts last night?"

Mr. Akoko went red as a tomato. He snatched the photo away and roared, "How dare you! I invited you into my office as a courtesy to the police and you turn around to accuse me of murder? Get out!"

It was exactly what Bola expected, and they exited without protesting, saying they would be back.

Toni kicked at the earth. "Try to be a little less heavy-handed with your accusations? We could have gotten more out of him."

"We don't need more out of him that we can't get with a warrant. The picture establishes a previous connection with the victims and we can get their school records unsealed because we have reasonable cause that we can find a connection with the murderer there. We need those lab techs right now." Her phone rang. "Just in time."

District 10 was a small district. It fell behind the other districts in many areas. It was for the less privileged, and it showed. The streets weren't taken care of; the roads were filled with potholes. There were hardly any street lights. Children lay in the streets covered in rashes, with severe fevers. People were on the corners waiting to attack. Still, it was home to many.

Bola leaned against the door and spat. The stink from the drains hung around in the air and assaulted her nose. She and Toni hurried into the police lab. The phone call had been from the lead technician calling with great news about the murders.

The suspicion surrounding toxins had allowed for a court order demanding the release of the bodies of the previous victims.

The lead technician, Mr. Kunle Ward, waved them over and displayed his findings on the table.

"You were right, Bola. The victims all had high levels of potassium. Nothing much was out of the ordinary regarding Mr. Ogunro's bloodwork, but he did die from a cardiac arrest. As did the others. The chemical on the skin wasn't the cause of death. I am now 90% sure that the paralytic substance is potassium chloride. Their hearts spasmed furiously until they died."

He turned the papers over. "The poured chemical was a bit more difficult. The skin was black as if all moisture had been sucked out. The degree of burns could be caused by a variety of things, but given the speed with which his skin reacted, it could be sulfuric acid. Drain cleaners or battery acid are commonly used chemicals that contain sulfuric acid. This version was highly concentrated, so it would have been very painful."

Bola asked, "Is it possible that the assailant could have gotten some on themselves while attacking Mr. Ogunro?"

The technician nodded. "Mr. Ogunro was huge. The angles of spilling on his skin are more defensive, downward and erratic. The assailant would likely be suffering some burns as well."

Toni interjected. "Any information on the blood?"

"It didn't match any of our records for now."

They needed that blood. It was a simple way to identify the attacker, but they couldn't find a match. Bola wracked her brain. So far, the only thing tying all the victims together was District 10 and the school they had all attended. Miss Tinuade had also mentioned a school when recounting the change in Mr. Ogunro. Something about the school was important. They were so close; they just had to figure out what the missing link was.

"Try checking the database for school officials and teachers both present and past for the school in Boni District 10," she said. "Someone with a personal vendetta against them could have attended the same school, and could have been working there before the school got shut down. We need to check out some of the stores in that area and find out if anyone has been purchasing large quantities of drain cleaner or battery acid."

Hours later, they had driven to five stores, but none of them had any unusual charges in their accounts of excess amounts of drainage cleaners and battery acid. Their logbooks of sales were balanced, and everything looked clean. Also, none of the storeowners remembered any suspicious figure trying to buy up any noteworthy items. Without CCTV in many of these shops, they had to trust that the owners weren't lying.

Toni was at the wheel, and Bola lay in the passenger's seat with her head thrown back.

Toni glanced sideways, He opened his mouth, but then shut it and shook his head. He did this several times, until Bola's voice cut through the silence. "What?"

"It's been some days since the Ogunro incident, and I think you're realizing that this might have something to do with all those children dying from typhoid all at once. Something is shady about the connections the victims had with Mr. Akoko. Are you okay? I know it must be hard to come so close to the disease again after what happened with your family." When Bola said nothing, Toni continued, "If you need to take a step back, just say the word. I've got your back."

Bola spat, "I'm fine. I don't need to wallow in my feelings. We have a case to solve. Let's solve it."

Her tone was final, and Toni dropped it.

He parked at Siesta and Sons, and they got out. It was a small shop, a little rundown but still standing strong. There was an older man at the counter. A much younger man who looked like his son had his headphones stuck in his ears, ignoring everything around him.

"We're detectives from District 10 Boni." Toni flashed his badge. "We have a warrant to search your log books; hand them over, please."

The old man grunted. "Why would you need my log books? This is a private business, not a government-run facility."

Bola slammed the warrant on the desk. "That's why we have the warrant. Inspect it and hand over your logbooks."

The man grunted again and laid his logbook on the table.

Bola flipped through and frowned. "You barely had any sales last month? And the month before that? You stopped making many sales six months ago. Can you explain the sudden drop in your sales? It's unexpected."

The man grumbled, "I guess people just don't want to come into the store."

Bola squinted. "Show me your supply of goods."

Despite the reported lack of sales, the supply room had ample goods with a large quantity and variety of drain cleaners.

"Explain yourself. Who has been ordering these?"

The man shook his head.

"Sir," Toni pleaded, "you could be arrested for obstructing an investigation. Someone paid you and asked you to order these large quantities of drain cleaner. Just tell us who it is."

The man shook his head once again.

Bola slammed the handcuff over his hands and led him away from the supply room. She was still reading him his rights when the son shouted, "STOP! Let him go, please." Tears streaked down the poor boy's face.

"I can't," Bola said. "He is refusing to cooperate with an active investigation."

"I know who ordered the cleaners. Just let him go. Please."

Bola stopped in her tracks.

The old man screamed, "No! Don't say another word."

His son ignored him. "She comes in very late at night to

order it. She always wears a shawl over her head and she walks with a recognizable limp. She wears dull colors all the time, and she stands so still it looks like she has blended into the walls. She doesn't speak much; she just hands over the money, more money than the cleaner is worth, and I help her load the acids."

A sob escaped his father. The old man was crying. "She ain't a murderer. She is a savior. She is a goddess sent by the Orisha Yemoja herself to save us from people like Mr. Akoko. Let her do what she was called to do. Please." His sobs shook his body, and Bola couldn't hold him any longer. She took off the handcuffs.

Her phone chimed: a text from the technician with the identity of the owner of the blood. "Would you recognize this woman if you saw her again?"

The son nodded in assent, and Bola showed him the photo of their suspect, whose blood had been at the scene: Naziri Babajide, a young woman who had formerly been employed at the school. He froze for a second, drew closer, and then nodded again. As they left, he was speaking gently to his weeping father.

Toni drove. "I can't believe someone so innocent-looking would murder all those people that way. Her smile was so bright. What could have caused her to turn so insane?"

"Well, when we get to her house you can ask her. Take another turn."

This was it. They had found their murderer. They could finally put the case to rest. As they drew nearer to the house, Bola cocked her gun. Naziri was a smallish woman, but she was also intelligent and had managed to kill six people, one of which was a huge man who played basketball. It was wiser not to take any chances.

Her profile fit perfectly. She worked in the school where over one hundred children had died from a case of typhoid. The school had been shut down despite rumors still floating that around the time of the deaths, the water had been polluted. Soon after, the killings started. Naziri was a chemistry teacher who had knowledge of the best way to purify sulfuric acid. It also meant she knew what sort of chemicals would cause untraceable heart attacks. She must have felt wronged by the loss of her job and angered by the deaths of her students. They still needed more to complete the case, but they had enough to bring her in.

Naziri's house was rundown and overtaken by weeds. But for the light at the window, Bola would have assumed she wasn't home.

Toni knocked on the door. A raspy "Come in" came from inside the house. Toni pried the door open slowly. Both Toni and Bola swept through the doorway expecting some resistance, but there was none.

"In here," the voice said. It came from the bedroom upstairs.

On the bed lay Naziri Babajide. The room was bare, the windows were shut, and the blinds drawn. The figure of Naziri was shrouded on her bed. The woman on the bed had a resemblance to the woman in the picture, but the version of Naziri before them was a shadow of her previous self. Her eyes were sunken; her skin hung at her bones. Her hair was disheveled, and her lips were cracked. Her hands shook as she gestured for the detectives to come in. Toni and Bola didn't let their guards down; they entered with their guns ready.

"Naziri Babajide, you're under arrest for…"

Before Toni could finish, Naziri held up a hand to interrupt. "I confess to killing the six victims with a mixture of sulfuric acid and potassium chloride. I'm afraid I won't be going to prison, though."

Bola recoiled at the threat, but Naziri's statement held no animosity. It was said with a resigned acceptance. Bola spotted the syringe on the bedside. "What did you do?"

Naziri answered simply, "Administered the potassium chloride to myself. I did it as you walked in. I got some of the acid on my hands because of John. I've been in pain ever since. This will be a nice way to go. No pain, no fuss. I never planned to pay for my crimes, although I am ending it sooner than I thought. I knew from the moment John scratched my legs that I would be caught very soon, but I never planned to pay for my crimes. What I wanted to do, I did. I accomplished my purpose. I'm done."

Bola latched onto her words. "What was it you hoped to accomplish?"

Toni dialed for the ambulance. Naziri's face was peaceful, just as if she were sleeping; her voice was clear. "Mr. Akoko used those people to push his agenda for building his manufacturing plant in District 10 Boni, despite the fact that it is incredibly close to a residential area and close to many families. Despite protests by the parents, and teachers like myself, he won. The plant was built. And then everyone died because of his carelessness. So many people, children...dead. And me? Partly paralyzed from the infection. We couldn't be saved quickly enough. So many people didn't react to the drugs. A new strain of the disease we were told."

She pointed a finger straight at Bola. "What happened after? We submitted the claims to people like you. But we didn't get justice. Everything was hushed up and more money was given by Mr. Akoko."

Bola's heart sank. This story was too close to home: losing everything and everyone in the blink of an eye to a disease that was preventable. Being one of the few survivors.

She had a job to do. The chemical was fast-acting and it was unlikely the ambulance would arrive in time. "You reported this to the authorities?"

"I did. I didn't have enough evidence, and I was dismissed. I sent many letters urging those dead fools to confess and turn themselves in, but they ignored all my messages. They begged me, when they knew they were dying. It was too late. Just like it was too late for my students."

Bola dropped to her knees and clasped the woman's hands. "Why is Mr. Akoko still alive?"

Naziri's voice was harsher now, more strained. "He was the one with the power to change everything. I knew he would panic when he saw the patterns of deaths. It was my intention. I left John Ogunro for last."

"And now?"

"He has reversed his decision to have his plant in Boni. A little too late, but it was what I wanted. He announced it on the news today."

Bola still grasped her hands, but the force in Naziri's hands was failing. "How did you get him to do that?

Naziri smiled. "I sent him a letter."

Bola started asking another question, but Naziri's eyes unfocused, and her jaw went slack. Her breathing stopped.

The ambulance arrived soon after but there was nothing they could do. She was dead.

Toni and Bola waited at the scene until the lab techs swept through the residence. Bola waited outside, sitting and kicking rocks.

It had been twenty years since she had lost her own family. All became infected with typhoid, and she was the only survivor. It was horrifying to remember watching them die, watching the life ebb from their faces as they tried to fight the disease but failed. No drugs could save them. It had been a stronger variant, just like what killed the children. The perpetrator was a wealthy businessman, just like Mr. Akoko, and she had never gotten justice.

Toni stood behind her, watching her think. "What is it, Bola?"

She sighed and stood. "I understand her. I understand why

she did what she did. No one fought for her, so she did what she felt she had to do. It was a tough spot she was in."

Toni nodded. "I understand her, too. But murder is wrong, isn't it? We have to do our jobs. We would have arrested her if she hadn't killed herself. Right?"

But Bola didn't answer.

◆

End

"I WANT TO SPEAK TO YOU ABOUT WATER."

The call was undoubtedly from a phisher; I could see from the number. Everyone wanted something from the salting, or, as certain people say, "the assaulting." Austral was a town with money, and money was worth phishing for. Another form of assault. I wish the phishers rang about bushrangers. Some forms of assault are less annoying than others.

"Everyone wants to speak to me about water," I replied. "I need to know *why* you want to speak to me before I answer. Why me and not someone who has higher clearance. Are you a journalist?"

A journalist rang me earlier today. I spent all their precious time recounting the complete long and glorious history of our water. In the early twentieth century, for instance, thousands of Murray cod died here, in Lake George itself, when the water levels fell to almost nothing. Later, there was contamination from mine workings. Then we magically transformed to become the national capital. Australia was so proud of its inland capital with its naturally salty lake. But from 2002 to 2010, Lake George contained no water at all. Locals made sheep jokes instead of water jokes. The government response to this was to build expensive pipelines. Due to a certain number of really stupid errors, all the water delivered through the pipelines is as saline as Lake George. The government has been working towards a desalination plant for nine years. Even the new government can't get the senate to vote on it. We all steal bottles full of fresh water when we go to meetings at Parliament House. And that's the short history of water in Austral. Not the one I gave that journalist.

We were not taught this history in school. The history we were taught in school told us that this is old bushranging territory. It was a haunt for outlaws and for "Stand and deliver," way back when it was merely Lake George. The other name for Lake George is Werriwa. It's a shame that the national capital wasn't called "Werriwa." One of the meanings of Werriwa is "Bad Water," which is perfect for our current situation.

The water in Lake George is undrinkable. These days "Stand and deliver" is probably the only way to get fresh water without going into debt.

"I'm not a journalist," he replied. "I want to sell you..."

"Water," I said. "I know. I still need an explanation. Why me? Why not the head of our organisation?" I didn't tell him where I was from, nor that he'd rung a government department. I knew who he was, but he didn't know who I was.

Before Austral became Australia's magnificent capital city, beloved by... almost no-one... Lake George was a depression in the ground that became a lake from time to time. When it was a lake, it was a big lake. That was no reason to build a city here. The city was built, anyhow.

Lady Denman had announced the city in 1913 while standing on a podium right next to whatever water was in the lake on that particular day. The podium was in the middle of a field that had held sheep the day before. That field is now always a lake: saline and annoying and water. Not water for drinking. The water for drinking belongs in the part of society that used to do bushranging. Phishers take advantage of that water corruption.

I wrote a paper on some of this for the Minister, just last week. The papers don't get anywhere. Nor do the phishers, to be honest. I kept pressing this one to help me understand why anyone should ring me about water. If he'd used the official listing, he'd know I was one of the many specialists in it in government. I specialise in the community ramifications of a problematic water supply.

He had no idea and argued that he didn't need to explain anything to me. He was here to...I interrupted and explained that he should probably speak to my boss.

What we need in Austral is a water supply. One that Sydney can't steal. One that was never, ever saline. If I had wanted salt, I would have moved down the coast somewhere nice. Somewhere I could fish and not be phished.

I'm into the history today. My task, as a good public servant, is to find out why everything's gone wrong and to recommend yet another possible solution. Preferably a solution without salt.

Moving the city to another river would probably solve everything, but no-one's willing to move a nation's fine (small) capital to another location where no-one is willing to live. Sydney wants us to change the constitution and make it the capital. Everyone else hates Sydney for this, except us. Australs hate Sydney for taking our water. Nor is anyone willing to battle Sydney for the region's water, not Austral, not Goulburn, not any of the towns that were delightful in the nineteenth century when Sydney was smaller.

The newspapers talk about this incessantly. We don't talk about the water itself. And yet, there is a crisis. Water poverty is a terrible thing, and my job is to explain how it affects people when it ought to be possible to find more water. Somehow. Somewhere. Someway.

All the venerable answers are revived over and over. Zombie ancestors to a pressing question. Money is spent on arguing water, not on obtaining water, or even fighting Sydney's use of our water. Sydney voters are more numerous than our dehydrated poor. We don't talk about their hurt or their deaths. We are the nation's capital, and it's easier to argue than to do something that will lose the government its precious votes. We do (I spoke to the policy officer responsible for this last Christmas) make sure that graves don't make the water problem worse. Our problems are not those of London in the nineteenth century: what water we have does not (yet) spread disease.

There is a joke name for the situation in my workplace. "Water margins" we call it, in honour of Chinese literature. It's far easier to honour Chinese literature than to give unemployed and underemployed Austral residents enough water to drink.

It's also easier to bait a phisher.

"Are you trying to sell me water rights?" I finally asked.

The big unsolvable problem is Sydney. Austral might have politicians, but Sydney is and ever will be the Emerald City... with our water. Also, with Goulburn's water, but that's not going in my report. We stole Goulburn's water first, you see.

"Everyone has a right to fresh water," he said. "I can help you."

"I know," I replied, filling my voice with adorable compassion. "That's why I want you to ring the Minister."

"The Minister?"

"My boss. I keep saying you should talk to my boss." There was a silence. Normally phishers hang up considerably earlier, but this guy was incapable of giving up, I think. During that silence I thought about things and started writing this note. It began as one of my notes to self in case I need to explain something. Dated evidence can make or break a career right now. I create more dated notes than most because I no longer trust being a public servant.

The days when Australia was the second most trustworthy country in the world are long gone. It began with two corrupt politicians and then the water became a problem and now... we're a different country. Rich and also suffering. Glamorous hurt.

I hope I don't need my notes. I'm moving to Melbourne just as soon as I get clearance for a job. Melbourne has water restrictions, but even the tap water is still drinkable. This means it's less corrupt and no one has to write notes to themselves in case there are issues with a White Paper. To be honest, it's not an "in case" for my White Paper; it's "Can I be out of town before it's released?" And I can, and I will, and I realise that this whole note is never going to be saved. I will write another note with the usual things and attach it to the regular file. I will protect myself even if I'm no longer part of the salting of Austral.

All my friends have already left. Most of my capable colleagues are, like me, leaving soon. Some of them work for state public services, which is not the safest route, but the easiest and has good pay. Some of them have jobs in international organisations, where the pay is even better and the job security terrific.

Blame will be laid when things get desperate. Right now, things are merely rather difficult. They're at the point where grumpy Australians give our work numbers to phishers, to show us what they think of our job and because they think we're water guzzlers and time wasters. It's a database of "private numbers" carefully leaked without our proper names and without any indication that every single one of them is political staff who works on water, public servants who work on water, or, best paid of all, consultants who work on water. All of our Ministers are expected to walk on water, so their phone numbers are sacrosanct. No one on that carefully compiled and leaked list will be around when Australia's national capital ceases to be a viable city.

I'm writing this angry note at this angry moment because water cost me ten percent of my salary this month. I don't know how the less-well-paid manage. Me, I manage by leaving.

I didn't tell the phisher about this. I spoke into the silence and reminded the phisher that they had rung a workplace and that I knew the water policy and knew my rights and if they wanted to speak to anyone about it, they could talk to my boss.

The phisher put on his best world-weary voice and said, "You're making me tired." I was wasting his time.

I am wasting my own time. I shall wander down to the waterfront and wonder how our depression-that-could-be-a-lake had turned into a permanent body of water, and how, when a city was set on its shores, it became the water nightmare for millions.

◆

Note: This story was inspired by a visit to Lake George (I have pictures!) and also by a visit, partly thanks to Sydney's needs, to a famous Goulburn brewery. It was a dry year and Goulburn's water supply was down to 5%. The brewery was fine, they told me, because they had their own water supply. This was the water that Australia would have tapped into if the option of a city on Lake George had been taken up. On our Earth, Canberra was chosen partly because of the water supply. The actual phisher who I exhausted by suggesting he talk to someone else was interested in telephony.

◆

End

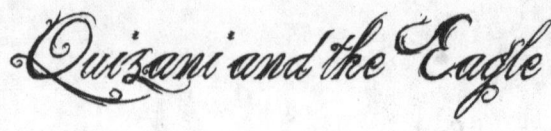

Quizani and the Eagle

[*Quizani* and the Eagle]
[Alfonso Arteaga Rodríguez/Alfonso Arteaga]

AT THE FOOT OF THE SNOW-CAPPED *IZTACCÍHUATL* volcano, there was an immense forest, almost entirely covered by huge pine trees. Animals of many species lived in them, such as the deer, the heron, and the mockingbird, known as the bird of the four hundred voices. Among all of them, the majestic golden eagle, who is an important part of our story.

All the animals lived freely and in harmony with nature. The deer lived on the slopes of the volcano, the heron in the beautiful lagoon that had formed by the thawing of ice, and the eagle together with the mockingbird in the treetops, and both came down daily to feed and chat with other animals of the region. On a certain occasion when the eagle and the mockingbird were talking on the shore of the lagoon, the eagle said:

- Well, the obligation calls me, I must retire, because I must take my children their food.

- And how many kids do you have? said the mockingbird.

- I have three beautiful chicks, which like fish very much, replied the eagle. You can't imagine how much they eat! OK, goodbye!

The eagle flew towards the beautiful and great lagoon, which still had its clean and transparent waters, and with certain precision took an enormous trout with its talons, to later rise into the air towards its nest.

- I have arrived, it told its chicks and began to feed them lovingly, and instead of saying, "Thank you mom," they just said, "I want more, I want more."

Sometime later, the eagle perched near the heron and said:

- Friend, days ago while I was flying, I saw that the humans were doing a big excavation into the mountain, and they were taking water from the river. Shortly after, they returned the water, but it no longer had its transparency and it smelled bad.

- Yes, I had noticed, the heron answered. The fish are disappearing everywhere, as if they have vanished or perhaps, they are dying. What will become of us?

- I think I know the cause! the eagle asserted. Since the humans have arrived, they take our water and then they pour it back into the river with another aspect. That is the reason for the disappearance of the fish, and if we don't do something they will end up destroying the forests. However, I must keep looking for how to feed my young.

The eagle rose into the air to see if it could find another source of food. After several turns furrowing the skies, it saw a little dog slowly walking through the forest and thought: what moves slowly is my food. But as it plummeted to catch the little dog, the eagle saw a human child walking near him, who, seeing the eagle's intentions, went out to defend his friend the little dog, asking the eagle to leave his dog alone and declaring that he would not allow it. The eagle, seeing how a human protected a being that was not of its kind, was so moved by the actions of the child that it approached him cautiously, because it knew how dangerous humans could be. The boy saw that the eagle was getting closer to him, but he was even more surprised when he heard it speak.

- You speak? the boy asked.

- Desperation made me learn your language, the eagle

answered him, but I didn't think you would listen to me. What are you doing here, human child? I was very surprised to see how you defended this puppy.

- He is my friend and partner, said the boy. My name is *Quizani*, and I am the son of the engineer in charge of the work on the mountain.

- You mean in charge of destroying the mountain, said the eagle. That mountain, like this forest of immeasurable beauty, is home to many species, which you call "animals." Here we live in harmony with nature, until your kind arrived. Look, human child, the eagle continued, that same river that creates this beautiful lagoon is the one that gives life to those who live in this beautiful valley. I am the bearer of the heartrending and pitiful voice that asks to put a stop to the extermination of my species and many others that live here.

- What are you talking about?

- I have heard of a human poet, the eagle answered, who wrote: "Man only wants his species to end, while we daily fight to perpetuate ours." The poet questioned which of the two species really was the animal. What is going on with you humans? Why this self-destruction? Why do you pollute the water? Don't you see that water is life for you and for us? Without water, the trees that give us the oxygen we breathe would die. We would die too, of not having water to drink. Your people who depend on water to irrigate your crops will die and the entire planet will die. Help us please! Man in his desire for wealth is contaminating the waters; every day toxic substances and garbage are dumped into the rivers to pollute the fish and kill the reefs. When these substances reach the sea, whales, dolphins, sharks, among others, stray from their routes and end up stranded on the beach sands, where many of them lose their lives.

Quizani could not help but cry when he heard the terrible reality that other living beings were experiencing because of the greedy decisions of humans. *Quizani* promised to take the eagle's prayers to his father and to all humans who were willing to listen, because he would become, for humans, the voice of those beings who share our world, and who claim their right to live, asking humans not to contaminate our vital liquid... water.

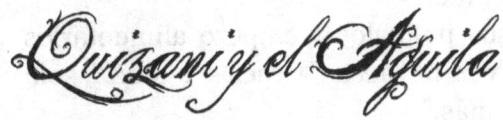

[*Quizani* y el Águila]
[Alfonso Arteaga Rodríguez]

AL PIE DEL NEVADO VOLCÁN IZTACCÍHUATL, existía un inmenso bosque, casi cubierto en su totalidad por enormes pinos. En ellos vivían animales de muchas especies, como el venado, la garza, el cenzontle; ave conocida como pájaro de las cuatrocientas voces. Entre todos ellos, la majestuosa águila real, quien es parte importante de nuestro relato.

Ahí todos los animalitos vivían libremente y en armonía con la naturaleza. El venado habitaba en las faldas del volcán, la garza en la hermosa laguna que se había formado por el deshielo, el águila junto con el cenzontle en las copas de los árboles, y ambas diariamente bajaban para alimentarse y charlar con los demás animales de la región. En cierta ocasión cuando el águila y el cenzontle platicaban a la orilla de la laguna, el águila sobresaltada se despidió diciendo:

- Bueno la obligación me llama, tengo que retirarme, pues debo lleva a mis críos su alimento.

- ¿Y cuántos críos tienes, le dijo el Cenzontle?

Tengo tres hermosos polluelos, a los cuales les gusta mucho el pescado, y ¡Vieras cómo comen! Bueno, ¡hasta luego! contestó el águila.

El águila voló hacia la hermosa y gran laguna la que aún tenía sus aguas limpias y transparentes, y con certera precisión tomó con sus garras una enorme trucha, para después elevarse por los aires con rumbo a su nido.

- Ya llegué, les dijo a sus polluelos y empezó alimentarlos amorosamente y estos en vez de decir "Gracias mamá," solo decían: "Quiero más, quiero más."

Tiempo después, el águila se posó cerca de la garza y le dijo:

- Amiga, hace días mientras volaba, vi que los humanos estaban haciendo una gran excavación en la montaña, y tomaban agua del río. Poco después la regresaban, pero está ya no tenía su transparencia y olía mal.

- Si me había dado cuenta, le contesto la garza; los peces ya no aparecen por ningún lado, como si hubieran desaparecido o quizás se están muriendo. ¿Qué estará pasando?

- ¡Creo saber la causa! El águila contesta aseveradamente, casualmente desde que llegaron los humanos, toman nuestra agua y después la vierten nuevamente al río con otro aspecto, esa es la razón de la desaparición de los peces y si no hacemos algo terminaran destruyendo los bosques. Pero por ahora tengo que seguir buscando como alimentar a mis crías.

El águila se elevó por los aires para desde lo alto ver si encontraba otra fuente de alimento, después de varias vueltas surcando por los cielos, vio a un perrito que lentamente caminaba por entre el bosque y pensó: lo que se mueve lento es mi alimento, pero al dejarse caer en picada para atrapar al perrito, alcanzó a ver que caminaba cerca de él un niño humano, quien al ver las intenciones del águila, salió a defender a su amigo el perrito, le pidió al águila que dejara a su perrito en paz y que no permitiría se lo llevara, el águila al ver como un humano protegía a un ser que no era de su especie, la conmovió tanto que se acercó cautelosamente, pues sabía de lo peligroso que podrían ser los humanos. El niño vio que el águila se estaba acercando a él, pero más se sorprendió al escucharla hablar.

- ¿Hablas? Le pregunto el chico.

- La desesperación me hizo hacerlo, le contestó el Águila, más no pensé me escucharías, ¿Qué andas haciendo por aquí cachorro humano? Me sorprendió mucho el ver como defendías a este perrito.

- Él es mi amigo y compañero dijo el niño, yo me llamo Quizani soy hijo del ingeniero a cargo del trabajo en la montaña.

- Será destruyendo la montaña, dijo el águila, esa montaña al igual que este bosque de hermosura intangible, es el hogar de muchas especies, a los que ustedes llaman "animales" aquí vivimos en armonía con la naturaleza, hasta que llegaron los de tu especie. Mira cachorro humano, continuo el águila, ese río que forma esta hermosa laguna, es quien da vida a quienes habitan en este hermoso valle. Yo soy portadora de la voz desgarradora y lastimera que pide parar ya el exterminio de mi especie y de las otras tantas que aquí vivimos.

- A que te refieres? Le contesto el niño.

- Supe de un poeta humano que escribió: "El hombre solo pretende a su especie terminar, mientras que nosotros a diario luchamos por la nuestra perpetuar" El poeta se cuestionaba cuál de las dos especies realmente era el animal. ¿Qué está pasando con ustedes? ¿Por qué esa autodestrucción? ¿Por qué contaminan el agua? ¿Que no ven que el agua es la vida tanto para ustedes como para nosotros? Sin agua morirían los árboles quienes nos dan el oxígeno que respiramos, moriríamos nosotros al no tener que beber, morirán ustedes que también dependen del agua para el riego de sus cultivos y morirá el planeta entero. ¡Ayúdanos por favor! el hombre en su afán de riqueza está contaminando las aguas, todos los días vierten en los ríos sustancias tóxicas y basura que hacen que los peces se contaminen y los arrecifes desaparezcan. Cuando esas sustancias toxicas llegan al mar, las ballenas, los delfines, los tiburones entre otros se desvían de sus rutas y quedan varados en las arenas, donde muchas de ellos pierden la vida.

Quizani no pudo evitar el derramar su llanto al escuchar la terrible realidad que están viviendo los otros seres vivos a cause de las decisiones avaricias de los humanos. Quizani le prometió llevar sus plegarias a su papa y a todos los humanos que estén dispuestos a escuchar, pues el sería la voz para los humanos de esos seres que comparten nuestro mundo, y quienes reclaman su derecho a la vida pidiendo no contaminen nuestro líquido vital ... el agua.

◆

End

The Ship of Sisyphus

[The Ship of Sisyphus]
[James Morrow]

FÁTIMA IS FALLING. From her airy vantage an upside-down Gulf of Mexico spreads in all directions to meet a circular horizon. Whitecaps and spindrift dance atop the waves. A seagull glides beneath her, scanning the water for food, oblivious to the descending woman.

Her arms are extended above her shoulders, palms pressed together. But Fátima is not praying; she is calculating. Unless her head and trunk strike the water at a nearly perpendicular angle, she will break her spine or, worse, become a piece of humanoid driftwood.

In the seconds that remain before she intersects the sea, she anticipates the common phenomenon whereby a falling person will see her entire life flash before her. Her expectations come to nothing. Perhaps the phenomenon isn't common after all, she decides. Perhaps it never even happens.

◆

Her parents called her El Bebé del Agua, the Water Baby. They joked that she was the incarnation of Chalchiuhtlicue, the Aztec goddess of seas, rivers, streams, and storms, though as reasonably serious Mass-goers—her parents described themselves as practicing Catholics who frequently fell out of practice—they didn't spend much time thinking about pagan deities. Throughout Fátima's infancy in the Yucatán, if there was a pond, lake, lagoon, sinkhole, swimming pool, or ocean within a hundred meters of her, she would be splashing through it before anyone knew she was gone. Shortly after her fifth birthday she decided that only a vain person would style herself the incarnation of Chalchiuhtlicue, so instead she gave the goddess a set of animal companions and appointed herself their keeper. She named the basilisk Alejandro, the gryphon Rafael, and the sea serpent Ximena. Where other children had imaginary friends, Fátima had imaginary fauna.

Given her aquatic girlhood, it was perhaps inevitable that Fátima would one day work as a lifeguard. Her summers found her sitting in a lofty wooden tower on various Cancún beaches, wearing a Panama hat and a white spandex swimsuit while scanning the surf through high-powered binoculars. She brought to her duties a gift for concentration and an aptitude for daydreaming. When not looking for wealthy tourists who'd taxed the patience of Chalchiuhtlicue and now needed rescuing, she pictured the goddess's sea serpent plying the waters beyond the horizon—not the present Ximena but a Ximena from the early eighteenth century, magnificent in her opalescent scales and conical horns, domesticated by Blackbeard the Pirate to serve as his organic frigate, faster and more maneuverable than any vessel in the West Indies.

Guarding lives was a paradoxical occupation, offering interminable stretches of tedium—her sea serpent reveries provided only limited entertainment—punctuated by the adrenalin rush that comes with playing God. By the time she'd graduated from the Universidad Nacional Autónoma de México and made it through her first year of medical training at the Universidad Autonoma de Guadalajara in Jalisco, Fátima could claim that, had she not on four memorable occasions scrambled down from her aerie and sprinted into the surf, a famous Italian actress, a misanthropic British diplomat, a beloved French chef, and an American financial advisor specializing in pyramid schemes would no longer be walking the Earth.

Playing God paid well, but not enough. By banking most of her salary, Fátima guaranteed that in her second year of medical school she could once again meet her tuition bills—government subsidies made higher education costs negligible for Mexican citizens—likewise the charges for housing, textbooks, and computer time, but she'd have to scrounge when it came to clothing, carousing, and non-dormitory food. She deeply resented the social norm whereby lifeguards never received tips, even though a person so employed had to be as vigilant and capable as any waiter or cab driver. Once she tried placing an aluminum bucket labeled GRACIAS POR LA PROPINA at the base of her tower, only to have it spirited away by an insufferable nine-year-old boy from Nebraska. She lost no time replacing the bucket, which the sunbathers, surfers, and volleyball players furtively filled with bottle caps throughout the day. Fátima was not amused.

Like many young Mexicans who benefitted from the international boom in Cancún tourism, she commuted to work by boat. At dawn every morning she would leave her parents' house on Isla Mujeres and singlehandedly pilot the *Estrella del Norte*, her Tío Rodrigo's coastal cruiser (a ramshackle vessel with a raked prow and a reliable Volvo engine), across the bay, arriving at the Nichupte Marina an hour before the beaches opened. There was always time for black coffee and salsa-enhanced eggs at the Café Por Favor before she slathered on the sunscreen and took up her perch above the dunes.

Throughout her ninety-first day of patrolling Playa Delfines, Fátima had no intimations that a disaster was in the making. At sunset she descended from her tower, sprinted to the marina, and set off for Isla Mujeres in her uncle's boat. She had gotten halfway across the darkening bay when an immense fog bank, thick and palpable as the smoke pouring from an active volcano, engulfed the *Estrella del Norte*. Instinctively she turned on the forward searchlight, but the beam failed to penetrate the massive shroud. She pulled back the throttle. A mountainous shape loomed out of the cloud. She shifted into neutral. The amorphous intruder grew larger yet. She shifted into reverse—too late: the intruder crashed into her, raising an obscene cacophony of splintering fiberglass and ripped aluminum, and then the universe went black.

♦

She awoke to a low, dense humming, as if a colony of immense bumblebees had adopted her as their queen, but she soon realized this was the sound of a motor. Was she being evacuated by helicopter to a hospital? Had she been kidnapped and thrown into a semi-rig trailer? Most probably she was hearing a diesel engine sending vibrations through the steel hull of the ship that had run her down.

A peculiar sensation washed through her. Even as the surrounding objects—cans of paint, drums of lubricant, spools of nylon rope, jumbles of moldering life vests—acquired utter clarity, her body likewise seemed to come into focus, sentience spreading horizontally from her feet to her shoulders. Evidently someone had improvised sleeping quarters for her inside a storage locker. She was resting on a pallet piled high with canvas. Her back ached. Her temples throbbed. Her white spandex swimsuit was dry, doubtless owing to the hot, gluey air.

"If you're wondering whether you're still alive, I can assure you that's the case." A male voice, low and mellow. "If you're wondering where you are—"

"I collided with your ship, and you rescued me," said Fátima as the sweet scent of canvas penetrated her nostrils.

"An astute deduction, but to survive aboard the good ship *Paraíso*, you'll need agility as well as intelligence. I'm the bosun, Damién Gutiérrez. You slept through the night."

"And my uncle's boat, the *Estrella*...?"

"Lies at the bottom of the bay," said Gutiérrez in a plaintive voice.

A tremor shot through El Bebé del Agua. Had her stomach been full, she would have hurled its contents onto the floor.

"Mierda."

"I quite agree," said the bosun. "Did your parents give you a beautiful name to match your face?"

"I am Fátima Lucia Zuniga."

"How lovely. Thirsty?"

She grunted in the affirmative. Gutiérrez proffered a tin cup, and she gulped down several ounces of bitter water. "If it's not too much trouble, I'd like to be dropped off where I was headed, Isla Mujeres."

"It's too much trouble."

She glanced at her watch, which had come through the disaster unscathed. 9:10 a.m. Inch by inch, limb by limb, she climbed off her pallet. The cavernous room was lit by a single naked lightbulb dangling from the ceiling on a frayed electrical cord. Harsh shadows framed Gutiérrez, a stout and grizzled sailor with a beard resembling a clump of dried seaweed.

"'Too much trouble?'" she protested. "Your captain bears more than a little responsibility for this calamity. The foghorn was silent. The running lights were off."

"It pleases Capitán Suárez to operate the *Paraíso* as a phantom ship. No horn, no lights, no drunken chatter on the weather deck. I must tell you that in Suárez's view every castaway like you is a Jonah, a bringer of bad luck."

"He would have fewer Jonahs—and Johannas—on his hands

if he followed maritime protocols."

"Your situation is undesirable but not hopeless, Señorita Zuniga. Each of our castaways is given the same test of stamina and fortitude."

"Test? What? That's crazy."

"Everyone who passes is no longer a Jonah but instead becomes an AB—an Able-Bodied Seaman."

"And then Suárez lets them go?"

"And then he permits them to stay on board and help keep the ship functioning. The *Paraíso* is renowned for delivering its cargo ahead of schedule. Suárez will not jeopardize that reputation by changing course."

"And those who fail...?" asked Fátima.

"They're locked in the brig until we reach the shark-infested waters of the West Sargasso Sea, and then ... you can imagine what."

Rage, resentment, and sheer terror convulsed El Bebé del Agua.

"I would like to speak with your Capitán Suárez."

"He doesn't talk to his Jonahs. If you pass the test, he might deign to spare you a minute."

Gutiérrez indicated three spherical rubber bags, black and bloated, lined up along the far wall, each the size of a weather balloon.

"Your task is to haul one of those bags to A Deck, whose occupants will by this evening have an acute need for potable water. Today, Señorita, you are a *Bhisti*, a *Wasserjunge*, a *portadora del agua*—a water carrier."

"Those bags must weigh a hundred kilos each."

"A hundred kilos, yes. A hundred liters of vital water. The first landing you'll encounter opens onto P Deck, twenty risers above our heads."

"P Deck? *P Deck?* You mean I have to drag one of those

things up sixteen decks?"

"Sixteen decks, sixteen landings, sixteen companionways, three hundred and twenty risers. The *Paraíso* presents to the world a profile more reminiscent of a skyscraper than a merchant freighter. Needless to say, if you ask for help from any humans you meet along the way, you automatically lose the game, and the sharks will receive their entrée."

Fátima flashed on her Tío Rodrigo's great guilty pleasure, the Luchador Enmascarado—Masked Wrestler—movies of the 1960s. "Demonio Azul or El Santo could drag a hundred-liter waterbag to A Deck, but not a wiry medical student like me."

"Perhaps you'll surprise yourself."

"It wouldn't be for the first time," said Fátima.

Gutiérrez sauntered to the door and set his hand on the latch. "Speaking of entrées, I imagine you're hungry. I'll see what our cook can spare."

"Suárez can't get away with this."

"I admire your nerve, but he has already gotten away with it, again and again and again..."

The bosun slipped out of the room, and the next sound Fátima heard was the thud of a deadbolt sliding into place, canceling her fantasies of escape.

♦

At least they fed their prisoners well aboard the *Paraíso*. Within the hour a gristly young man appeared at her side bearing a tray laden with fresh fruit, buttered toast, and scrambled eggs.

"What sort of cargo does the *Paraíso* carry?" asked Fatima.

"Don't ask me. I'm a Seaman Third Class, the lowest of the low."

"Petroleum from the Sureste Basin?"

"Matías Ortíz at your service." He indicated an aluminum

urn. "I suspect you want coffee."

Fatima nodded. "Zacua electric microcars?"

Seaman Ortíz decanted hot black coffee into a translucent spherical mug etched with the Earth's continents.

"Tequila from Tamaulipas?"

Ortíz slipped out of the room.

Fátima hastily consumed her breakfast and then approached the nearest waterbag, which in her imagination became a proximate neutron star, its black rubber sucking up light. Although the bag offered a wooden handle affixed above the spigot, she discovered she couldn't drag the thing without abusing her rotator cuff and risking a hernia. A better method, she soon found, was to place both palms on the equator of the ponderous sphere, bend her knees, tighten her shoulders, firm her abdomen, and push, thereby enlisting a majority of her muscles in the task and causing the bag to roll forward like an immense beach ball.

The doorway easily accommodated the sphere, but the companionway beyond was lamentably narrow. She inhaled, closed her eyes, and pushed the bag upward, so that it now lay across five adjacent risers. No sooner had she accomplished this feat than the bag began slipping toward her.

"Quetzalcóatl, give me strength!" she cried, surprised that a pagan sentiment would spring so easily to her lips. "Nuestra Señora, hear my plea!" she quickly added. "Santa Catalina, watch over me!" she continued, covering another base.

Before the sphere could knock her over, she set her shoulder against the equator and stopped its descent. She gave the thing a mighty shove. It rolled forward 90 degrees. She redoubled her efforts. The waterbag kept rolling, traversing fifteen risers and arriving on the P Deck landing. Arms splayed, she threw herself face down across the bag and, panting like a sheepdog and sweating like a goaltender, indulged in a ten-minute time out.

"Heave-ho, dear Fátima!" she told herself, setting her feet squarely on the platform. "Heave-ho!" she cried again, hands on the equator. "Heave! Heave! Ho! Ho!"

She attained O Deck sooner than she'd expected.

"Ho! Ho! Fo! Fo! Go! Go! Lo! Lo!"

N Deck proved no match for her desperation.

"No! No! Ro! Ro! Wo! Wo! Yo! Yo!"

On reaching the M Deck landing, she again embraced the sphere and caught her breath.

A stately, tawny woman wearing a white lab coat strode through the door and joined Fátima on the landing, a stethoscope dangling from her neck like a pendant. The name *Aguilar* was stitched on her lapel.

"What's all the commotion?" asked Dr. Aguilar. "Is that a waterbag?"

"Y-Yes." Fátima wiped her brow with the back of her hand, removing a tiara of sweat. "One hundred liters."

"Come inside, and you'll see why we need every drop."

"This water is marked for A Deck," Fátima protested.

"We've never met Capitán Suárez, but we've heard about his Jonah obsession and his ill-treatment of castaways."

"If I fail the test, Suárez will—"

"I know," said Dr. Aguilera. "Please step this way."

Against her better judgment, Fátima abandoned the rubber sphere and crossed the threshold. A startling scene presented itself. The salon had been converted into a nursery featuring a grid of twenty variously complected newborns lying in bassinettes, some sleeping, others babbling, most crying. Three women wearing antique Red Cross nurse's caps scurried about, supplying their charges with milk from nipple-topped glass bottles.

"Their mothers will probably never see them again," said Dr. Aguilar. "Each of these infants represents a forced birth, abortions being almost impossible to obtain in the Caribbean, to say nothing of those benighted U.S. states along the Gulf. Thus far none of our clients has regretted giving us the procreative results of being raped by a stranger or, far more commonly, her uncle, brother, cousin, husband, or boyfriend."

Stern of face and robust of frame, the nearest nurse sidled up to Fátima. Her surname, according to the embroidery on her pocket, was Herrera. "Even when no violence attended the moment of conception, we offer our services, helping those who know that unsolicited motherhood will drag them deeper into poverty and despair."

"So the *Paraíso* is a floating orphanage?" said Fátima.

"Quite so," said Nurse Herrera. "The problem with all the non-floating orphanages in the Caribbean is that sooner or later the Asociación Antifornicación de Santa María impounds their records. Armed with this information, they track down the birth mothers and chastise them as sluts and whores. But the AASM would never imagine there's an orphanage aboard the *Paraíso*. We've been in business three years now, and so far no morality guardians have shown up."

"In the absence of wetnurses we must rely on powdered formula to keep our babies alive," said Dr. Aguilar, "a reasonable expedient for any orphanage, assuming it has a good supply of concentrate and—"

"And plenty of clean water," said Fátima. "Midterm exam. Multiple choice. An infant fed contaminated formula will typically contract meningitis, salmonella, giardiasis, or all of the above?"

"You sound like a medical student," said Nurse Herrera.

"That's probably because I'm a medical student."

"The nurses and I are quenching our thirst with plastic bottles of cold-brew coffee, but you can't feed that to a baby," said Dr. Aguilar. "We have no facilities for boiling our tainted water, and our potable reserves will be gone by this afternoon."

"Can't Capitán Suárez find some for you?" asked Fátima.

"He doesn't even know this place exists," said Nurse Herrera. "If he did, he would shut us down."

"You'll be pleased to hear there are two more waterbags in the storage room," said Fátima.

"And we dare not commandeer either one," said Dr. Aguilar. "If we're spotted pushing a bag up the companionways, Suárez will show us no mercy."

Fátima clenched her teeth and exhaled, whistling through her incisors. There was no question what Chalchiuhtlicue would have her do. While the idea of rolling a second unwieldy sphere from the storage room up to M Deck distressed her, those 80 risers seemed negligible compared to the 240 that lay between M Deck and A Deck.

"Very well," said Fátima. "My hundred liters are yours, starting immediately. I can easily deliver a different waterbag to A Deck."

"Easily?" said Dr. Aguilar. "Not so easily, I should think."

"True."

"Bless you," said Nurse Herrera.

"You will not regret this," said Dr. Aguilar

"Unless, of course, by substituting one bag for another I'll be breaking one of Suárez's rules, and he'll declare me a loser—in which case I'll have no regrets whatsoever," said Fatima. "I'm told the dead are at peace with themselves."

◆

Fátima is still falling. The indifferent wind shrieks in her ears. The unfeeling sea rolls ever onward, radiating waves that will in time break against the shores of western Florida.

She remembers the course in evolutionary biology she took

during her senior year at the Universidad Nacional Autónoma de México. The professor had devoted an entire lecture to the immense celestial body that had crashed into the waters off the Yucatán peninsula, sealing the fate of the Cretaceous dinosaurs.

As Fátima braces for impact, she realizes she may be following the same trajectory as the Chicxulub asteroid. Although she doesn't believe in panpsychism, she imagines the impossible rock knew what was about to happen and wished it might be otherwise.

◆

Fátima returned to the storage room, where she drank cold coffee from Ortíz's urn and took possession of a waterbag. She spent the balance of the morning fighting gravity and cursing Suárez. Riser by riser, push by push, groan by groan, she wrestled the second black sphere to P Deck ... O Deck ... N Deck ... M Deck. She entered the floating orphanage, lingering long enough to savor the sight of the nurses working the spigot on their black sphere, decanting clean water into the glass baby bottles. Dr. Aguilar offered her a thumbs up and a smile. Fátima made an about-face and resumed her struggle with her rubber nemesis.

Throughout her subsequent ascent, riser 81, riser 82, riser 83, riser 84, riser 85, riser 86, *ad nauseam*, Chalchiuhtlicue's companions—Alejandro the basilisk, Rafael the gryphon, Ximena the sea serpent—became chimerical presences by her side, whispering encouragement. By noon she'd conquered L Deck. By 12:15 p.m. she'd added K Deck to her list of triumphs. Twenty minutes later she reached J Deck. At one o'clock precisely she found herself on I Deck, where a broad-shouldered, white-suited golem of a man dressed in green surgical scrubs stood on the landing as if he'd been anticipating her arrival.

"We'd heard that one of Suárez's Jonahs was on board." The surgeon pointed to the rubber sphere. "My dear *Bhisti*, we shall be pleased to take those hundred liters off your hands."

"If you know about my bargain with Suárez," said Fátima, wheezing and coughing, "then you know this water isn't for you."

"I'm Dr. Peña," said the golem, ignoring her protest. "Behold."

The instant the physician opened the door, Fátima was assailed by a cyclone made of pain. Screams, howls, wails, moans. Reluctantly she entered the salon, where a distressing spectacle met her gaze. At least thirty men and women lay on the floor, most wearing shredded remnants of combat fatigues and all displaying ravaged flesh and bloody dressings.

Dr. Peña had only two assistants, a weary, rawboned man and an equally haggard, equally gaunt woman, both wearing rubber gloves and green surgical scrubs. Everywhere Fátima turned, she saw bandaged stumps. The soldiers had lost hands, arms, feet, legs.

"Last month the tensions on Hispaniola erupted into a full-scale border war, Spanish-speaking Dominicans versus French-speaking Haitians," Dr. Peña explained. "The *Paraíso* functions as a politically neutral hospital ship. Whatever their nationalities, we patch them up and return them to Hispaniola, whether they want to go back or not. If this ship were to acquire a reputation as a sanctuary for deserters, the generals on both sides would order their gunboats to blow the *Paraíso* out of the water."

"'The first line of defense against sepsis,' that's what my clinical pathology professor called clean water," said Fátima. "She told us that using seawater to clean open wounds amounts to malpractice, since the world's oceans are laden with bacteria."

"Then you understand why we need your hundred liters. I'm thirsty, my assistants are thirsty, our charges are thirsty, and we have to irrigate their wounds immediately."

"My waterbag is supposed to go to A Deck."

"No, it's supposed to go to this clinic—assuming there's still a modicum of justice in the world," said Dr. Peña.

Never had Fátima felt more divided against herself. "Basilisk, gryphon, sea serpent," she chanted in a singsong voice. "Basilisk, gryphon, sea serpent."

"What are you talking about?"

"If they were here, they would tell me that their queen, the goddess of water, expects me to help these soldiers."

"She sounds like a sensible deity," said Dr. Peña.

◆

Fátima's frantic sprint down 160 risers to the storage room left her winded, but she lost no time appropriating the remaining waterbag and rolling it into the first companionway. Throughout the climb to M deck, pain screwed through muscles and bones she hadn't even realized she owned. Arriving on the landing, she paused briefly to observe the feeding of the infants. Dr. Aguilera pointed to her new rubber burden and smiled in approval of Fátima's apparent decision to mitigate misery somewhere between M deck and A Deck.

Now came the second half of her agonizing 160-riser journey back to I Deck, where she lingered, caught her breath, and observed, with profound satisfaction, the surgeons using the second waterbag to irrigate the soldiers' damaged flesh.

She continued on her vertical Via Dolorosa, retching, gagging, and weeping all the way. Once again the ephemeral voices of the basilisk, the gryphon, and the sea serpent offered encouragement, but Fátima's greatest ally proved to be herself. Evidently her soul commanded resources of which she'd been previously unaware, an inner Azul Demonio, and so it was that she accomplished the torturous ascents to Hell Deck ... Groin Deck ... Fatigue Deck ... Excruciation Deck.

A door swung open and two athletic women, wearing yellow jumpsuits and fixed faces, appeared on the E Deck landing. Without saying a word, they hoisted Fátima upward by her elbows, ushered her past the waterbag, and carried her into the salon.

"Put me down, damn it!"

"I am Señora Muñoz," said the heavyset woman, relaxing her grip. Her self-presentation included a holstered Glock semiautomatic pistol like the one Fátima's Tía Sofía owned.

"Call me Señora Castillo," said the rangy woman, likewise relinquishing Fátima and likewise armed.

Several dozen men, women, and children of presumably Caribbean heritage jammed the room, most of them sitting on the floor in postures bespeaking shock and misery. A dozen of Muñoz and Castillo's charges were lined up outside two portable latrines standing in the far corner.

"But for our crude sanitation facilities, the atmosphere on E Deck would be intolerable," said Señora Muñoz. "All these people are facing a choice between drinking contaminated water or being tormented by thirst, but thanks to your hundred liters, that's about to change."

"If I don't deliver my consignment to A Deck, Suárez will cruise into a shark zone and throw me overboard," said Fátima.

"Suárez doesn't know this, but for the past three years the *Paraíso* has been the most effective rescue vessel in the Caribbean, taking aboard victims of catastrophic weather," said Señora Castillo, as if Fátima hadn't just spoken of being eaten alive. "Last week Hurricane Ivan visited itself upon these waters, bypassing Cuba and Jamaica but devastating the Lesser Antilles before moving out to sea."

"'Rescue vessel,'" muttered Fátima. "By other accounts the

Paraíso is a merchant freighter, an orphanage, and a military hospital."

"I have no idea what you're talking about," said Castillo.

Never before had Fátima felt so depleted, a condition tracing partially to Castillo's remark—what sort of mind-game was the señora playing with her?—but mostly to her battles with 240 remorseless liters. She knew her inner Azul Demonio had deserted her. Her knees buckled and she dropped to the floor, pressing her shoulder blades against the wall.

"Such a catch-22," she muttered. "A community whose water is polluted with rotavirus or pathogenic strains of *E coli* will suffer a plague of acute gastroenteritis that invariably brings life-threatening dehydration that can only be treated with the community's nonexistent supply of clean water."

"Catch-22—I never thought of it that way," said Castillo.

"Final exam," muttered Fátima. "True or false? Over 760,000 children die each year of preventable diarrheal disease."

"Our faithful *portadora del agua* knows a thing or two about scientific medicine," said Muñoz.

"Here's something else I know," said Fátima. "The plight of these refugees is horrific, but conditions on A Deck are probably even worse."

"Except you're not on A Deck," snapped Castillo. "You're on E Deck. Without your water, the souls in our keeping will soon succumb to the dehydration clause in your catch-22."

"Here's what's about to happen," said Fátima, heartened by the return of her resolve. "This faithful *portadora del agua* will haul her waterbag up to A Deck and assess whatever catastrophe is unfolding there." She sucked in a breath and gained her feet. "Depending on what I find, I'll either surrender my burden or send it tumbling down the companionways. I suggest you station yourselves on the C Deck landing, so you can take possession of the sphere before it rolls all the way back to the storage room."

"We would rather take possession now," said Muñoz.

"Good señoras of E Deck, if you'll consider Suárez's threat against me, you'll realize my terms are astonishingly reasonable."

◆

Hastily she did the grim arithmetic of the day's ordeal. After factoring in her two Sisyphean returns to the starting place, she figured she'd climbed from one riser to the next 480 times. And now a mere eighty untrod risers stretched before her.

She set her shoulder against the wretched black sphere and pushed. Eventually she attained Death Deck ... Curse Deck ... Bloody Deck ... Anguish Deck. Having reached the summit of her woes, she collapsed on the boards and gasped, sweat stinging her eyes, thirst racking her throat.

The A Deck landing offered two archways leading to presumably luxurious salons. A roly-poly man in a gaudy steward's uniform, all brass buttons and gold piping, was waiting for her, standing beside a serving cart holding an aluminum ice bucket. A green bottle of San Pellegrino sparkling water peered above the rim like a periscope.

"I am Hernando," said the steward, pouring San Pellegrino into a glass tumbler. "Let me be the first to congratulate you. You must be thirsty."

"How did you guess?" rasped Fátima.

She snatched the tumbler from Hernando and drained it in one gulp.

"Another," she said.

The steward refilled the glass.

Leaving the waterbag on the landing, they proceeded though the left-hand archway and into the ballroom beyond. Dozens of hyperkinetic revelers, male, female, and indeterminate, danced to the music of a marimba band while blowing into tin horns and slide whistles. Their cardboard hats variously resembled tricorns, fezzes, busbies, and traffic cones. Squalls of confetti poured down from minions deployed in the balcony. A detachment of waiters roamed the room ferrying trays holding canapés and champagne flutes.

"My dear *Bhisti*, allow me to introduce myself," said a lantern-jawed officer in dress whites, striding up to Fátima. "I am Señor Vázquez, the first officer. Everyone here appreciates your efforts, though I must admit we expected you much sooner."

"I was detained by newborn babies, war casualties, and hurricane refugees."

Señor Vázquez scowled and rolled his eyes. "Fortunately for you, our ice-making machine gets the job done in less than an hour. Capitán Suárez will almost certainly gauge your mission a success and give you a berth on the *Paraíso*."

"So you'll be using those hundred liters merely to make ice?" asked Fátima, aghast.

"Nobody on A Deck would put the words 'merely' and 'ice' in the same sentence," said Vázquez.

"Ice? Really? Goddamn *ice*?" said Fátima.

"This festivity will soon be fueled by Scotch on the rocks, Black Russians, James Bond shaken martinis, and margaritas abrim with crystalline cubes and tequila."

"Even if it goes on till midnight, you won't consume a hundred kilos worth of ice," Fátima argued.

"Midnight? You don't understand. The *Paraíso* is the largest party boat in the region. The A Deck festivities never end. My job is to insure they don't get out of hand."

"Party boat? *Party boat*? No, the *Paraíso* is an orphanage and a hospital and—"

"This conversation has turned tedious, and so I shall now

take leave of you," said Vázquez, inflicting a whole-body sneer on Fátima. "As for your babies and soldiers and refugees, they must have been figments of your enervation."

An uncanny force began building in El Bebé del Agua, flowing outward from her heart to command her blood, bones, flesh, and mind. She lurched away from Vázquez, charged past a knot of revelers, and, reaching the landing, jammed her shoulder against the waterbag.

She pushed. It didn't budge. She pushed harder. Nothing. She pushed still harder. It moved.

Thump, thump, thump, thump, thump.

Thud.

"*Muchas gracias!*" cried the señoras in unison, their buoyant voices echoing up the companionways between C Deck and A Deck. "Are you there, Capitán Suárez? Here is what a warning shot from Valentina Muñoz sounds like!"

A bullet ricocheted off the archway to the A Deck ballroom.

"And here are what three warning shots from Renata Castillo sound like!"

Three more bullets whizzed through the air.

◆

The consequences of Fátima's impulsivity were not long in coming. Hissing and swearing, a half-dozen revelers fell upon her. They blindfolded her with a cloth napkin, bound her wrists with zip ties, and frogmarched her across the landing toward the right-hand archway, or so she presumed.

"I demand to speak to Suárez!"

"'Of all them blackfaced crew, the finest man I knew, was our regimental *Bhisti*, Gunga Din,'" quoted Vázquez—pointlessly, in Fátima's view.

The parade continued for a full fifteen minutes along a

succession of corridors, their carpets so deep and plush Fátima imagined she was walking on mud. She tried keeping track of the left turns, right turns, and straightaways, but in her dazed state she lost the Theseus thread of her salvation, and she realized that returning to the ballroom and pleading her case before Suárez would probably prove impossible.

A door swung open on hinges in need of oil. The revelers' insolent hands pushed her into a chair and unbound her wrists. The heady scent of orchids sweetened the air.

"When you hear the door close, you may take off your blindfold," said Vázquez. "Remain seated until you're told to stand."

The hinges shrieked, and the door slammed shut. Fátima reached behind her head, untied the dinner napkin, blinked, blinked again, and, craning her neck, looked in all directions. She was seated on a cane-back chair facing away from the door. The suite was spacious and lavishly furnished. Potted orchids arrayed along the walls filled the room with primary colors and heady perfumes. The central dais supported a saltwater aquarium holding iridescent tropical fish.

Again the hinges shrieked.

"You may stand now."

The man's voice was resonant but coarse, as if he were using a corroded bell as a megaphone.

"Keep staring straight ahead. Take ten steps forward. Don't look back."

Fátima stood up and strode past the aquarium toward the rear wall, its bamboo curtains framing a wrought-iron veranda overlooking a tract of open, placid water. A sliding glass door sheltered the suite from the vicissitudes of the Gulf of Mexico.

"I've never had a Jonah do that before," said the bell-voiced man, appearing at her side in the dress blues of a merchant vessel commander. Capitán Suárez was stunningly handsome, his soft brown eyes and cleft chin organized around a Roman nose. "Pushing your waterbag off the landing and letting it roll down to C Deck—what were you trying to accomplish?"

"The *Paraíso* serves many worthy purposes, but your A Deck bacchanals are not among them," said Fátima. "I suggest you reward my benevolence toward the hurricane refugees by taking me back to Isla Mujeres."

"What hurricane refugees?"

"You know what hurricane refugees."

Suárez slid back the glass door and stepped onto the veranda. Ocean breezes brought the tang of brine and intimations of mist.

"I have no desire to reward your benevolence, Señorita, only to punish your impudence. When my first officer returns, he'll lock you in the brig. By morning we'll be in the West Sargasso Sea, home to the planet's most accomplished predators."

"Is that my cue to beg for my life?" said Fátima, joining Suárez on the veranda.

"I'm the Capitán. I give orders, not cues." He placed one hand on the balustrade and pointed toward the sea. A flat, dark mass, at least thirty kilometers away, broke the horizon. "Aklins Island. I was born there. By age ten I was tacking around it in my sailing dinghy."

"Have you no compassion for the infants on M Deck?" said Fátima. "The casualties on I Deck? The victims on E Deck?"

"There are no infants, casualties, or victims aboard the *Paraíso*."

"Descend and see for yourself."

"I never descend."

"Only condescend."

Suárez snorted and clucked his tongue. "God doesn't automatically know everything that's happening in the universe—that's why people pray—and I am likewise incognizant of many events aboard this ship. My childhood on Aklins was idyllic. I once built a sand castle as large as a wishing well."

"I'm curious, Capitán. Do you *choose* not to visit the world below—or are you *incapable* of going there?"

"Of course I'm capable. I'm the master of the *Paraíso*. I pity you, Señorita. You could have joined this ship's company. Instead, with one rash act, you squandered away your entire future."

"I have not exhausted my repertoire of rash acts, Capitán."

Abruptly Fátima scrambled onto the parapet. Struggling to maintain her balance, she took a deep breath and sealed it in her lungs.

"Very well, then, *drown*, why don't you?" cried Suárez.

El Bebé del Agua faced the horizon, reached for the sky, brought her palms together, bent at the waist, and jumped.

◆

Fátima continues to fall. Her pressed palms and raised arms puncture the Gulf like an arrowhead, and instantly the rest of her drills into the water and keeps descending. She has reckoned her pike-position dive will send her twenty meters down, and that's indeed what happens. Still holding her breath, she slows her fall by throwing out her arms, then changes her orientation by 180 degrees, using her palms like oar blades.

Kick by kick, stroke by stroke, she rises. She praises herself for having inhaled so deeply on the parapet; her buoyancy is a thing of beauty. She tilts her head back and surveys the uncountable kilograms of Gulf water, lit by the setting sun, that lie between her lungs and fresh air.

Now the surface looms up, and she breaches it like a circus dog jumping through a paper moon. She exhales ferociously, inhales greedily. Gasp, inhale, exhale. Gasp, inhale, exhale. The

Paraíso is still obscured by fog, but she can infer its skyscraper proportions. Aklins Island is a speck on the horizon. El Bebé del Agua feels confident she can cover all thirty kilometers in under three hours.

Drawing in a large helping of air, she strikes out for the island. The water is cold, but the exercise keeps her core temperature close to normal. Her preferred technique becomes the breaststroke, for it allows her to hold her destination always in view. In time Ximena the sea serpent appears at her side, or so it seems, scales coruscating, barbels undulating, horns thrusting heavenward. Blackbeard the Pirate's erstwhile organic frigate assures her she can make it.

The kilometers melt away. Sooner than she expected, the lighthouse on Salina Point appears, and within the hour she discerns massive black rocks arrayed along the beach. She wades through the moonlit surf, water sluicing off her swimsuit, and comes ashore, gasping, shivering, teeth chattering. A wooden bench commends itself to her exhaustion. Excited voices emerge from the darkness. Local inhabitants, deracinated Bahamas tourists, the lighthouse keeper's family: it doesn't matter—her escape is now complete.

She sits on the bench and waits for the strangers to arrive. The crashing waves soothe her, the night wind serenades her, and the starry vault spreads before her like a spangled curtain behind a proscenium arch, even as she plots the imminent return of Fátima Lucia Zuniga and her animal companions to the *Paraíso*, bearing hope, justice, wisdom, and water.

◆

End

Ocean Scourge

[Ocean Scourge]
[A.E. Fonsworth]

The world's womb is a tomb
That of a woman scorned
And forced to watch her tongue
Scrubbed from the mouths
Of a dozen generations
Creolization's
Born and—
Worn in her ebb and flow
Degraded into the white froth
That once foamed in dissipation at her shores
Words whispered on the winds of changing tides
Of time
In currents that reflect a past still plaguing our present
Called a gift
A dream
The dream
Thee dream
And yet I am still naught
Absent and blank
Named and defined
Thirsty
Dehydrated
Emaciated
Of truth
In crisis

A. E. Fonsworth

In tandem with another self
They that belong
She that can
Her that will
Him that cannot
We that will not
Do refuse
To forget
The salt scouring of our lips
As we search for water between the breaks

♦

End

143

Inmates of Ikenga Point

[Inmates of Ikenga Point]
[Uchechukwu Nwaka]

Act I

AZU PEEKED OUT OVER THE EDGE of the loading crates to find two sentry-droids by the hangar doors. Their pulsing green eyes swept across the compound and he snapped his head back behind his hiding place before they could spot him. The sentry-droids were armed with rifles that had enough stun rounds to incapacitate a whale. He took a nervous breath.

"How many?" Mayor asked beside him.

"Two," Azu whispered in response. His drill gun felt heavy in his hand. "You'd think they'd disengage the security protocols on their robots in a situation like this."

"Yeah," Mayor grunted in response. His voice was strained, and Azu could see the effort it took the man to keep his weapon steady. The dehydration was getting to him. Hell, it was getting to *all* of them. Mayor might have been a big man, but he was also old. Working for too long on this forgotten rock.

"Guys, we're in!" Isioma's voice broke the silence through their intercoms. Azu lets himself exhale in relief. While he and Mayor were making a run for the station's hangar, Isioma and some of the other inmates had tried to take the Point's central hub.

"Great," Mayor said. "Any casualties?"

"A few injuries. We were able to overpower the sentry-droids on this end, but just barely."

"Okay," Azu cut in. "Can you hijack the controls to the sentry-droids?"

"No. Their controls are decentralized. However, I can hack the service bots around the compound. Once they attack the sentry-droids, you'll get a window to get to the hangar."

"Isioma, we'll get our sentences extended if we destroy any more government property," Mayor said.

"We'll be lucky to even live out the rest of our sentence at this rate," Azu hissed drily. He was parched, and his tongue felt like an old rag. The last bottle of water he had had was as brown as gin. And that was over twelve hours ago. Not even the makeshift filter they'd rigged could remove the rust flakes from the water. All the pipes on Ikenga Point were rusted and broken beyond repair. Even the maintenance bots were all busted. The water filtration systems had long fallen into disrepair. Supply dropships were few and far between, almost completely stopped.

Maybe the government forgot there were still humans serving sentences at the facility.

Or maybe they forgot what system their favourite remand facility was located in.

There was a sudden crashing noise. Azu turned, in time to see scores of small, saucer and spherical-shaped service bots swarming across the loading compound. They zig-zagged around empty loading crates and dead pieces of machinery, in a bee-line for the sentry-droids. The sentry-droids' green eyes pulsed in some sort of machine communication to the bots, but Isioma's programming seemed to override the commands. The bots crashed into the sentry-droids and their eyes switched from green to red, drawing their weapons to fire.

"Now! Go! Go!"

Azu didn't need to be told twice. The two men ran into the stretch of compound separating them from the large hangar doors. The sentry-droids had whittled the service bots to a handful, but it was enough distraction for them to cover the distance. One of the sentry-droids locked on Azu, red eyes pulsing in warning. It lifted its rifle and Azu ducked under the barrel, driving his drill gun upward. There was a sickening crunch as the hand-held machine whirred in ignition, embedding itself destructively into the robot's skull. Azu grabbed the droid's gun and turned to acknowledge his partner.

Mayor was on the ground.

The second sentry-droid loomed over him. Azu panicked, emptying the clip on the droid's back, and it crumpled in a heap. He rushed to Mayor's side. The man was still breathing, but his breaths were shallow. His breath smelled sickeningly sweet. Ketosis. Azu placed his hand on his neck, and his pulse was weak.

"Isioma, Mayor is down!" Azu yelled.

"Shit."

"When last did he have anything to eat, or drink?"

"I-I don't know. Two, three days? The hydroponic farms are gone. And you know how Mayor is. He'd rather make sure everybody else ate before he did."

Azu cursed. Mayor was like that. Fancied himself like some sort of father figure. Nobody knew how long his sentence was, but everybody met him when they first arrived at Ikenga Point. Mayor was the one who showed everyone the ropes. Some of the inmates had even joked that he probably had a life sentence. Unlikely. All sentences on the Point came to an end.

This time, it seems like all our sentences will end with us as desiccated bodies inside body bags.

"Azu, you have to go now," Isioma urged him.

Azu bit the inside of his lip. This was *not* supposed to be a one-man job. He took Mayor's small supply sack and headed for the hangar.

"Please get someone to get him out of here."

146

The hangar doors slid open. Pale yellow lamps lit three small, first-generation spacecrafts. Shadows shrouded the ships in sharp angles. Azu swallowed the lump that had formed behind his throat. The last time he really flew a craft, there were casualties. The last time he tried to fly a craft, he was remanded to Ikenga Point.

His gaze fell on the small supply bag in his hand. It contained a small ration of water, filtered by their slapdash rig for four days straight. He *had* to find the supply ship.

"Where was the supply ship last seen?" Azu asked, strapping into the pilot seat.

"I'm sending you the coordinates now." The ship's engines grumbled to life. Panels lit up as the ship's controls activated. Azu took another deep breath. After months of one-sided communications that received automated bot responses, and unanswered help requests, the government eventually sent a supply dropship. But, like one epic joke, the dropship with the Point's water, food supplies, and new maintenance droids was hit by a solar storm on entry into the system, completely incapacitating it.

The government said that was now *our* problem.

Azu steadied the control yoke as vibrations shook across the body of the ship. Did they understand what it meant to be stranded on a moon that was lightyears from the nearest civilization point? To be unable to even *drink* water? Ikenga Point was dying. Many of the solar panels and generators had broken down ages ago. The hydroponic farms barely yielded harvests. The station was once something to behold. A novel enterprise for the Nigerian government, in association with the Western world, to mine exoplanetary rare minerals and exploit the booming space business. All Nigeria had to provide was the manpower. Send offenders there, let them serve sentences. Worked like a charm.

Now the market was oversaturated. Humanitarian groups now pushed for automated labour, and the government was left with a station nobody wanted to have anything to do with. Understaffed, under-maintained, under-everything, in one obscure corner of the galaxy.

Our planetary coffin.

Azu gritted his teeth as the craft shuddered, rising over the facility. From above, he saw Ikenga Point stretch across the moon's surface. Towers of steel and domed compounds were visible within several man-made craters. Indeed, a multinational project, which the Nigerian government was left managing alone. Many sections had crumbled. Pipelines had been compromised. There were even several shuttles in wrecked heaps all around the surface. It didn't help that the planet was magnified before him. One of those planets nobody bothered enough to give a proper name, besides some odd alphanumeric designation. The surface was dark, tremulous with storm clouds. From what Azu knew, the atmosphere was so dense, probes couldn't make it deeper than a few hundred miles.

No water there either.

Azu wondered about the dozen prisoners in the station, all dealing with starvation and dehydration. If he couldn't find the lost dropship vessel, then they would all die of dehydration. *If the water poisoning didn't do them in first.* The farms would never recover either, and only God knew if anybody would even give a rat's ass about some no-name troublemakers.

The coordinates to the stranded dropship pinged on his display.

"It'll take a while to get there," Azu said. The first-generation ships travelled at only sub-light speeds. He was on a timer, but if he pushed the craft too hard he would risk imploding the flying heap of scrap with him in it.

"We'll manage until then," Isioma replied. "And Azu, be

careful. The flares from the solar storm are still coming in hot. It *will* be dangerous."

Azu bit his cracked lip grimly. "It's not like we have a choice."

He pushed the yoke forward.

◆

Act II

In another life, Azu used to be an emergency pilot.

The population on Earth forced expansion into orbiting annexes. There were no real sustainable exoplanetary colonies yet, save for mining facilities on asteroid clusters and farther-off systems. The construction of these annexes unavoidably involved accidents, and Azu was one of the pilots who flew the ambulances. It was a good job. The pay was great too. All in all, stuff was looking good.

Until he suffered a stroke behind the wheel.

Two lives were lost and he was discharged. No more spacefaring. Stuck on one of Earth's many slums with dwindling savings, and unable to land a job due to depression, Azu wasted away. One day, in a drunken stupor, he'd tried to hijack a shuttle, only to crash it before it could even lift off the landing pad.

He got seven years on Ikenga Point.

"How's Mayor?" Azu asked.

"We got him on some infusions," Isioma replied, her voice riddled with static. "You're getting close."

Azu gulped the last of the water in his supply pack. It tasted like iron. "I know."

"Hey, did I ever tell you how I got to Ikenga Point?"

Azu's eyes rolled to the back as he tried to remember. "I think so? Weren't you a hacker or something?"

"Yeah! I sold a piece of lunar real estate to an Alhaji in Dubai."

Azu snickered. "What? That's nuts."

"Too crazy," she laughed back. Static almost muddled her next words. "I'm on parole this year. But I'm worried, since it's been years since anyone ever left this rock."

Azu sighed. He had two years left himself. He was one of the last set of inmates to reach the Point. Even then, it was in serious disrepair, but at least there'd been water to even bathe with.

"I see the ship!" he exclaimed into the comms, but he was greeted by static. He tapped the controls furiously, but there was nothing on the other end. Azu cursed. The large supply ship hung eerily in the void, pieces of debris floating about it like a broken children's toy. In the distance, the twin suns that served this system burned bright. Azu had to squint at the glare. The shuttle rocked, making uncomfortable sounds as he drew nearer the supply ship.

He checked the control panel. Solar readings were normal.

For now.

With much difficulty, Azu guided the ship through a hole in the hull. The dropship was a frigate-class vessel designated as the *Kunja*. Possibly second-generation. Little wonder why it didn't make it. Cost-cutting was synonymous with Nigerian government policies. Azu thought that if they could no longer manage the Point, then they should bloody abandon it.

Azu secured the helmet of his spacesuit over his head and exited the smaller ship. The dropship was dark, without any signs of a secondary power source. He floated through the corridors, his breaths loud in his helmet. The light from his space suit swept across the steel-walled passages. It took some time, but he was able to access the cargo bay.

His breath caught in his chest at the sight.

There were pods all across the room. Each cylindrical

structure was ceiling-high, made completely out of steel. Over each surface were panels displaying a number of parameters. Azu drew closer.

H_2O (Gas). $X°C$

Azu screamed, hugging the pod. His eyes scanned through the rest. Everything was intact. There were ports on the pods for pipes to go through. Elation ballooned in his heart and he screamed some more. On the floor were numerous crates labelled as machine and replacement parts.

That was when sudden cold realization needled through his chest, permeating into his bones until the dread suffocated him inside the tight confines of his suit.

There was no way he could transport all of this back to Ikenga Point with just his small craft.

Even if he could get a few of the replacement parts, they would never be able to get the water systems back online on time. If at all.

Azu slumped, and even the absence of gravity did not help the weight that pressed his shoulders down, crushing him in defeat.

♦

Act III

"Azu... Azu... Azu can you hear me?"

The ghost of a sentence materialized from the static of the comms embedded within Azu's spacesuit. He blinked, trying to adjust to the near-darkness of the cargo hold. He must have nodded off. The voice broke through his speakers again. "Azu, are you there?"

Azu jumped. "Isioma, that you?"

"Oh thank God. Thought we'd lost you. What's up?"

151

"I found the ship, but I can't transport many of the supplies here." Azu tried to fight the panic creeping into his voice but failed. "I... I don't know what to do."

"Can you fly the ship?" It was Mayor's voice, deep and gravelly.

"M-Mayor! You should be resting!" Azu yelled.

"I'll rest when I'm dead. Seems like you're going through a tough time, Azu."

Azu bit his bottom lip. He was glad that Mayor was okay, but he wasn't sure anything he could say right now could calm the storm in his heart. "The ship's hull is damaged. I don't think there's any power left on the ship either."

"Azu!" Mayor's voice was stern. "You absolutely cannot give up now! It's not over, you hear me? Take a deep breath. Think rationally!"

"B-but..."

"It's an automated ship. Is there no way you can get it back online?"

Azu shook his head, as though to clear the confusion from his thoughts. "Tell me what's in the hold," Isioma said quickly. Azu described the contents of the hold the best he could. Isioma made a small sound on the other end. "Azu, there just might be power left on the ship."

"What?"

"The water tanks are still functioning. Plus, it seems the solar generators are still fine. You just have to redirect those inverters to auxiliary power."

Azu blinked as her words sank in. "But the hole in the hull. I can't fly the ship with that."

"Activate the maintenance droids. Let them work on the hull. Azu, I don't mean to pressure you too, but you have to hurry—" static cut her short suddenly. "Time... storms... Azu?"

"Isioma!"

The ship suddenly groaned, tremors wracking its body. Flares! Azu waded towards the crates with the maintenance droids and forced them open. The droids were squat machines with saucer-like heads. There was no way to activate them.

Shit.

Maybe, if he got the systems back online, they would also come online. Azu swore, turning back to the corridor. He'd passed by a circuit box on his way down, and so he headed towards it. Another quake rocked the ship, and he nearly crashed into a steel beam jutting out of the wall. He panicked. A headache was pounding behind his eyes. The corridor split into two, then four, his vision swimming. Fatigue pulled on his bones, his limbs feeling like blocks of concrete. He couldn't give up now, not after he'd come this far. Everyone at the Point was counting on him.

Azu kept going.

He flipped the circuit board open as another quake rocked the ship. He flipped a set of levers and a hum greeted his ears. Lights filled the ship instantly. An automated voice announced the ship was at 30% functionality.

The droids?

But it seemed his gamble was spot on. The maintenance droids scuttled along the corridor, heading for the fault in the hull. Azu dared a sigh of relief, before heading to the bridge. There, control panels beeped on and off with life. Through the viewscreen he saw streaks of vermilion spiraling across the void, originating from the twin suns like flailing tentacles. His blood ran cold. He waded to the comms console and furiously worked the panel. Nothing seemed to get past the static. The solar readings were recording dangerous spikes.

He had to get the ship out.

In another stroke of luck, the gravity engines kicked in and Azu fell to the floor. System analysis revealed that the droids had managed to seal off the section of the ship with the hull breach. Functionality was rising. Azu took off his helmet.

The *Kunja* was an automated ship. He worked the command console. It was still locked onto Ikenga Point. It made things easy.

"Computer, initiate jump protocol."

"Cannot initiate jump," the system announced. "Insufficient energy reserves."

What? Azu scanned through the schematics again. Some of the solar panel arrays had been damaged by the initial accident. Questions of what to do buzzed angrily in his mind. There was another tremor and the ship lights flickered. This was probably what Isioma was trying to warn him about. Was there really no way to get this ship out of harm's way?

His eyes met the flares burning across space.

Flares were mostly electromagnetic energy... but there was something different about these flare storms. If the flares were powerful enough to rip a hole in the *Kunja*'s hull, then, maybe, he could somehow harness all that energy to make the jump to Ikenga Point.

"Computer, delay jump protocol." Azu gritted his teeth as he said the words. He took a deep breath, willing himself to be braver than he felt, then said. "Record message."

The idea was crazy, but it was worth a shot. Azu dashed out of the bridge, sprinting at top speed to the cargo hold. He disengaged the conduit cables that fed the water tanks. If he failed, then nobody would be drinking anything anyway. The landing craft was beyond the sealed section of the *Kunja*. Azu floated towards the ship's engines. He worked the conduit cables onto the engine's outflow plugs. Then, circling around the *Kunja*'s damaged outer hull, he found the damaged array of solar panels.

Azu undid the panels.

He worked the cables into the circuitry.

Then he boarded his craft.

"Computer, do you read me?" he said, sweat rolling down his face, neck, palms. The pinprick points of stars had been replaced by streaks of divine yellow. Like the branches of some heavenly tree. Photons of pure energy travelling across the infinite distance of space.

"Affirmative," the computer replied.

In his vessel, the solar readings were going haywire. Azu pushed against the control yoke and the craft sluggishly eased away from the dropship. Everything felt heavy. Like the ship itself was rejecting his resolve. A bright streak of crimson fire split into a thousand mini-flares just above his head. The explosion sent shudders through his ship and he feared the craft would buckle. It did not. Azu gulped, pushing the craft even higher, until the cables connecting his engine and the *Kunja*'s damaged solar array were stretched taut.

Then, Azu fixed the yoke.

Fired the engine.

His terminal rang in alarm, the radar flashing a warning red. An icon flashed over the screen, three words in bold black.

<WARNING! IMPACT IMMINENT!>

Golden light filled the cockpit as a flare ejection struck his ship. Azu cranked his engine to the max, bones shuddering together with the hull of his small craft. Blinding white energy coursed through the body of the ship. If this failed, Ikenga Point would die from certain drought-induced collapse.

"Computer, initiate jump protocol."

"Initiating—"

The world burned into static.

◆

Act IV

Is this recording already? Oh, all right. Yeah. Um... this is Azubuike Abarah. Azu for short. I've been trying to get the Kunja to jump for the past hour, but no joy. One of the power relay systems is busted, and there's no more time. There's a flare storm on my neck, and I don't think this ship can survive another strike.

I have a plan, but I'm not very sure it'll work.

Before I get to that though, do you guys remember that time I first arrived at Ikenga Point? I was really angry, haha. I'm pretty sure I was a handful, even for Mayor. Thank you man, really. I never said this, but that time, I really needed someone who was not going to give up on me.

Isioma. Thanks for the many lessons on rerouting circuits and all that. Funny how we kept rerouting pipes from different parts of the station until there were no more pipes. Or water.

Do you think cables can conduct enough of a solar flare's energy to power a jump?

My ship will be the receiver. I'll pass the energy through its engines to give it some sort of vector control. Even if it's all theory, I can't delegate this to a droid...

I'm going to miss you all. I'm going to miss that blasted rock. I hope y'all can throw a party tonight and drink clean water to your hearts' content.

...

I hope, somewhere along the line, I atoned for my sins... Damn, I think there's something in the air. My eyes... ha ha.

...

Don't... don't come looking for me.

♦

End

Fanon and Soyinka on Traditional African Ecoharmony, Colonial Greed, and the Mystic Functionality of Water

[Fanon and Soyinka on Traditional African Ecoharmony,
Colonial Greed, and the Mystic Functionality of Water]
[Mingle Moore, Jr.]

IN HIS STUDY *BLACK SKIN, WHITE MASKS*, Frantz Fanon applies his own distinctive form of psychoanalysis, incorporating psychoanalytical theory to present a clear understanding of the dependency and inadequacy that the Pan-African community experiences. Bringing a plethora of arguments, Fanon speaks to the divided perception of the Pan-African person who has lost touch with his or her cultural origins by embracing the culture of a colonizing European country. Analyzing an inferiority complex that may have become embedded in the minds of the colonized

Pan-African collective, Fanon illustrates what takes effect when the cultural code of the colonizer is indoctrinated into a collective colonized community: an inferiority complex entrenched in the overall colonized group's self-perception. Conversely, Fanon deduces that:

> The Blacks represent a kind of insurance for humanity in the eyes of the Whites. When the Whites feel they have become too mechanized, they turn to the 'Coloreds' and request a little human substance. (Fanon 108)

This acquired mutual dependency that Fanon is referring to leads to a deeper yearning for acceptance, on the part of the colonized African, in hopes of finally becoming recognized in the eyes of the European collective. Fanon postulates that when it comes to the individual: "Hatred is not a given; it is a struggle to acquire hatred, which has to be dragged into being" (Fanon 35). Hatred needs to be taught to the subconscious mind; when it eventually arises, it will co-exist with feelings of guilt that result from harboring that hatred. Fanon identifies the complication of fear as well as rejection of the Pan-African person who wants to co-exist within the European collective.

In works of twentieth-century African literature, micro-nations explore how they cope with Europeanization. Characters and plotlines are negatively influenced by invasion and dominion and demonstrate feelings of dependency and inadequacy in the abandonment of their own social orders. In Ngugi Wa Thiong'o's *The River Between*, repudiation and corruption are the results of European influence on both the Makuyu and Kameno villagers, illustrated by a flowing river evidenced by a permanent split into two different belief systems that will never become one again. Wole Soyinka in *Myth, Literature and the African World* asserts, "Economics and power have always played a large part in the championing of new deities throughout human history" (12). Soyinka hypothesizes that traditional African nations have lived in harmony with nature for generations by utilizing the resources made available to them in their homelands. This harmony with nature remained constant until European invaders brought foreign dictatorship through deception, and an insatiable greed. The theories of Soyinka manifest themselves in twentieth-century African plotlines, illustrating that Europeanization and Europeans play a harmful role in African life even in their absence: Okot p'Bitek's *Song of Lawino/Song of Ocol* depicts a passionate discussion that title characters Lawino and Ocol have over Mother Africa's future through the lens of one woman's trepidation among the colonized Acoli. Ben Okri's *The Famished Road* illustrates how post-European colonization is responsible for the miseries of post-independence as a spirit child deciphers deceptive ways left in the colonizers' wake. Ngugi Wa Thiong'o's *The River Between* illustrates how European religion and traditions that the Gikuyu people are forced to recognize divide those who fear this sudden change and those who embrace it, causing the downfall of the entire nation. The conclusion demonstrates how the European belief systems that Africans embrace are destructive. European belief systems are intended to divide and conquer African nations by forcing them to dispose of traditional ways of life that include ecoharmony.

In Thomas Mofolo's novel *Chaka*, the titular character's fall from grace is due to corruption as power clouds his judgment. Europeanized literature portrays snakes as omens of evil, deception, and negativity. However, the serpent was welcomed and even celebrated in many traditional African societies: Mofolo writes, "he who kills a snake is regarded as insulting the gods and showing them disrespect because snakes are known as their earthly messengers" (2). Snakes served the purpose of healing: "it is understandable, then, that the snake should be an ingredient in all medicines of Bokone, because there is no way in which such an important thing could be left out" (Mofolo 3). Finally, the appearance of the serpent also served as a symbol of good fortune: "when a snake enters a house, the owners at once begin to express their thanks, or to ask for forgiveness from their gods who may be angry with them. Snakes are abundant therefore, since they are not killed" (Mofolo 3). Serpents are symbolic of Chaka's advancement to manhood: "While Chaka was looking over there in the deep where the water was rippling, he saw the huge head of an enormous snake suddenly break surface and appear right here next to him" (Mofolo 22). The Lord of the Deep Pool is the deistic entity who determines when the exiled young prince is prepared to transition into kingship. The colossal and elongated mighty monster of the water (Mofolo 24) anointing Chaka with his dual tongue represents rites of passage into both manhood and kingship and unites the physical and spiritual worlds through the flow of water. From this meeting, Chaka realizes that he is the chosen one of his people's gods. Chaka controls his people's destiny, as their king:

> This land is yours, child of my compatriot,
> You shall rule over nations and their kings
> You shall rule over peoples of diverse traditions
> You shall even rule over the winds and the sea storms
> And the pools of large rivers that run deep [. . .] (Mofolo 24)

Mofolo uses Chaka's and his father Senzangakhona's yearning for respect to represent dependency and inadequacy, writing, "even as he first arrived, the son of Senzangakhona, he made a name for himself by killing that madman, and all the people respected him" (Mofolo 51). Frantz Fanon explains:

> Man is human only to the extent to which he tries to impose himself on another man in order to be recognized by him. As long

as he has not been effectively recognized by the other, it is this other who remains the focus of his actions. His human worth and reality depend on this other and on his recognition by the other. It is in this other that the meaning of his life is condensed. (Fanon 191)

Dreams are important, as life is governed by the interpretation of dreams. Fanon explains that "the dream fulfills an unconscious desire" (Fanon 79). The enlightened African may turn to dreams for guidance in his or her life. Mofolo's delirious Chaka serves as the enlightened character who prophesizes about the European invasion: "You are killing me in the hope that you will be kings when I am dead, whereas you are wrong, that is not the way it will be because *umlungu*, the white man, is coming, and it is he who will rule you, and you will be his servants" (Mofolo 167). In this relationship between need, dependency and inadequacy, Fanon concludes: "Let us have the courage to say: *It is the racist who creates the inferiorized*" (Fanon 73).

Ngugi Wa Thiong'o's *The River Between* shows a destructive juxtaposition of European faith and African traditions. Fanon explains, "Inferiorization is the native correlative to the European's feeling of superiority" (Fanon 73). Through exploitation, feelings of dependency and inadequacy enter colonized communities. Wa Thiong'o utilizes the African male, cultural change, and European adjacency to create the characterization of inferiority. Europeanization takes place in one of two villages divided by a mighty river. Each village is indoctrinated to believe that the other is corrupt. As a result, this nation is split between two different belief systems: Makuyu is headed by Nyambura's father Joshua, who supports the European invaders' religion, while the land of Kameno is led by the protagonist Waiyaki and focuses on traditional rituals.

Fanon parallels Wa Thiong'o by postulating that, "to teach

Christianity to the people of Alor would be a quixotic undertaking [....It] would make no sense as long as the personality remains composed of elements that are in complete disharmony with the Christian doctrine" (Fanon 75). The introduction of Christianity in *The River Between* acts as a catalyst into Europeanization while traditional Gikuyu customs conflict with the imposed religion. The two communities are unable to coexist without prejudices driving them apart once again. Joshua illustrates Fanon's notion that "[t]he feeling of inferiority by Blacks is especially evident in the educated black man who is constantly trying to overcome it" (Fanon 9). Joshua doubles as the enlightened African in the eyes of European colonialists as he uses his acquired knowledge to brainwash traditional Gikuyu into embracing the beliefs of the Europeans. To escape his own sense of inferiority, Joshua passes this down to the Makuyu people, who ultimately present it to the people of Kameno; this act results in a never-ending spiral of intensified cultural whitewashing.

The Christian religion is associated with Europeanization, and it is Joshua who converts most of the Makuyu people to this belief system, which further aids Europeans in obtaining power over the Gikuyu. While Joshua has given in to the newly-acquired religious beliefs of the Europeans, Waiyaki holds the honor of being the representative of his people by "putting oneself to the test in order to prove it" (Fanon 57). Waiyaki proves that the motives of the Europeans are corrupting only if weak-minded individuals allow them to be influential; Fanon states that "you need to retract your pseudopodia and behave like a man" (Fanon 16).

In terms of colonized Europeanization, Wa Thiong'o demonstrates that if two communities are split into two belief systems, then the merging of the two is destructive and will ultimately cause the collapse of both. Wole Soyinka's *Myth*,

Literature, and the African World points out that African art has been distorted in an Americanized world: "the African world of the Americas testifies to this both in its socio-religious reality and in the secular arts and literature" (1); deistic symbols of African origin not only lead a promiscuous existence with Roman Catholic saints but are intermingled with twentieth-century technological and revolutionary expressionism (1). According to Soyinka, "The essential problem is that the emotive progression which leads to a communal ecstasy or catharsis has been destroyed in the process of re-staging" (5-6), the self-alienation experienced by Waiyaki in *The River Between*.

In Ugandan Okot p'Bitek's epic poems, *Song of Lawino/Song of Ocol*, Lawino's husband Ocol acts as the liaison for European influence as he demands her acceptance of Europeanization. Initially, Lawino's only option is to depend upon Ocol for self-validation: "He says I am silly/Like the *ojuu* insects that sit on the beer pot. My husband treats me roughly. The Insults! Words cut more painfully than sticks!" (p'Bitek 35). Lawino sees Ocol's Europeanized lover Clementine as an embodiment of England's oppressive demon familiars, keeping Ocol under an evil enchantment, "similar to Isanusi's assistants in Thomas Mofolo's *Chaka*" (Brooks de Vita, 2011). Ocol's fascination with Clementine prompts Lawino to question and recognize her own customs, belief systems, and overall existence in a liberated Africa. Soyinka determines that Lawino embodies the notion that "the symbolic disintegration and retrieval of the protagonist ego is reflected in the destiny of being" (36). The aftermath of European colonization is shown in Ocol's conformity, as the European community helps him reject his former customs and rituals to embrace those of European colonists. Lawino poses the question, "I do not understand/The ways of foreigners/But I do not despise their customs. Why should you despise yours?" (p'Bitek 41). Lawino deliberately holds on to her heritage, unlike her husband. Lawino arrives at the conclusion that every individual is born to carry out a specific purpose; Lawino defines traditionalism as her destiny.

The Acoli people believe that medicine is viewed as a substitution for natural ingredients from the Earth; Europeans have used their creations to brainwash the Acoli into thinking that Europeans are able to manipulate death. Instead of death being the end of individuals, death in the perspective of the Acoli is envisioned as an eternally flowing river that never stops as it approaches an unknown ending. Death is personified as a feminine figure, while humanity is personified as her children: "When Mother Death comes/She whispers/Come, /And you stand up/And follow/You get up immediately, /And you start walking/Without brushing the dust/On your buttocks" (p'Bitek 102). Soyinka's theorization that "the fragmentation of the original godhead may be seen, however, as fundamental to man's resolution of the experience of birth and the disintegration of consciousness in death" (27-28) mirrors the Acoli notion that all of humanity, as Death's children, is metaphorically in debt to Mother Death, a debt so enriched with symbolic importance that humanity is capable of repaying it only with their lives.

Novella Brooks de Vita's "Abiku Babies: Spirit Children and Human Bonding in Ben Okri's *The Famished Road*, Edwidge Danticat's *Krik? Krak!*, and Tina McElroy Ansa's *Baby of the Family*" defines the spirit-child as "a vessel allowing those in the spirit world to communicate with and affect the world of the living" (18). Okri's *The Famished Road* begins with the premise: "You have to travel many roads before you find the river of your destiny" (6). Azaro, a spirit child, and his family endure a series of trials until their destiny is revealed to them. Soyinka states, "Destiny is the logical result of the aesthetics of estrangement that defines reality" (25). Azaro recalls stories of European visitations and the destruction that came along with them.

Brooks de Vita writes that "spirit-children provide a gateway for spirit and human to interact within self, with the surrounding environment, and with the possibilities of existence" (19). Both worlds are made available simultaneously, and the only entities that account for these happenings are spirit-children. While the Europeans' first visit to Africa was based on acquiring information about an unknown land (Okri 282), the terms of their subsequent visits were guns, theft, fire, abduction, greed, indoctrination, machines, slavery, corruption, and hatred (Okri, 282). Europeans imposed their religious beliefs:

> Several people gathered outside the barfront, and stood with ostentatious Bibles. Their leader had the biggest Bible of them all. It looked like an instrument of vengeance. They evoked visions of fire/brimstone, sulphur/torment/damnations. (Okri, 375)

Fanon surmises that, "Yes, European civilization and its agents of the highest caliber are responsible for colonial racism" (Fanon 70). Fanon's theory manifests itself in the critical interpretation of twentieth-century African fiction: the need of the African to belong to the colonizing European community that subjugates his own. Okri's *Famished Road* explores nature restoring a society's way of life, a defining aspect of traditional African lifestyles, in which each person is responsible for the well-being of himself/herself and the totality of that person's community.

Race relations transcend the boundaries of critical theory and permeate works of African fiction to illuminate how the European belief systems that Africans embrace are unreliable, unnatural, and in disharmony with nature-based religious beliefs and practices. Colonizing European belief systems conquer traditional African nations by forcing them to destroy eco-harmonious belief systems and reject their traditional ways of life.

[Works Cited]

Brooks de Vita, Alexis. "Afterword." *Mythatypes: Signatures and Signs of African/Diaspora and Black Goddesses*. Connecticut: Greenwood Press. 2000.

Brooks de Vita, Alexis. Lecture for English 532-01. Martin Luther King Humanities Building, Texas Southern University, Houston. 7 Sept. 2011.

Brooks de Vita, Novella. "Abiku Babies: Spirit Children and Human Bonding in Ben Okri's The Famished Road. Edwidge Danticat's Krik? Krak!, and Tina McElroy Ansa's Baby of the Family." *The Griot* 24.1 (2005): 18-24.

Fanon, Frantz. *Black Skins, White Masks*. New York: Grove Press, 1952, 2008.

Freud, Anna. *The Ego and the Mechanisms of Defense*. West Haven: International Universities Press, 1979.

Keats, John. "Ode on a Grecian Urn." *Poetry X*. Ed. Jough Dempsey. 16 Jun 2003. 22 Jan. 2013.

Mannoni, Monsieur Octave. *The Psychology of Colonization*. Athens, MI: University of Michigan Press, 1990.

Mofolo, Thomas. *Chaka*. London: Heinemann, 1981.

Okri, Ben. *The Famished Road*. New York: Anchor Books, 1991.

p'Bitek, Okot. *Song of Lawino, Song of Ocol*. London: Heinemann, 1984.

Soyinka, Wole. *Myth, Literature and the African World*. Cambridge: Cambridge University Press, 1976.

Wa Thiong'o, Ngugi. *The River Between*. Johannesburg: Heinemann Publishers, 1965.

◆

End

The Turning Part

DRENCHED IN HUES OF LIGHT DUST, cerulean and crumbling sand, the engineer stirs from a tense slumber. His eyes, thick with the weight of numerous awakenings, blink open. Before them rests a cluttered desk and at its center, a big device. It buzzes with a soft, resonant energy, casting a flickering ring of yellow and blue light upon the desk. The fan has been blowing hot on his skin, an old fan hanging on the ceil of that third floor where the lab is built.

The engineer sighs, his eyes still towards the device. *It's ready.*
His fingers gently dance across the strange dials and levers, their memory a mosaic of past attempts and failures.

◆

Did I fall asleep again here in the lab? Surely it was a dream. The people in the manholes with water on their feet. That part of the city, with water, dirty water on the floor that people were trying to drink. Surely it was a dream, although not far from reality. This city is dying. The markets are nothing now but stalls abandoned to ghosts, their colorful wares replaced by a lingering emptiness. And that is the part I think about the most. All the damage that we did to the world, the things we took for granted. Water. I have no idea what is going to happen if this does not work.

◆

The blue, yellowish flashing light keeps coming back at him and he senses, somehow, *this has been going on forever*. A sudden sound vibrates through the lab and through every inch of his bones.

It's just the door. He clears his voice. "Yes; come in?"

Two familiar figures enter the lab. The first man, Nhabas, is short and ruffled. The second guy, Dzimukhe, is tall and sharp, and has his hands in his pockets. Both wear blue jumpsuits.

"Are we interrupting?" Dzimukhe asks. He looks uneasy.

"Not at all; come on in," the engineer replies, perceiving, however, that their faces show some concern.

"We have not seen you for a while," Nhabas says, hanging his head low.

"Yes, or so, but I have been quite busy. You know that."

Dzimuke raises an eyebrow, a frown pulling his face. "We are here to find out if you have made any progress. Everyone is waiting, you know."

"I... wait, what do you mean, everyone is waiting?"

"I mean," Nhabas turns towards him in all seriousness, "you realize that this thing you're doing will change the course of the Alliance? It's important that you deal with this carefully."

The engineer is lost for a second. They know his position. He told them why he had to move, why he left the MajiMlezi

168

Alliance. "I'm well aware, but I'm not dealing with them, not after all these years of fiasco."

Without asking, or any notice, the two men approach the desk. The sun has been gone for a while. The streets are a glass of silver rays.

The engineer feels cold as he speaks: "Don't touch it. I told you I will not share it until I am ready to do it!"

"We understand that," Nhabas says, looking away. "Man, I'm sorry. We have orders."

Dzimuke holds a syringe out of the engineer's viewing angle. "What the—"

◆

The turning part is hard and clenched.

Drenched in hues of light dust, cerulean and crumbling sand, the engineer stirs from a tense slumber. He sighs, eyes drawn back towards the device. *Wait. What? Was I dreaming with the people in the manholes with water on their feet?* His heart spins as he sees the blue yellowish flashing light. He is not sure of what's happening. Is the crisis over? Did he also dream of his colleagues entering the lab? Distantly, he hears steps in the corridor. There's barely time and his eyes widen in horror as the door is knocked and two guys walk in.

"Nhabas."

"Hello, my friend."

They practically grew up together. Same street, same school. Those kinds of friendships that you feel lucky to find. The engineer even remembered the day Nhabas turned to his father and said: "I will not join the service father, even if that makes you..."

The old man did not speak to Nhabas for some time after that. For him, his son was never going to be a true man.

The engineer shakes his head. That does not really matter now, not now that he is staring at Nhabas scared, as if staring at a venomous snake.

"What are you doing here?" the engineer asks, turning off the device.

"We came to see it."

"It's not ready. I know you have been sent by the Alliance. I..."

◆

The turning part is hard and clenched.

Drenched in hues of light dust, cerulean and crumbling sand, the engineer stirs from a tense slumber. *No.*

The engineer has a frightening realization that rebounds through his ears. Holding his breath, he wipes the trickle of sweat off his forehead. The door will be knocked on. A device that captures humidity from the air and condenses it into clean water shouldn't pose any threat. And yet, they see it as a threat to their authority.

He thought of that invention as a means to redeem himself after watching the water dry, after seeing his people and his city dying. After so many years of connivance with a state-owned company incapable of meeting the people's demand for water. After so many years of being one of them, benefiting from illicit loans and corruption.

Should I resist now?

But the door is already bursting and...

◆

The turning part is hard and clenched.

The fan has been blowing hot on his skin, an old fan hanging on the ceiling of the third floor where the lab is. *I'm stuck. There must be a way to prevent them from reaching me. Could I maybe jump in and end this madness?*

The lab starts to shake a bit and the engineer notices his balance wavering as he runs to the window, holding the device in one hand and the cellphone in another. There is a knock on the door as he rapidly texts his wife with the codes he still remembers.

♦

The turning part is spotless and plain. From crisis deep, the city rises and he rises, together. With innovation's guiding hand, it has regained life, a stunning land. A thriving haven takes its place.
Here I stand.

♦

End

"THREE WISHES."

At the corner washing machine, the old woman in black is whispering to herself. Maureen spares a glance in that direction, then fishes around in her purse for the roll of quarters she brought from the bank. She is fifteen, and dressed in black herself, with a black henna rinse covering her blond hair and thick dark mascara that is starting to irritate her eyes. The laundromat is littered with cardboard coffee cups, cast off sections of the *Boston Globe*, and stacks of the free circulars that carry TV listings for people who don't get cable. She'll have to remember to bring one back to the apartment for Dad.

Maureen hates being sent to the laundromat. Poor people use laundromats, poor people who wait with a basket full of wet clothes for an empty dryer, and then fight over who is next in line. Just last week Maureen got into a shoving match—some stringy-haired woman with a smoker's voice and the brown teeth of a meth-head—all because of a dryer. Maureen would have kept shoving, too, if it were not for the two-year-old clinging to the woman's leg. Today, though, it is just Maureen, the woman in black, and the guy who sits next to the change machine, always with his t-shirt riding up over his hairy belly. He only looks up from his magazine if someone from outside tries to come in and get quarters for the parking meter. Then he'll bark,

"Customers only," and go back to flipping through his copy of the *Victoria's Secret* catalogue. That is if you are lucky. Other times he might be looking at the kind of magazines that come in brown wrappers and have names like *Swank*.

"Threeee wishesss," the old woman keeps repeating, just loud enough for Maureen to hear above the rumble of the laundry machines and the faulty speakers piping in the same 1980's pop songs every hour. (Of course, Maureen forgot her own music today. Stupid ear buds are still in her raincoat pocket at home). The woman is wearing a black kerchief, black dress and thick-soled black shoes, like the ladies Maureen sometimes sees walking to morning Mass, carefully, as if their feet are made of porcelain. They live in narrow houses wrapped in red brick and vinyl siding, with overgrown grape arbors in the back yard and trellis roses surrounding cracked statues of the Virgin Mary. Their kids drive in from the suburbs every weekend to eat baked ziti and beg them to sell out and get an apartment at the Little Sisters of the Poor, or move into the "in-law" that is all ready for them in Wilmington or Melrose.

Maureen turns away, places her quarters in the tray and starts the dryer. The old woman is staring at her. She can feel it at the back of her neck, but when she looks around, the woman is standing hunched over the washer, folding clothes into a cracked plastic laundry basket -- clothes that probably used to be white but now are stained a rusty brown. Has she even cleaned them?

"Three ... wishes. Three ... wishes. Three ...." She's saying it over and over.

On a winter day like this, the laundromat is a closed world, one without bathrooms and with no food allowed. Signs to that effect are posted everywhere, despite the scattered coffee cups. Maureen sits down in one of five orange plastic chairs, connected to each other by a metal bar. Outside, the city sky is gray against the faded triple-decker buildings that line the street. Cars and people move slowly past the plate glass window, unheard beneath the crackling speakers, the rattle of the laundry machines and the whispers of the woman in black.

"Threewishesthreeswishesthreewishes ..."

As Maureen focuses on her clothes spinning round and round in the dryer, the old woman's words seem to accompany its motion, becoming more and more insistent. Maureen has heard many old people talking to themselves—on the street, in the park, riding the subway—repeating the same words over and over like a chant. Those people are never really talking to anybody but themselves, but the strange repetition in the old woman's words is beginning to feel directed at Maureen, like an offer. She looks up and this time, the old woman is looking straight at her. The woman has high cheekbones and a pointed chin and is perhaps not as old as Maureen thought. The woman's skin is pale, her eyes dark, with dark circles underneath. Even as she watches Maureen, her blue-veined hands keep moving, folding and refolding what Maureen can now see are not just dirty, but bloodstained clothes.

◆

After the thing happened, she found herself here, this rattling room occupied by bored and lonely people. Mostly, people do not notice her, or when they do they see no one but an old crone at her washing. Once in a while, though, there is someone tired or angry or sad enough to stare a while in her direction, just long enough to really see her. Or maybe the person hears her first and looks around to find the source of the voice. Either way, when this happens, she speaks to the person, makes her offer. The same questions every time; and always three wishes. She does not know why she has been doomed to this existence, to wash her clothes over and over, never getting the blood out,

and to tend to other people's hearts's desires. If she believed in
fairness ... but then again, the thing that happened was not fair.

◆

"Three wishes," the woman says again, firmly this time. Now that she is not whispering, her voice is deeper than Maureen expected. All around her the room has gone quiet. Even the change machine guy is asleep, his magazine fallen face down to the floor beside him. "Three wishes for you. Anything you want, but only if you answer my questions."

The woman's gaze is steady, her dark eyes unblinking.

"Okayyyy," Maureen says slowly, trying to humor the strange woman, even as she recoils from her. From where Maureen is sitting—despite the neatness of the woman's plain black clothes—there is a smell noticeable beneath the heavy odors of detergent and floral fabric softener that overpower almost everything else in the room. It's the smell of wet bathing suits and clothes left too long in the washer. Mildew. Still, the woman's face is familiar, and also kind of ... plaintive. Maureen sighs. The quicker this is over, the quicker the woman will leave her alone. Besides, Maureen can always lie. It's not as if the woman can actually grant wishes. "What do you want to know?"

The first question is simple. "What is your full name?"

"Maureen O'Hare."

"Full name," the woman in black says sharply.

Maureen rolls her eyes. "Maureen Anne Deirdre O'Hare." She leans back in the orange chair and it squeaks, making her jump a little.

The woman smiles slightly, revealing a chipped front tooth. That feeling of familiarity nags at Maureen again.

"And your first wish?" the woman asks

This is so stupid, Maureen says to herself, but seeing the

woman's expectant face she just says, "I wish for sommmmme ... more quarters."

A pile of quarters appears on the seat beside Maureen. She blinks.

◆

Sometimes she feels as if she's been in this place forever. It can't be that long, though, because the girl is still quite young. She waits for the girl and always watches her carefully. The girl used to come in with her father when she was small; sometimes she'd look in the woman's direction and wave, smile. Once she even tried to get her father to look, but he shook his head and kept reading his newspaper. Now, that the girl is older, she usually comes in by herself, dragging her black garbage bag filled with laundry and always bringing a magazine, and a small music player. Her hair is dyed black and she never smiles. She has stopped looking in the woman's direction. Her eyes are rimmed in black and her mouth a thin line, sometimes angry, sometimes sad. She sits staring at the dryer, with the wires from her music player coming out of her ears. Her face is set, her shoulders hunched forward, and she never looks up. Until today.

◆

It's not a huge pile of quarters or anything, not like the woman said a magic word and the room was filled with glittering coins. It is just enough quarters for a couple of loads of laundry.

"Really." Maureen just stares at the woman. "They probably fell out of my purse."

She checks her purse. Half a roll of quarters, still wrapped in brown paper. Maybe I'm dreaming, she thinks. I fell asleep staring into the stupid dryer and now I'm dreaming.

Outside, the sky has gotten darker. The laundromat's fluorescent lights are ghostly and turn the woman's face a kind of blotched and greenish color, pale and dirty as the stained sheets in her basket.

"Tell me something you're afraid of," the woman says out of nowhere.

Maureen finds herself answering without hesitation. "I'm afraid this dream won't end and I'll be stuck here forever like you." She tries to sound sarcastic, but she is telling the truth. She doesn't know how she knows the woman is stuck here, but she does.

"What is your second wish?" The woman's face is expressionless. The air in the room is heavy and thick. The mildew smell fills Maureen's nose and throat.

"I wish I had my music," Maureen says, because she really does. Then she could put in her ear buds and ignore this crazy old woman with her basket of blood-streaked clothes.

Maureen doesn't get her ear buds. Instead, above her head the silent speakers come alive with the sound of a secondhand guitar, of her own voice singing songs she has written herself, the ones she plays alone in her room when Dad isn't home. Tears form in the corners of her eyes. "That's me," she says. "I sound so sad."

◆

She died on this spot, collapsed onto the floor beside an empty laundry basket. She'd been having terrible headaches all day, and then her water broke in a stream of pinkish yellow fluid, all over the blue-flecked linoleum. Then there was sharper, shooting pain in her leg and she just ... crumpled. A doctor might have told her to stay on bed rest to keep down her blood pressure and the swelling in her legs, but she couldn't afford a doctor, and anyway there was no one else to do the laundry

*and make the meals. She lived long enough to hear the
paramedic tell her she'd had a daughter. She'd been hoping for
a daughter.*

◆

As the room fills with the sound of Maureen's high trembling
song, the woman in black asks her final question, softly, as if she
is afraid to know the answer. "What is the worst thing you've
ever done? Remember. It has to be the truth."

The look in the old woman's eyes is deep and sorrowful, a
look that means no harm, a look that can wait, has waited,
forever. So, in that lonely, empty room, where poor people wait
and fight and sometimes even die, Maureen repeats the terrible
thing Dad told her. He only said it once, a year ago now. They
were fighting, about her grades or her hair or her friends. She
isn't sure. Dad looked stricken right after he said it, as if he
didn't know where the words had come from, and he tried and
tried to apologize. Maureen said it was OK, but she hasn't
forgotten. He meant what he said, if only in the moment, and
Maureen knows he was right. He only confirmed the thing she
always suspected. Maureen looks into the old woman's eyes and
tells her heartbroken truth.

"I killed my mother." She says it in a whisper, although there
is no one but her and the old woman to hear it. There aren't even
any cars going by outside. "I killed her," she says again. "It was
my fault."

The woman in black doesn't say anything. Nor does she try to
contradict Maureen's words. Instead, the old woman's eyes are
deep and shining with pity, and Maureen knows where she has
seen that face before, the curve of that small mouth, the chipped
tooth beneath the old woman's trembling upper lip. There is a
picture on the mantel in the apartment, a summer's day and a

woman—younger than this woman—standing next to a green metal railing with the ocean behind her. She is looking straight into the camera with serious, forgiving eyes.

As the dryers start to rumble again, as the too-loud Top 40 music starts playing again from the hissing speakers, Maureen makes her third and final wish.

♦

"There's a change machine in there," Mama says. She has parked the car in front of the laundromat and Maureen sees them both reflected in the plate glass window. The day is bright but cold. "I'll watch for the bus while you get the quarters."

Maureen shakes her head. "Come on, Mama. I hate going in there alone. That guy's a creep. Plus he never..."

"You'll survive." Mama gives a flicking gesture with her mittened hand. Her cheeks are pink from the wind, her dark eyes shining. "And hurry up. The store's going to close."

Maureen walks away with a theatrical sigh, pulling at her tight black jeans to straighten them. Her blond hair is streaked with the black henna her mother pretends she doesn't hate. As Maureen opens the door to the laundromat, a strong smell of detergent hits her and she coughs a little. The man at the change machine puts up a hand, eyeing the dollar bills she's carrying.

"Customers only." He is wearing dark washed jeans with gold stitching and a tight t-shirt over his round stomach. On his lap is a lingerie catalog.

Maureen sighs again. "My *mother*," she says to the man. "I tried to tell her."

"Three wishes..." Maureen turns her head sharply. A song is cutting in and out on the laundromat's speakers, something about three wishes. A whiff of mildew hits her nose. In the far corner of the room, a longhaired guy in his twenties, dressed in

179

black, is putting his darks and whites into the same washing machine, without bothering to sort. She stares at him a little too long, then smiles and walks out into the winter sunshine.

◆

End

le mot, la mort

[le mot, la mort
for Edmond LaForest, Haitian Poet (1876-1915)]
[Albert Uriah Turner, Jr.]

Edmond, mon Edmond, *la parole faite dieu,*
 "the word made god" must imprecate you,

must construe, must conjugate, must make you.
Caught in *langue's* gross weight, you find *parole*

in hemp rope; no tempest spent in plundering
their word can sunder that bridge from your fate.

Wait. Was that Nago Shango now heard thundering
in your chest? Or is it your new wine-ridged voice,

rhyming Kreyol? Your now too-old head bent down,
the estuary will roll brown, free but betray the flesh.

Your keening soul lent to brackish mix of fresh, of
ocean, your name wracks my tongue with old song:

air, made of crimes, that expands the lungs, banned words
heard best through faults of time when some confess

to know the Artibonite (en Kreyol, Latibonit) in songs
that are free, are whole where river ghosts rest, children

de Dieu, who knowing, will raise you (the spirit
that sits now on the riverbed) to haunt, to quest.

♦

2.

Wait, why is Nago Shango now heard thundering?
Or is it you, bloated with the sounds heard

the same as words murdered by their Motherland--
one blunder *leur gros dictionnaire* defines as free?

Edmond, *la parole faite chair*, "the word made flesh,"
cannot wrest you from where you've seen bodies

(Égalité, Fraternité) to be; you are words (become
sound) to dull guillotines, a dreaming command

to strike at Liberté, that word, that thought enjambed
within your wants, entombed within Toussaint's land.

Wait, is that now Nago Shango again heard thundering?
Or is it you, who breathes Kreyol through borrowed songs?

In longing, you move to below making their words whole,
soul-sounding beneath dark. Drowning the meaning of free,

the word made flesh is weak; speak of the willing word
made god. The word made god (it is) is weak. Speak now

of why the word can cut the flesh blacked by no birth, you
god of poet's earth, of sky lost to hue, of stories we have
heard.

◆

3.

There is a spirit in the Artibonite, mermaid Mami Wata,
traveling in her trail of black plaits and burnt sugar skin.

There is a spirit in the Latibonit; it is not mermaid Mami
Wata
who unravels your tangle of brown cords and bloodless skin.

Simbi Dlo slithers in this so far away deep, beneath reach of
rest
you still wait in the Latibonit. Will that serpent bless you,
keep you

whole? Wait, from god have you plundered old words? Sing!
What could you have made unheard that is heard after you
spoke

and *parole*, greedy for your soul, demanded sacrifice?
You spoke. What could you have made unsaid that is said

to be the precise word (oh, can Shango be heard
thundering?)

183

as the other god, greedy for blackness, demands sacrifice?

Bon Edmond, qu'es-tu? What wonder had you, construed,
brooding? What word, *un gros dictionnaire* lashed to your
neck,

forced you to depths below surmise, made you rise into
waiting?
What word to forget, made to reconstrue *la parole est chair*,

made you rest from fleshing truth, made your riverbed
request
weighty like dreams of death, free of breath that made you?

♦

End

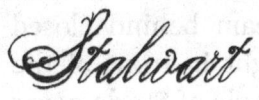*Stalwart*

[Stalwart]
[MultiMind]

HERE, THE SUMMERS ARE HOTTER, the winters aren't colder, and the city is still as corrupt as City Hall tries to normalize.

The city of Storla was on its third mayor in seven years— there was even an "interim adjudicator" once. He was the walking and breathing definition of incompetence, and no one, not even City Hall, was sure if it was corruption, abject stupidity or a baffling combination of both. He didn't count as Mayor, but he was thrown out of office roughly as fast as one.

It was hard to keep someone in office. Every election year, they would all spin such pretty little promises and say such darling, wonderful things. That they're nothing like the last person, oh how that person was so evil, double-talking and corrupt. That they, dear citizen, are different! Jobs! Opportunities! Honesty! Maybe a lower murder rate. Perhaps only crack 100 dead bodies instead of the usual 300+. Possibly. Without doctoring numbers and cooking the books. Maybe. Might possibly. Ma'haps.

And then the new person would be the exact same as the one before them. Sometimes they'd even tag-team behind closed doors for a better bounty to pocket, but fight in front of the public to provide a thrilling show that the people of Storla never needed and certainly didn't for.

Once a local artist circulated a comedy poll online, and that elected an actual ferret named Mockie. Mockie had a landslide of support and became the online "Honorary Mayor" of the city. Even City Hall thought the whole thing was funny until the Mayor's webpage was hacked so that Mockie could be listed alongside the mayor's portrait with a detailed oil painting of its own and a banner underneath: "Honorary Mayor: Grand Lord Sir Thaddeus 'Mockie' Thurgood III". Then it was all declared "vandalism and a punishable lack of respect for the Mayor's office." It had been fun while it lasted.

If anything, it was a reflection of how tired the people were. With every new mayor, there would eventually be another mysterious black hole of missing money in the city's budget, usually uncovered by some hyper-sleuth news team. There was sometimes also an intriguing multi-part documentary to watch as a companion piece, filled with award-hungry panning shots and well-dressed talking heads all chatting from tall chairs and comfortably furnished rooms.

The world would gasp in mostly pretend shock and horror, pass their judgements in countless comment sections, and keep scrolling to the next algorithm-picked cute picture or unfolding disaster.

That was how Shawntae found out about the current issue du jour: something was wrong with the water, so sayeth Mayor Something-Something.

Shawntae had stopped paying attention to their names a couple of mayors ago. They just weren't staying in office long enough to justify the brain cells. They were all just "The Mayor"

186

to her. She did, however, remember the name of Honorary Mayor Mockie. She felt Mockie ran on a fairly solid platform, and had voted for him. It had been a yes/no poll, but still Mockie ran on a more stable ticket than the actual human contenders. She appreciated that Mockie had his own party, the Wonder The Future party—the WTF party, for short. She even had a small flag of the party's symbol, a futuristic and explosive-looking question mark.

As for the regular, human mayor, Shawntae didn't care much. She did hear the current mayor was a lame duck do-nothing that seemed nice and meant well, like the others before him, but at least he didn't do anything corrupt. There was even chatter he might be able to do a full term without controversy; he only had a year and a half left of a four-year term to go.

Shawntae didn't really care; that was still a year and a half left of potential cock-ups to be revealed. Right now she was looking at a local meme of the current mayor smiling in a mock political ad that read:

> "Vote for me! I'm not corrupt! I don't do anything!"
> Citizen: Oh, cool. Will you fix the schools?
> "I don't do anything! *thumbs up*"
> Citizen: Uh, what about jobs?
> "I literally do nothing! *thumbs up*"
> Citizen: ...
> Citizen: Can you at least help me not die? At *least* not become a cold case, bare minimum?
> "I do precisely nothing! I don't do corruption. I don't do work. I'm basically a seat-warmer! And *that's* why you should vote for me! I take nothing and I give nothing!"

Shawntae just sighed to herself at the sight of the meme and thought, *In Mayor Mockie we trust.* She kept scrolling on her phone.

The meme was above a news report that was a day old. It detailed a mysterious bacterial outbreak in the city's water system. Shawntae briefly checked her ad-blockers to make sure she could read the article without pop-ups and in one piece, and tapped the news report. She read in the brief byline that the outbreak affected only a few neighborhoods, just a small cluster.

Including hers.

Freakin' great, thought Shawntae as she scrolled along, reading more. A few more taps around the internet and she saw that everywhere the story was posted, there were massive sparks in the comments among the regular digital squabble. The general consensus matched hers: nothing made sense and everything caught everyone unaware.

According to the article, the water quality had been bad since Thursday, as told by a source close to the matter that requested anonymity so they could talk freely off the record. The article had come out Monday morning and it was currently Tuesday.

A brief visit to the city's social media showed that the city hadn't really made any big all-calls yet, just a couple of cryptic "water boiling advisory in effect for certain areas" posts and a small map with affected neighborhoods marked in transparent red. The posts had been made late Monday night and before dawn Tuesday morning.

Now that there was an article out, it was time for the city to do what it usually did anytime a local crisis hit the papers: first hand out little dribbles of information, eventually building into a heavy dead sprint as if the city had been on top of things all along. This first article just so *happened* to look early. Happened *every* time. From riots to corruption, that was the tactic.

Shawntae was not looking forward to this.

A brief refresh on the city's social media proved her suspicions right. There were now more posts, but they were still varying levels of cryptic and "we will present you with more details when we get them. Thank you for your understanding and cooperation." They always talked as if the citizens had a choice in the matter. And whenever citizens aired grievances, these fell on indifferent ears and received canned replies.

The only things Shawntae knew for sure were that her neighborhood was indeed part of the small cluster of the affected, and that a mess storm was brewing.

City Hall always seemed to need one of those, a mess storm to make the problem look harder than it actually was, so they could justify all the sluggish reactions, blatant inaccuracies, and rushed out non-responses, and have magnificent baskets of plentiful blanket excuses on hand—everything from painting cover-ups as "slow responses of overwhelmed systems" to addressing their favorite people, the dead. The dead were always perfect: never complained or protested, and their backstories were more malleable than wet clay. Just bring them up, play the part, try to guilt the population into quieter compliance, and hope it all works until the next hiccup. Simply perfect.

Shawntae worried for a moment, with a familiar pang, if she was about to be future perfect. She'd always worried about getting future-perfected by a germ of a rampant virus or a germ of a raving person. There were times she'd tried to future-perfect herself, but that was a different matter altogether. She simply didn't want someone else or something else to do it.

Paradox? Perhaps, but Shawntae got the pang all the same.

She tried to make a mental register of everything she'd done since Thursday that had involved water.

Her apartment was postage-stamp small and she barely went out, so she thought recollection wouldn't be too hard a task, but alas, it was. Her brain always operated on low memory. Probably because of the overclocked processor constantly running in the background. Shawntae had good hardware for a head, but the software was all jumbled and fairly solution-proof, for the most part. Not from a lack of trying; it was just that Shawntae would always somehow land back at square one, or have another try at making herself future perfect. Sometimes both; every day was always a mixed bag with her.

But still, Shawntae tried to recall her water use since Thursday.

She tried.

She tried again.

The past few days were simply a foggy 404, Memory Not Found.

Her brain did that from time to time, just cut out, or delivered jumbled-up memories. She would probably forget she had a head if it wasn't attached. Shawntae suffered from too many bad memory files clogging up her head, slowing down her system, and sometimes getting stuck in feedback loops.

But she sighed and tried again one more time.

Had she done laundry? Yes, but that was on Wednesday because that was the day a favorite gamer streamer of hers had dropped a new video. The hour-long video had given Shawntae a useful timer to work alongside.

Had she watered her glowflowers? Yes, yesterday, but with the water collected in her dehumidifier. Shawntae didn't know if dehumidifier water was fine for the softly beaming yellow-aqua flowers staked in the lava stone and tree bark mixture, but they had flowered, and were emitting their heavy cinnamon-candy smell just fine, as they had since she'd had them.

Had she drunk water? Not sure, 404. But she didn't feel thirsty, so she guessed she may well have done so. Besides, she got her water from her filtered, bottom-spout cooler in her fridge, which she had refilled the day before laundry. It held over 30 cups, so she figured she would be fine—for now.

That realization gave her a thought. She wasn't sure what the thought was, but she was sure she was thinking. Shawntae could feel her head beep and whir softly as it did the best it could with such a bogged-down processor running who-knows-what in the background.

It dawned on her that she hadn't showered since Wednesday, something she did to spur herself to do laundry.

Augh. Yukkers.

It wasn't the thought her brain was thinking of, but it *was* a thought and a salient one, at that.

She now only had the option to bathe in contaminated water.

Augh. Double yukkers.

Showers were all her frazzled brain could handle, and that was on a good day. She had once gotten bath bombs as a spur-of-the-moment purchase, and had taken a week of self-cajoling and mental preparation to use them.

Add having to boil massive amounts of water to bathe in? With*out* somehow mentally blipping out to discover later that she'd added spaghetti to the water?

Shawntae decided to just stay grotty. She didn't feel too grimy anyways; some days she hardly moved from her random blip trances, where she would slip into silent stillness for unknown amounts of time. She couldn't help them; they always took her unaware. Other days, time slipped by unnoticed. Part human, part machine, Shawntae simply didn't know how to keep herself together.

Besides, she rarely left her apartment. Too terrified to. Used to do it for years, then the ways of the city eventually messed up her head too much. Shawntae got tired of having new defects and traumas added on top of the ones she already had. She wasn't the only one like this in the small city of Storla, not by a stretch. She just was one of the few who would rather bow out of society altogether and stick to her tech projects. Machines had fewer problems than people, and fewer problems was exactly what she wanted.

But now, she had to figure out her water dilemma.

Shawntae checked the city's social media. It seemed like a regurgitation of what had been said before, except there were new blue spots on the map. They were apparently "Water Stations" where anyone with an ID could get a big jug of water. One post said citizens just had to show up; a different post said citizens had to call ahead to make an appointment. It didn't matter which post had come first; the city preferred to play plinko with the truth, and citizens would find out after the fact what had been the right answer all along. Though, a good rule of thumb was to pick the worst and/or least convenient of the two options; that would be right a solid 60 – 70% of the time.

Shawntae didn't like either option. Both involved going outside. To her, that was where the danger lived.

I need a break, Shawntae decided. She got up off the neon pink recliner tucked in the corner of her little box of an apartment (that was priced like part of a mansion) and shuffled the short distance to her fridge, on the other side of the pint-sized place she found too cramped and expensive to call a "home."

The apartment was stuffed with all that she needed to function and keep at least a couple of specks of some degree of sane. She had her virtua-box, a virtual-headset-turned-full-immersion-booth that had taken a week to build, blip-outs included. The outside was covered in random paint pen scribbles and errant stickers. In there, she could run, she could exercise; she could look and experience any landscape on Earth, in space, or from anyone's imagination: from the billowy, scented fields of a distant meadow to the cold, brisk diamond rain of Neptune. Her recent preference was a gray, aged wooden dock on the lip of a brisk, churning sea under a moody sky filled with ominous towers of rolling dark clouds. She loved the racing of the raging wind and the coolness of the sea air. It had always been a good location for idle musing. Even if she blipped out, Shawntae at least had something soothing to come back to.

Opposite the booth was a Grand Materializer, version 1.0.4., sitting on an old repurposed desk. It wasn't the latest and greatest, too expensive, but it had been frankensteined into something close. It could materialize anything solid from the digital world. Wood, resin, iron filament, biodegradable marble. (Well, the marble *said* "biodegradable" on the box and the ad, but it turned out to have nearly a quarter of the life of regular plastic. A makerspace streamer tested it and cracked the math via livestream. The comments had been interesting—especially when the creators of the marble showed up.) The Grand Materializer could spit out anything Shawntae constructed or found on the internet, from cups to slotted planters for her glowflowers, or anything she needed for her plentiful tech projects and tinkery. Whenever she felt okay enough, she would make and tinker. Otherwise, she just researched and bought. Tech made Shawntae's life easier.

Such as her fridge. It was plain and rinky-dink, but it didn't need to be much more than that. Keep food cold, hold ice cream. Simple tasks.

"Runnin' low on juice and sodas?" Shawntae mused to herself as she took a long gander inside.

In the crisp, bright light of the soft cold, the fridge was fairly bare. On the bottom rack, a triplet of big jugs of juice sat, only two opened and roughly a third of each used. Two big bottles of soda lay on their sides beside the jugs, both blue tropical-punch-flavored. They filled up the rest of the bottom rack and were unopened. Shawntae usually didn't get sodas, but they were an impulse buy as she picked the groceries she wanted delivered. And now, they were an ironic lifesaver. It reminded her of a story told by a comedian from her youth: he'd been at a club and low on cash. He saw that a bottle of water cost a dollar-fifty but shots were fifty cents. He hadn't intended on drinking alcohol, but he'd ended up having his fill of shots. Couldn't afford a cab so he drove home. Tried to, anyway. When the officer asked, "Do you know why I pulled you over?" the comedian slurred out, "Officer, I'm drunk because I'm poor."

She had always found that joke humorous and poignant, but now the poignancy outweighed the humor. The city treated honesty the same way they treated ethics: something meddling and offensive. Shawntae wondered how long it would take for the water to genuinely become uncontaminated again. On the middle rack was her tall water cooler; it shared room with a nearly-empty container of rice pudding she couldn't decide whether to toss or keep. The cooler had a six-month filter (that was a month overdue, too expensive to keep up) but Shawntae knew it was for impurities, not bacteria. Special filters like that were hard to get, pricier to have, and sometimes too slow and frustrating to use.

And she guessed if there were bacteria in the water, it was most likely from fecal matter. The city ran on incompetency; it wasn't a leap of logic to believe a city worker had busted the wrong lines and tried to hide it, and now everyone has a "surprise" water advisory.

Shawntae closed the fridge and checked her phone. No city all-calls yet. She checked the city's social media; there were hardly any new details.

She then checked the social media of Honorary Mayor Mockie.

The profile picture was the oil painting in a circle frame. Underneath read the byline "Honesty. Integrity. Cute. Unofficial Duly Elected Mayor of Storla."

There, Shawntae found much more info, including some contextual information. She'd figured Mockie would have more information; whoever ran the account was quite diligent. The local artist who'd come up with Mockie admitted it wasn't their doing—but they were indeed glad it was done and wholly supported it.

Shawntae guessed if she'd been saner, she would have gone to this account first, but shouldn't an official government account be the first place a citizen ought to look before a parody account? Because of the reasonable expectation of accurate, first-hand information and all that jazz?

Not here in this city.

On Honorable Mayor Mockie's timeline, Shawntae's suspicions were confirmed: on Wednesday road work had broken a sewage line and a water main, and a rough patch-up job was why everyone in the affected areas now had to figure out how to not die from what came out of their taps.

In adorable bubble letters, the account said:

Good News: This should take about a week to fix!

Bad News: We haven't factored in the corruption, stonewalling and "miscalculated setbacks" so expect two weeks, rough estimate.

By the by: Rain is expected later today but remember: you can't drink rainwater. Too many impurities. Upset? So am I! Pollution is such a washout. Watch the video below that explains Rainwater, Drinking & You!

There was a little thumbnail below of an animated kitten scientist in a soft rainfall, holding a glass of water in one paw and the handle of an open red umbrella in the other. The umbrella bore the title, "Why Can't I Drink the Rain?"

Shawntae had seen it before; it was as informative as it was adorable. It explained acid rain and air pollution. The rain served as the washwater for the air and atmosphere to clean out the nasties in it, but now the impurities and toxins hanging in the air rendered rainwater unsafe to drink. The kitten would muse at the end that it hadn't always been this way; rainwater used to be safer, but corporations and eco-unfriendly politics had done a lot of damage—but! It was all reversible; just takes a little effort on everyone's part.

Shawntae wondered if the actual mayor had seen the video, thought "This is stupid," and found something else to watch.

She also saw that Mockie had shared personal accounts from the street: not all water spots had water, but there were pyramids of water jugs at places not marked out on the map, and several water spots were run by people who were some shiny boots and a few goosesteps away from being a historical throwback. Nothing short of rude, crude and vicious.

Classic city workers, in other words.

There was another post from the Mayoral Ferret:

Getting reports that people from unaffected neighborhoods have tried to get free water. Please abide by the map below. We got citizen scientists on the case!

If your neighborhood isn't blue, don't come through!

Below was a map of the city. The affected neighborhoods, in transparent blue, matched those on the official map. However, some neighborhoods that bordered the affected ones were in barred blue, as "possibly affected/still testing." Shawntae's neighborhood was still a solid block of blue.

Shawntae sighed yet again. She saw the water spots, marked with black dots. Those were the confirmed water spots, according to the legend at the bottom of the picture. The grey dots were water spots the city said existed, but "No Water Found/Never Arrived." Barred black dots meant "Depleted/Ran Out."

She saw that she was surrounded by several dots. The closest ones to her were a couple of gray dots, but there was a barred black dot and a couple of solid black dots a little further out.

All this map spelled out was that she would have to go outside. The city already was dangerous, unpredictable and traumatizing in the best of times, the result of incompetent policies by incompetent leaders. Now, there were lives on the line and the crisis was being handled by the empty-headed, who were supposed to be serving the fed-up, tired, and agitated. She knew the city wasn't as bad as outsiders depicted it, but she still had a head full of busted software from living there. Everyone did.

Shawntae looked at her large dehumidifier. It cleaned the air, dried it out and, if it were particularly hot, spat out the processed air as frigid cold. It only dried and purified today.

She wondered if she could be fine with drinking the collected water of the dehumidifier. All it did was pull water from the air, right? Just run it through the filter on the water cooler and drink.

Then her brain finally pinged her: this was the thought it was trying to think all this time. That the dehumidifier was a potential option.

As soon as that ping arrived, another, more disagreeable ping followed behind it.

The disagreeable ping had with it an accompanying memory clip from back in college. Shawntae had been younger, lazier from just taking the last of her finals, and thirsty. She remembered how she'd been slopped upon the couch of her friend Naia, who was trying to find something decent to watch beside her. Shawntae had wondered aloud if dehumidifier water was safe to drink.

Naia looked taken aback by Shawntae as she channel-surfed. "Even if you filtered it, there still would be whatever bacteria and mold breeding down there!" She gagged briefly and continued, "And a regular filter probably isn't even classed for all the metal and stuff."

"Penicillin came from mold," Shawntae mumbled back, muffled by a couch pillow.

"You don't need to try to discover new penicillin through lead poisoning," Naia scoffed, still flipping through channels. "Safe enough for plants you don't eat, not safe for you."

Memory end.

Well ... nuts, thought Shawntae.

She *really* didn't want to go outside. Shawntae knew she needed to work on this; it simply wasn't living. She used to never fear the world outside, but as the city got worse and worse over the past seven years, so had she. Staying in was at least a marginally better option than the poor mental health services the city ran. Shawntae had already tried reaching out for help. Between brusque cops sent on mental health calls, and the mobile mental care workers who sometimes came cheerfully flinging around misdiagnoses in their stead, Shawntae would rather stay in and rely on her tech. The last thing she wanted was to go outside and have an episode, or attract bad attention she never asked for. Inside was simply safer. Small, cramped, and a verdant tech-filled step above an actual cell, but it was safer. She tried to keep up weekly therapy appointments with an AI therapist. They seemed fairly accurate and helpful. At least they cost way less than the human variety.

Yet again, Shawntae sighed. "Time to test new tech," she mused.

Shawntae pocketed her phone and pulled down her left pajama sleeve. On her deep brown skin was a glowing field of numbers, her biokeypad's screensaver. It was an old addition from college after she saw a movie with one and thought it would be cool. She had spent the lion's share of her quarterly scholarship stipend on it, but it was worth it. Especially now.

Shawntae typed in her passcode to slide the keypad up and reveal a small octodrone. It was pearly black and a replacement for the older drone her digi-arm came with. Shawntae had modded it to have even quieter propellers, heavier amped motors, and a retractable hook in its belly.

She plucked out the drone and tossed it into the air with a spin, where it took flight.

"You're up!" commanded Shawntae as part of her vision became whatever the drone could see.

The drone hovered for a moment as Shawntae took out her phone. She explained while she uploaded the water maps, "You need to tell me where the actual water spots are. Lemme know how much is there, if the routes are walkable, and which has three people or fewer." She didn't think any water spot had fewer than three people standing there, but she would still rather try. If she had to go out, she would rather there be as few people as possible. Or she would devise an alternate solution.

The drone went to the window by the recliner, dematerialized through the glass above the glowflowers, and materialized itself on the other side before shooting off out of sight.

The sensor readouts and drone camera revealed a coming storm, but no rain. Shawntae hoped it was probably a bluffing cloud, something dark and ominous-looking that produced no rain, but she didn't want to take her chances. The drone was built to be waterproof, but it would still automatically seek shelter if it rained anything more than a medium drizzle.

◆

A citizen scientist finished submitting her hourly water safety test. It still came up contaminated.

"What a mess," Naia grumbled to herself as she reviewed her results once more. The person they sent the results to was shrouded in mystery. Naia had no idea if it was one person or a cadre of people but she worked with them all the same. She had seen the email posted on Mockie's account, read the call from yesterday for citizen scientists to submit their data, and gotten to work. Naia had a hard time trusting the city because of all the failures of the past and the problems so far. Besides, she had the schooling and the kit for the task.

She wore plain clothes, so city workers wouldn't hassle her; the city was already aware of Mockie's penchant for revealing whatever was discovered, and not simply what sounded good. (Want to see City Hall work fast? Check their math and post the numbers. Something the Mockie account did often.) Naia had already watched another citizen scientist livestream themselves getting ruthlessly shooed away; she didn't want the same to happen to her.

Naia was already moonlighting as a water handler at a "surprise spot." She had come across the pyramid first as she saw it being built early that morning by city crew workers. When she noticed that all the crew workers piled back onto the bright yellow city truck and no one stayed behind, she ran up to the driver side of the truck as it was taking off, and banged on the door, yelling, "Who's gonna give these out?"

The driver only slowed down to yell back louder, "Not my problem! Not my *problem*! We're just deliverers; talk to City Hall!" They then sped off.

The scientist had looked at the water pyramid, exasperated, and decided to be the water handler. It was close to a prime water testing spot, so she could stay and try to make the best of everything. Naia didn't have an official city worker black shirt, but she also thought that might have been for the best. She didn't want a citizen screaming at her; the city workers could keep that, as far as she was concerned.

Times like this, she wished the city wasn't so dysfunctional.

A wide array of people came up to get the water. Some were young. Some were old (she tried to call rideshares for the ones that really had a hobble to their walk), some were calm, quite a few were frustrated, and only once did a fight nearly come to blows. One of the fighters had cursed at her directly as she tried to mediate and cool tempers; the rest of the crowd forced him to apologize.

"We're all angry!" one random mother of three tired kids snapped. "No need takin' it out on her! She ain't got a black shirt on! Ain't no one say nothin' 'bout this spot! Everyone here is in the same boat as you! Includin' *her*!"

The fighter had grabbed his jug with a quasi-heartfelt apology and stormed off.

That had been Naia's morning. Things died down in the afternoon, where it was just her ... and behind her, a soft whirring she could have sworn she had heard before.

She turned around to find a pearly black octodrone hovering steadily over the top of a jug. It carefully lowered down a carbon steel hook attached to a black titanium chain. The top of the hook had a hand-drawn smiley face with afro-puffs on it and the scrawled phrase "Mine Now." She recognized that handwriting.

The scientist just stood there in gobsmacked shock until the clinking of the chain brought her back, as the drone tried to hook the water jug handle.

"Shawny!" yelled Naia as she ran up to the drone, which maneuvered its hook quicker now. "No!"

Naia clapped her hands on the bottle the drone was attempting to airlift. "Shawny!" She looked for the camera on the drone and spoke into it. "I will *get* you a bottle!"

It was basically college all over again. Shawntae had tried to airlift a tray of curry goat at a cookout. Shawntae thought she was being sneaky; she didn't have a camera on her previous drone, only sensors and running numbers. Everyone else, including Naia, had just watched the drone, simply to see if it could. The drone eventually moved to the much smaller tray of plantains instead. Someone even sneaked over to help attach the tray when they saw it was about to slip.

That had been roughly around the time Shawntae became more withdrawn. She didn't do cookout socializing, but she went with Naia all the same for the free food. Naia didn't really know what exactly had set off the hermit-living, but that was Shawntae now.

And now, Shawntae had tried to airlift a three-gallon jug of water behind her back.

"I will *get* you a jug!" Naia repeated as she tried to free the water. She didn't want Shawntae to fly the water above people or cars in case it slipped off the hook. Plus, she had no idea how the drone would be able to materialize a jug of water through a window without bits of window winding up in the jug.

The drone stopped trying to lift the jug, and lowered so that it was eye level to the scientist. It was listening.

"I'll get you *three*, ok? Three!" bargained Naia, holding up her dark gold-brown fingers. "But you gotta wait! Gimme an hour and I'll bring 'em to you!"

Naia didn't want to abandon her post, but she reasoned that she already did so to test the water. This wouldn't be much different. Shawntae didn't live too far away, only a few blocks.

Patters of rain struck Naia's shoulders. She didn't have an umbrella, only her car parked down the street. Naia surmised that she probably would have to call it a day and let the mystery person behind Mockie know, so they could find someone else. There was already a waiting list; one of her friends told her about it after they signed up on it.

The drone started to warble a little in response to the rain drops. It needed to get back. It did a quick drop-spin as an affirmative and rocketed itself into the sky, drawing in its hook.

Naia watched the drone zip back the way it came, a quiet black dot that banked sharply around a random rowhouse's corner and out of sight.

She looked up at the sky. It was pregnant with thunderclouds illuminated by crawling cracks of lightning. Looked like a heavy cloudburst was due soon.

If only the town could drink the rainwater, Naia wished. She sucked her teeth at the situation as she set aside bottles for herself and Shawntae.

"Water, water everywhere," the scientist grumbled to herself, "and not a single clean drop to drink. What a *mess*."

◆

End

Finding Water to Fish with

Friends and Family

[Finding Water to Fish with Friends and Family: *Daybreak*]

[James H. Ford, Jr.]

I AM SOMETIMES FRIGHTENED by the thought that one day I will have a car accident because I am looking out of the window and not paying attention to the traffic while looking at a pond, a slightly hidden waterway, or the ocean waves jumping each other as they find their way to the beach. As far back as I remember, my family always searched for water bodies—to fish with family and friends, or just to hang out. Whether my love of water is inherited or I was trained by family to care about it, the love for water is now in my blood.

My mother's side of the family loved to head to Louisiana and find old antique boats hidden between trees in the swamp. When they found one, they would pull it from where it was lodged, load it on a trailer, bring it back to Houston, and repair it. That side of the family repaired everything, worked on every kind of motor, and did a good job. Big Papa told stories about fishing and riding on boats with his family. Often Big Papa used a word many of us thought was about bayous, but later found out it was about Baden Baden, Germany: "Bayouden" is the way he pronounced the word. Baden Baden, Germany, was apparently the hometown of a family member from the "White side" who had immigrated to America.

When we had a car, Daddy would regularly drive around looking for new and different fishing holes. Once, when Interstate 10 was being constructed, Daddy received a ticket while looking for a fishing hole. He turned under a freeway overpass that was under construction and decided to turn the wrong way on a one-way street. The street, too, was under construction, and no cars were using it. I was sitting in the backseat, and when I saw the one-way sign, I said, "Daddy, you can't go that way." Both he and Mom looked back at me. Dad frowned, and Mom had a smile. He turned anyway because there were no cars.

A police car was parked down a side street. Just as he passed the construction signs, the policeman turned his lights on and pulled Dad over. Dad was asked to get out of the car, and the policeman wrote him a ticket. When Dad returned to the car, he got in and looked back at me. He said, "Don't you say a damn thing." He drove to the pond.

When I was young, I remember my family going on crabbing trips at the drop of a hat. We could get to a body of water that was home to big blue paw crabs, only minutes away from Houston. We would go east on Market St., and then east on I-10 East, once the freeway was completed, to San Jacinto River. Our family would get out of the cars like we were going to the Great Gold Rush, and in a few minutes, we would put out eight to ten crab lines. Even on lousy crabbing days, we would fill up a number-ten wash-tub full of big blue paw crabs within an hour.

A bad environmental experience caused us to stop fishing under the I-10 Bridge. Oily discharge from the barges spilled into the river, filling the crabs with oil. There was no news report to inform people not to eat the crabs from that area. So, we only knew the oil-infested crabs were dangerous to eat once we began cooking them. The mercuric, oily smell invaded our house, and we became aware of the problem. I haven't crabbed at the bridge in years, but occasionally I see others still fishing and crabbing there as I pass on my way to Baytown or Beaumont. Even though warning signs are posted, people refuse to stop fishing for the damaged fish.

The U.S., being a country that refuses to give up its bad habit of supporting racism, finds discrimination even in its waterways.

The days when my Daddy and Mom could not stop and buy a burger, use a restroom, or even clean our catch at any fish cleaning table are over, but the memories still exist. Yes, the unmarked car of racism is still policing how, when, and who can speak about the U.S.'s history of racism. In the early days of me learning to fish and love water, I could only fish on "Black Beach" in Galveston. African Americans were not allowed to fish on Stewart Beach or unload boats at public boat ramps. Fish cleaning tables were designated for the use of Whites only. Depending on the personality of the person driving the unmarked car, cleaning crabs or fish along the waterway was prohibited.

Racism can be found even in some of the most wonderful places to fish in Texas. Anahuac, Texas, may not be one of the most popular destinations in Texas, but it is hugely significant in Texas's secession from Mexico, and a wonderful place to view the beauty of Texas waterways.

William Barret Travis, who became a part of the Anahuac Disturbances between 1832 and 1835, probably never fished in Trinity Bay. He probably did not have time for hanging out with friends in the bay area north of Galveston.

Travis had escaped arrest in Alabama, left his expecting wife, and arrived in Anahuac with Joe, who he enslaved when he purchased Joe. Almost immediately upon arrival, Travis became a lawyer for an enslaver whose men had escaped enslavement. Travis filed a lawsuit for their return. Later, after being arrested and confined for violating Mexican law, Travis escaped and then brought a small contingent of Texans to Anahuac to turn control of the then-Mexican garrison over to the Texans.

In an essay entitled "Joe, Survivor of the Alamo" by Katie Bender, there is a suggestion that Joe did fish regularly. He fished with his brothers before Travis bought him, and fished after Travis enslaved him. Joe was purchased and sold several times, and purchased twice by William Barret Travis.

After the second time, Joe accompanied Travis to the Alamo. The Anahuac garrison, where a historical marker stands, is planted on top of the hill adjacent to Turtle Bayou and is now the entry to the boat-launching area that connects to Trinity Bay. Joe's name does not appear on the marker. He was only the body servant of Travis. Joe took care of Travis's clothes and his mule, drove his wagon, and managed all his personal details; and Joe watched Travis die at the Battle of the Alamo. Travis was killed in a battle against the army of Santa Anna, at which Joe was captured.

Joe hid away after Travis's death, as the Mexican military sought battle survivors. The Mexican military yelled out as they entered a barrack area, "Are there any Negroes in here?" Joe crawled out from his hidden location and surrendered.

There is more to the story of Joe. Of course, he disappears from history, as only a footnote to the life of William Barret Travis. But I wonder whether he had a chance to fish with friends after he survived his oppression and enslavement. I hope he did.

Anahuac celebrates the alligator during a festival each year. One can fish close to the boat launches, which provides an easy escape from the rough and tumble of daily life and allows people to breathe in the fresh, salty smell of the gulf. Squint your eyes, and you can see the island of Galveston to the south.

Carroll was one of my favorite fishing friends; we often fished in Anahuac. On our first trip together, Carroll pulled the control arm back to the neutral position and cut off the boat engine. As the engine gurgled to a stop, the nose of the boat nudged forward and glided gently onto the soft, sandy bottom of the bar separating Lake Anahuac from the main channel. Seagulls' white wings sliced the air as they disappeared from the deep blue sky and hurled themselves downward. Their bodies briefly indented the placid water's surface as they scooped up fingerling fish and went airborne once again to view the gallery of swimming fish below. Mullets leaped from the depths and splashed aimlessly into the murky Trinity Bay estuary, and the sun's eye peeked above the horizon as though observing its children at play. It was daybreak.

After drinking in the sights and sounds of the Texas Gulf Coast the evening before, Old Hanna, the sun, had a red, swollen eye the next morning. But white bulbous clouds toweled it off until her eye color faded to orange. Then the sphere danced like a white spirit upward until it was high in the sky on its throne, where it ruled the day.

We disembarked from the boat and stepped into the cool bay waters. Waist-deep now, but a few trudging steps later, the water was no deeper than the soles of our wading shoes. The tide was out, so the water was peeled back from the bar, exposing it like a wound on the knee of a young child.

Carroll and I were like two giddy young boys, trudging and sloshing along in the ankle-deep water as we made our way to the deeper water on the east side of the bar. Mussels littered the bar like forgotten hand grenade shrapnel, occasionally squirting water from their siphons. Beds of hundreds of flounder, who had spent the night gorging themselves on shrimp along the bar's apron, were now only an impression in the soft sand. I pointed the impression out to Carroll, who made a note that the same spot in the morning or the early evening would be an excellent place to gig flounder.

Carroll was the first to cast into the waist-deep water, and as always, he was the first to have his rod doubled up with a fish. The heavy red drum bowed the rod tip and strained the line as it aggressively sought to free itself from the hook embedded in its mouth. The drum was a mighty fighter as it stripped line from Carroll's Shimano Curado fishing reel. The fish swam rapidly away from Carroll and then stopped. Carroll reeled the line back onto the spool, and the fish swam hard in the opposite direction. Then, after every six or seven reel-turns, the fish undid the line again. The monofilment line sounded like angry bees fighting for a place in the hive as the fish stripped the line away. Carroll fought the fish for what seemed like forever, but it was probably not even a full minute.

Then, finally, the fish tired, and Carroll netted him and removed the hook. Nineteen inches long! He was not big enough to keep. Carroll let him go so that he might fight for his life on another day. We waded on for more than five hundred yards, occasionally catching a keeper, and throwing back the undersized drum.

Even though we were fishing for the red drum with gold spoons, other fish sometimes struck the lure. Golden croaker and sand trout were the usual takers, but even salt-water catfish, hardheads as we called them, would hit the spoon. By the time we turned and headed back to the boat, we had caught our limit of red drum. Other times, we would catch our limit of flounder or speckled trout.

This trip was the first of many fishing trips Carroll and I would share. Sometimes we would fish at night, and other times we would fish all day. But there is nothing liking fishing with a friend on the Texas Gulf Coast at daybreak.

There is something magical about fishing on a cool body of water at daybreak. Maybe it's the feeling of the air as it wraps its coolness around your warm body in the morning. Or perhaps it's the freshness the sun brings to the morning, but whatever makes this magic work, it has been shared between friends since time immemorial.

◆

End

Water Is Life, Water Is Death, There Is no Truth or Joy without Water

[Water Is Life, Water Is Death,
There Is no Truth or Joy without Water]
[Mary A. Turzillo]

YOU EVER GET THAT FEELING, like when you accidentally grab onto an exposed electric wire? Well, maybe you don't, because you're still alive. But me—

I was in the tub, having a nice soak after washing the car, rinsing the dishes and putting them into the dishwasher, sudsing a pretty new pink cami I got on Amazon (hey, that's a river, coincidence?) the directions of which said "hand-wash only" (or maybe it was that symbol I've never bothered to figure out), and sipping Earl Grey made from my Keurig, with milk.

Tomorrow we were going to Edgewater. Lake Erie is cleaner now, so I was taking my bathing suit.

I remember my mistake—I accidentally splashed some water in my do, and I knew it would make it all frizzy unless I dried it immediately. So I grabbed the rusty old hair-drier, right on the sink next to the tub. Don't you love a nice soak in warm water, with maybe lavender bath-salts? Right? Relaxing.

I turned it on, forgetting about something—some warning—and blasted those droplets of water. And caught it as it slipped into the bathwater (soap, you know). I remembered something, something about water and electricity—

And that funny feeling you get when—well, actually, it wasn't funny. I couldn't let go of the dryer. My whole body buzzed like Godzilla-bee. As if a stinging bug the size of a rhinoceros was singing, stinging. Kept buzzing until my lights went out.

You think I'm an idiot. I dimly remember reading that 290 people die every year by electrocution in the shower or bath, but most of them are suicides (ouch! Why didn't they use sleeping pills?). Still, it happens.

It had just happened to me. And it was not painless. The insides of my head burned, and my lungs screamed. Silently.

But as to myself, I couldn't scream. The buzzing paralyzed me. My boyfriend was in the bedroom. He probably found me, dead. I don't know.

When SHE appeared, I was surprised. If a dead person can be surprised.

I'm not an atheist. So the appearance of God was to be expected. I believe in God, or maybe a couple of gods. Or Loas. Or Orishas. I've read about Orishas. Back when I was eight, a boy in my school died of leukemia, and I started wondering about this one-God, all-powerful, all-knowing, all-good. Multiple gods, or divine spirits, started to make more sense to me, even back then.

But she didn't just *arrive*. First came the salty smell of the sea. The water under me rose up and I was borne on a huge swell, a tidal wave. Then an ominous rumble, then the deafening crash of a mountainous breaker.

♦

Which slams me as I stare at the tip of her delicate blue mermaid tail.

She rises up out of an ocean I suddenly see all around us, and I am rocked in a gigantic—what is this enamel thing?—cowrie shell.

She is beautiful. Of course, she would be. Or maybe my electrical accident acted like some drug that makes me see her that way. She is so exquisite that her features have to be obscured by a veil made of strings of pearls. She seems to have a mermaid tail, but when I blink, it's not there.

"Thank god!" I squeak. "Can you save my life?"

She smiles, an expression both sweet and somehow terrifying. "Ah, girl, you ask. I am your mother, Yemoja. The mother of all. Death is unavoidable, but before you are quite dead, have a few glimpses of the living world. Water killed you. But water is a good thing, girl. Here, see what happens when there isn't enough."

And I am floating, awash in a receding sea, my mouth and nose stinging with harsh salt water.

Then there is darkness and I am standing on dry land, smelling the odor of barn animals, dust, and dry grass.

Yemoja stands on a rise, looking down at a pasture. We are far from any ocean. The air is brisk and thin, so this is in some mountainous area. And it's dark, stars above us as sharp as the points of needles.

"Peru," says Yemoja. "Do you like alpaca scarves, girl?"

At the other side of a wooden fence, I see a winsome cream-colored animal, like a colt or a calf, lying with its legs tucked under it against the cold. Its eyes, closed, are surrounded in black, like makeup on some goth teddy bear. It has a short, cute

213

snout, and I think Disney must model some of their fictional animals after this thing. Its fur makes me want to reach out and pet it. "A goat?" I ask.

"It's called a cria. A baby alpaca."

My grandmother had a pair of alpaca socks. They had to be washed by hand, and she used to give me two dollars to launder them. Mom gave those socks to me a few years back, after Gran died. They were very soft and warm. I'm not sure where they are now.

"Well, girl, this cria is at a farm in Peru. But it is alone. Alpacas are very social animals, and it misses its mother and the rest of the herd."

"Where are they?"

"They were sold because there is a drought. As you see, the grass is dried out, not good pasture for alpacas. The family who owns him, the alpaqueros, have taken them to market. Someone will buy them and try to find good pasture for them. Or butcher them, for meat. This cria is named Kusi-Kusi. That means joy, or party-time."

To my right, I notice a small farmhouse—at least I think that's what it is. A boy of about twelve darts out with a blanket wrapped around his shoulders against the cold, closing the door behind him.

The little alpaca, about the size of a large dog but with long coltish legs, jumps to its feet and runs to the fence, to the boy. The boy leans over the fence and wraps his arms around the cria's neck, letting his blanket fall to the ground. He speaks to the little animal, calling it Kusi-Kusi, burying his face in its fur. The little alpaca nuzzles him and makes a sweet humming noise.

The boy pulls back and looks into the cria's eyes. He speaks.

Yemoja translates: "'This is the last time I'll ever see you, Kusi-Kusi. Tomorrow Papa will take you down to the market where he took your mother and the rest of the herd. There is not enough grass here for you, is there, little one?'"

The cria ramps up the humming.

"'—And Papa says the drought has destroyed our family business.'"

The boy caresses the cria's small, perky ears.

They stay that way, the boy's blanket forgotten on the cold ground. The boy is weeping. My vision fades as the darkness deepens.

A faint voice in my head says, *Well, that's global warming for you.*

"A minor tragedy," says Yemoja, "except that this family has lost more than just a beloved pet. The years-long drought has destroyed their livelihood. The boy and his family will have to migrate down to the market town and do hard labor for menial wages. Just like other alpaqueros, thousands of them."

But I'm alive. "I didn't mean to die," I tell Yemoja. "Can you please please revive me?"

My eyes roll up in my head. I feel myself borne in the cold above seas and continents.

When my vision clears, Yemoja is waiting. She is still radiant—literally, radiating light, but with her eyes the color of the space between stars. Now she is wearing silver bangles set with sapphires and diamonds. Her face is so lovely, I am afraid to look at it for long.

We are in another rural area, but this is not in my native Ohio. The terrain is very green and fertile-looking, and I see what I would call terracing, layered fields on the gentle slopes of hills. In the distance, I notice a bull-like animal with huge curved horns.

"Water buffalo." Yemoja is close by me, almost companionable, as if we were friends.

Can you be friends with a god?

In a flat area, near some sort of habitation, a group of people in white trousers and pants are gathered around a small—coffin? Oh, no, not another dead person. And a very small one. I catch a glimpse of the child's face—the mourners have given her toys and chopsticks. The women are wearing white tunics with Nehru collars. Flowers, white flowers, are everywhere.

A teenaged boy carries a framed portrait of a little girl.

Yemoja startles me by saying, "This is the third of the children to die in this family—the oldest was eight, the middle one six, and this one, a girl, Anh, 18 months."

I move to go closer to see the portrait, but Yemoja holds up a hand to stop me. "It is unlucky for you to be part of this funeral party."

"Why did these children die?" I ask. "Surely not from thirst; everything here is so green."

"These Vietnamese farmers use water from a borehole, something like a well. The lining of their borehole was cracked, and the water was contaminated. The organism was called B. pseudomallei. It causes an illness called melioidosis. The children were taken to the hospital, but the diagnosis came too late, if indeed the remedy was in stock. These parents are blaming themselves, but B. pseudomallei is very common in east Asia."

I think, *If I were in charge, I would have water testing programs*. Then, "Your godliness, I don't understand why you are here, or why you took me to these places. Is it because I'm dead, so I will have to live with them?"

She turns her luminous smile on me. "Why not?"

"But I don't want to be dead! Please! I have a boyfriend and a good job and friends, and I actually like my job. I want to live. Save me, please!"

She sighs.

And we fly.

Then I spy an island, and she says, "This is the tiny nation of

Tuvalu. Only about ten thousand citizens. The fourth smallest independent country in the world."

It's surrounded by water, the blue ocean. But I see that water is being doled out to a line of people. One is a woman carrying a tiny baby, just newly born.

The goddess speaks again. "They have little fresh water right now. Each citizen is allowed only a liter."

Why? Why an ocean—but I know. Salt water is not potable, of course.

She says, "The ocean is rising here, year by year. The people have lived on this isolated island for generations, and always there has been a lens of fresh water, caught from rain, under the island. But the ocean has risen up and made it salty. Watch what this woman does—her name is Mahana, and her baby is Hiwahiwa."

I watch. The woman named Mahana accepts her canister of water and gazes longingly at it.

"Mahana is very thirsty," says the goddess, or shall I call her an Orisha. "But her baby is dirty, needs a bath. The little one's skin is too delicate to wash in salt water. What will she do? If she drinks the water, her baby will get sick from being soiled, as babies do. But if Mahana uses the water to wash the baby's bum, she will become dehydrated. She will have no milk for her baby. What would you do, Anjelika?"

I have no answer, but where I live there is plenty of water. *Global warming hasn't touched our lake. Maybe that's why I voted for that jerk that supported pulling us out of the Paris agreement.*

Oh, how can I convince Yemoja to let me live? "Oh beautiful, powerful goddess, I want to go back. If you are so powerful, can't you turn back the clock, before I dropped the hairdryer in the bathwater?"

Vertigo and a whirlwind.

Now we are standing, like Jesus, on top of the water, as if it's a perturbed and frozen glass surface, as big as the whole earth. Then my feet are back in the cowrie shell, but unsteady. I am rocking in gentle waves.

—and a gigantic wave thunders over me, spilling me out of my cowrie shell.

When the tumult calms, I pull myself to my feet in the shallows of a beach that seems to extend forever, and I shake the water out of my hair and eyes. I see, marching down the beach, an army of people, many of them children. They are dressed in a variety of outfits. The older girls wear blue or yellow ankle-length frocks, plus matching scarves that cover their hair completely. Many of the women are similarly garbed, although a few are in American/European-style dress. The men are either in suits and ties, or jeans, or alternatively white cloth draped around their shoulders and lower bodies. They march past, flowing around me. Then they turn and walk into the ocean. Their clothing falls off their bodies and soon I see only their heads, sinking into the gently surging and retreating sea-water.

They march and march. They are an army.

"Hey!" I yell at one of the men in the passing army. In one hand, he is leading a little boy in a caftan, and in the other, a little girl in a yellow dress and veil. They march onward, unheeding.

"Do you know about droughts, Anjelika?" asks Yemoja.

"But—there is no drought here—"

"Just an ocean. A rising ocean." Yemoja sighs. "Somalia is suffering from a six-year drought. These are its victims. They have come back to me, back to my aqueous arms. You can shout all you like, but no one will answer. More than forty thousand, half of them children, have perished."

"Can't they—"

She smiles gently. "Can't they what? There is famine when

there is no fresh water to grow plants. Or drink. This happens in your country too, my child, but it is not so dire, because your area is a huge country and you have infrastructure to ameliorate it. But even that may not be enough, in the future."

I break. "Are you saying there's anything I can do? Is that why I'm here?"

For answer, she smiles one of her soft, pitying smiles.

A little girl's dress has washed up at my feet. I drag it out of the surf and in the little pocket find a doll, like a Barbie, but clad in a home-sewn yellow dress and veil.

I turn my gaze down the beach. The horde still surges forward. Endless.

She sighs. "I speak to each of you in my own way. In your case, you are on a journey from life to death. You humans call me by many names: Mami Wata, Sirène; some in South America even claim I am the mother of your Christian god. You are in a good position to understand my visions and my message."

"I understand, Your Supremeness. But I'm just one person. Why did you pick me out of the eight billion people on this planet? I can't do anything without the other 7,999,999,999."

Her lip curls, and I catch a glimpse of her mermaid tail as it flips, petulantly, beneath her gauzy blue skirts. "You live on the lip of the greatest source of fresh water on this planet: America's Great Lakes. You used 80 gallons of potable water—basically, to kill yourself, even if unintentionally. Yet you seem not to appreciate your privilege."

"There's Antarctica," I murmur. "I know—that's ice, and when it's melted, it'll be all muddled up with the salty oceans."

She doesn't answer, just stares at me.

"Could I at least be reincarnated?"

She rolls her beautiful black eyes. "Whining will get you nowhere."

And then—

—a vision of a White man with curly dirty-blond hair and a pierced ear. He's in his early twenties. And he is hunched over a printed sheaf of papers. He looks stressed to the max, breathing heavily, clutching a pen as if it were a poisonous snake and if he were to let go it would turn around and bite him.

All this time, it has seemed that I'm invisible in these scenes, so I creep closer and peer over his shoulder. The paper is an employment application.

He has filled out his name and address, but even in these routine responses, he's scratched out letters and numbers and reentered them. He's written "STRETE" for "STREET," for example. Elsewhere in the document, chaos reigns. He can't spell many simple words, and in some cases even writes letters backwards. I notice a wedding ring on his left hand. He must have found a wife who forgives him his illiteracy.

"He's trying to get an entry-level job at a grocery store," says Yemoja. "He has a wife—although their marriage is on the ropes at the moment because he has a few misdemeanor records. Drugs, bar-fights. He also has twin boys. He really needs this job."

"Why is he having so much trouble with this form?"

She sighs. "You do notice the form is in English. And the address is in your country—Michigan, I believe, on one of your Great Lakes."

"Well, he's sure not thirsty," I snark. Then I shudder. I really should be more respectful—or scared—of this spiritual being with the gorgeous face and body, plus supernatural powers.

She quirks a smile. "He grew up in a midsized city in Michigan. For most of his childhood, the water he drank was contaminated with lead. Nobody in authority wanted to take the blame—or correct the issue."

"He's—got brain damage?"

"You could call it that. Not all of those children grew up with such severe disabilities. He's one of the most afflicted."

"Please take me away," I snivel. I wonder if I want to go back to a world, and a country, with so little care for its children. I think, *Poor little kids. They didn't deserve this.*

Then I muster the courage to say, "Great goddess or Orisha, or whatever wonder you are, could you at least let me have a few more years on earth? Maybe ten more years? On this planet? I won't waste any more water. I'll take three-minute showers, honest."

Her resplendent gaze fixes on me. "Like that's going to do any good."

I stammer, "I could even, like, talk to people about this global water mess. No, wait! I could join Greenpeace."

And rain, a cloudburst falls on me. At first, I throw my head back and allow it to bathe me in delicious chill. Then it accelerates, becomes a tempest.

After the storm, the sun comes out and dries my astral face and body. It soon gets hotter. Hotter. I'm thirsty, I realize, dreadfully thirsty. And tired. Tired of this whole mess. Hallucinations. I am floating. The Orisha is not real.

And abruptly I land, hard, on dry earth, a hot sun broiling my astral body. A desert.

A crowd of people who look vaguely Latinx. Mostly youths and children, also some women. I zone in on two children. The boy is crying, "Mama! Mama!" while his older sister tries to calm him.

The kid looks a lot like my nephew, Tamir. About the same age.

This must be the US border, and the two children are refugees wanting to enter the US, maybe illegally.

From a distance, the refugees point; they see plastic cubes. Some charitable organization has left these for them! The group breaks into a run for the cubes, which my spidey sense tells me are full of water.

But as they scramble for them, a Hummer pulls up. Out climb men in olive-green uniforms, wearing tan headgear like cowboy hats. Something tells me these are not G.I. Joe cosplayers. Border patrol.

Two of the men point rifles at the crowd of children and adults, while others use machetes to slash the plastic water containers and let the precious water flood the dry ground.

The children wail. I want to help, but how?

I scream at the border patrol men, but my voice is swallowed by silence. I start forward but cannot move. And the men have rifles.

Where is Yemoja? I see her lingering behind a big cactus. Her skirt catches on its thorns, but she glides free of it, as if using her mermaid tail to swim though water, rather than walk on the dusty earth. She nods, affirming my thoughts about the refugees and the border patrol.

Then, as I look up, I realize it's night. One of the brightest stars looks red, like a bicycle tail-light a thousand feet ahead of me.

I blink, then I am in a dry arroyo, with the torrent of a river rushing toward me, slamming me down, carrying me away toward—

The roaring flood has turned to a river of wind. Another desert, another dry river bed. Then all is silent, though tiny whirlwinds rise up and fall.

"Mars," she says, and we're standing on a dry, cold plain, devoid of vegetation. The sun has risen; the sky is the color of a marmalade cat's fur, and the soil under our feet is various tints of butterscotch.

We're gazing at what looks like a dry river bed. In the distance, I can see part of a huge canyon.

She says, "Your scientists have sent robots here. And also

flying ships to circle the place and take pictures. They want to find out if anything is living here—or if it ever did. Their mantra is 'Follow the water.'"

I notice then that I'm not breathing. Although I see sand blown about by a stiff breeze—a tiny hurricane—the breeze does not touch me.

"I can't feel anything," I tell Yemoja. "Is it because I'm dead?"

"You are indeed dead. As to the scientists and their followers, they will find water here. Frozen, but maybe liquid at times."

"Is water going to be as much of a problem here as on Earth?"

It's the first time I've heard her laugh. "All water is my domain, and by water I rule all the universe. But much depends on you humans."

My mind races past the idea of people walking in this dry, cold desert. Looking for tiny springs? For pockets of ice under the surface? Wanting to live here?

"Come with me, back to Earth, girl."

—and we are flying through darkness, seeing the blue curve of Earth beneath us, then clouds over continents, and—what is this? We are falling fast, down to what seems to be Africa. I got good grades in elementary school Geography, so I think we are falling toward—without those lines between countries, it's hard to guess. We land, light as seagulls. We are in a huge tent city.

"This is Rhino Camp," says Yemoja. "Near the border between South Sudan and Uganda. And here comes Isaka."

Isaka is wearing a long dress and head-scarf. The dress must once have been colorful, patterned with vivid hues—red, green, yellow, like a butterfly. But now, it's torn and filthy, the hem dragged in dirt. My overactive fashion gland wants that dress—in its original condition.

Isaka is carrying a boy of about four and leading two little girls. I can see that the boy's slight weight is almost too much for the frail woman, who is maybe a little older than me. Isaka, starved and bruised, enters a line before a white tent.

A nurse approaches. Isaka grabs her arm and utters a volley of frightened, urgent words.

Yemoja says: "The boy is her son Taban. They were attacked in their village by insurgents. Isaka's husband was gunned down with all the other men and older boys, and her older daughter was seized as a prisoner—you can guess for what purpose. With a group of other widows, Isaka fled with her children and wandered, lost, unable to find food or clean water. They found this camp—they are now in Uganda, and it is called Rhino Camp."

I ask, "What are they saying?"

Yemoja cocks an eyebrow at me. "Go closer. Isaka knows English. It is a common language for the doctors and some of the refugees."

I listen. "He had diarrhea that wouldn't stop on our fourth day. After that—there was no food to feed the diarrhea. I have no thermometer, but he felt so feverish." Her voice became low and fearful. "Is it cholera? I know there are medicines for that."

The nurse takes Isaka, Taban, and the two girls into the tent, through crowd mayhem, into an area screened off from the rest of the clinic tent. A teenaged boy writes down their names. Another White nurse, an ancient woman wearing green scrubs and a sanitary mask, takes the little boy and lays him gently on a table. I notice that the sheet on the table is blood-stained, but since nobody can see Yemoja or me, I keep quiet.

The ancient nurse puts a stethoscope to Taban's little chest, then a thermometer to his forehead. She pries up one of his eyelids.

Isaka says, "He's so still. He's such an active child, always wanting to play basketball with the older children."

The old nurse raises pale blue eyes, clouded with cataracts, to

Isaka. "I am so sorry, Mrs. Makhauch. Your precious son has left this world."

"No!"

The nurse nods compassionately. "His body is cooling. My poor friend, there is nothing, nothing we can do."

Isaka opens her mouth in agony and keens, falling to her knees. The nurse comes around the table to her with a cup of water.

Isaka's wails soften. "I was afraid that was it. This morning, no fever—"

The nurse bends with difficulty and puts an arm around Isaka's frail shoulders. "I know. I have children. You had to hope-"

"I couldn't feel his pulse, or feel his breath, but I thought maybe he was just so weak—"

"I am so, so sorry." The nurse gently wraps Isaka's fingers around the cup of water and guides it to her lips.

Isaka sips, and then she has enough water to make tears.

I scream at Yemoja, "Why have you brought me here? I can't do anything about this." Then, softer, but not very nicely: "This woman could be me." And then again: "Why do you torture me with these horrible tragedies?"

"Well, girl, do you still want to go back to your life with your boyfriend and your rich city and your big, clean lake?"

Not caring that she has the power of life and death over me, I snap at her: "Of course, I still want to live! That thing with the hair-dryer was just a mistake."

"I am not punishing you. But remember, girl, you can change your world."

I said, "But I can't mail even a pint of water to anybody, even if I had their address."

She smiles, her beautiful and scary white teeth almost incandescent in the twilight of my death. "That's your problem to

225

solve, girl."

"But why me? What brought you to me? Drowning?" But no. I have a sudden, kind of stupid idea. "What, you want me to run for Congress?"

"Maybe you are capable of learning." She moves very near me, smirking slightly, and—this is the first time she has touched me—she places her lovely, strong hand on my abdomen. "There is sea-water inside you, Anjelika. It, too, is in my domain, like every body of water. And something else: I think it will motivate you."

A rogue wave surges from the astral plane, knocks me down, and drags me under.

Then I am nowhere, and then on my back, on a hard floor, I don't know where.

A jolt on my chest. I open my eyes and see, kneeling over me, a man and a woman in navy uniforms, the guy holding two things like irons, trailing fat curly wires. And Brandon, gripping my hand.

"Please, live, Anjelika," he says. "We need you!"

◆

End

Love, Temptation and the Downfall of a Water Rig in Kai Ashante Wilson's "The Devil in America"

[Love, Temptation and the Downfall of a Water Rig
in Kai Ashante Wilson's "The Devil in America"]
[Desireé Y. Amboree]

OPPRESSIVE SYSTEMS THRIVE on the status quo. Dominion over a cultural or societal other requires the apparent submission of that conquered group. African American writers W.E. B. Du Bois, Alice Walker, Zora Neale Hurston, Kai Ashante Wilson, and Octavia E. Butler demonstrate to their audiences the freedom made possible when that acquiescence is revoked. They offer a truth-telling that bends the very understanding of submission. Love is the driving force behind revolution. It is through love that the authors humanize their characters, themselves and the reader. This dialectical relationship gives rise to an extratemporal conversation of love and humanity. It leads to the question, if love humanizes, what does temptation do?

In his short essay, "The Souls of White Folk" (1910), W. E. B. Du Bois elucidates for the reader the realities of "whiteness"— that is, the colonial byproduct of imperial domination by Anglos and Europeans on societal structures and relations. Du Bois calls the reader's attention to the hypocrisy of a racist society's insistence on subjugating other human beings. Unfortunately, as Du Bois recognizes, none are immune to this false superiority: "The Middle Age regarded skin color with mild curiosity [...] the world in a sudden, emotional conversion has discovered that it is white and by that token, wonderful! This assumption that of all the hues of God whiteness alone is inherently and obviously better than brownness or tan leads to curious acts" (Du Bois, np). The division by which society is governed is by no means inherent to the people of the Earth. Racism is a system constructed to fortify abuse of the rest of the world. To accomplish this, offensive stereotypes were infused into every major institution of society, holding them all complicit, to conjure negative schemas of people whose skin was darker in hue and positive schemas of those whose skin is lighter. These attitudes have become internalized, used to organize civilization then as it continues to be today. This is where the true shame lies: racists and colonialists believe they are destroying the racial other—those belonging to colonized groups—and they are; however, they are also destroying their relationships to themselves. Because racists so believe in the truth of their own illusion, they are cut off from the reality of themselves. The rest of the world is not as naïve:

> Neither Roman nor Arab, Greek nor Egyptian, Persian nor Mongol ever took himself and his own perfectness with such disconcerting seriousness as the modern white man. We whose shame, humiliation, and deep insult his aggrandizement so often involved were never deceived. We looked at him clearly, with world-old eyes, and saw simply a human thing, weak and pitiable and cruel, even as we are and were. (Du Bois, np)

It is through the eyes of W.E.B. Du Bois that conquerors/

colonialists/imperialists/racists are humanized. Because, as Du Bois recognizes, the oppressed see themselves so clearly as human that they can also see the humanity in their oppressors. I argue that it is through love that Du Bois can humanize not only himself but the world. His own love for himself activates his self-determination, allowing for him to take a critical look at the state of the world and to call out a giant, with or without fear of retaliation.

Like Du Bois, Alice Walker offers up her own criticism of society at large. Her "Only Justice Can Stop a Curse" (1982) rages against the systems of oppression in the hope of their violent downfall. The original author of the quoted prayer-curse, already old when Zora Neale Hurston collected it in the 1920s (Walker, np), vehemently beseeches God for retribution for crimes committed against herself, her family, her people, and the Earth as they have suffered great wrongs at the hands of a relentless oppressor. Love, again, is the driving force behind this prayer: "My home has been disrespected, my children have been cursed and ill-treated. My dear ones have been backbitten and their virtue questioned" (Walker, np). The original author opens the prayer curse with this statement, signifying her reason for contacting the Creator. Though the prayer is angry, desperate, and indignant, the original author prays the curse because those she cares for have been wronged. It is her love that allows her to access feelings of anger that fuel and impassion the prayer curse. Likewise, Walker's love for herself and the world is at war with her cynicism and contempt for violence. She toys with the notion of mutually assured destruction, recognizing this may be the oppressed people's only chance at salvation. "Fatally irradiating ourselves," she writes, "may in fact be the only way to save others from what Earth has already become. And this is a consideration that I believe requires serious thought from every one of us" (np). However, she continues to assert that "Life is better than death" (np). Resolving to continue living, Walker affirms the beauty of—love of—life itself as reason enough to resist the dominant structures seeking to tyrannize her.

As with Du Bois, it is through love that Walker can humanize herself and her oppressor. Because she loves herself, she must recognize her own humanity, and because she sees humanity, she recognizes that same humanity in her oppressor. Walker and Du Bois are in conversation with one another in that they both have a firm grasp on the reality and hypocrisy of the world, and despite that knowledge—and because of it—choose to maintain resistance.

While Du Bois and Walker's works are resolute, factual, and even grim, Zora Neale Hurston's "How it Feels to Be Colored Me" (1928) is aloof, playful, yet solid in resolve. Hurston details her experience of growing up in Eatonville, Florida. Even as a child, she has astute observations concerning racial differences and dynamics amongst the residents and visitors in her small town. She pays them no mind, however. Hurston is not transfixed by the so-called problem of race. She enjoys life as she chooses to live it, with whomever she chooses to live it. It is her difference that makes her confident and sure of herself. Further, it is the love and validation she gets from her community, especially in her formative years, that makes it possible for her to be so self-assured. She writes, "The colored people gave no dimes. They deplored any joyful tendencies in me, but I was their Zora nevertheless [...] everybody's Zora" (Hurston, np). Her community sees and affirms her humanity, loving Zora Neale Hurston for the person she is and not what she can do or provide for them. Neither do they use their love to forgive her for her weakness—being Black. Love itself unlocks the chains of self-hatred before the lock has the chance to latch onto Hurston. This is an example of the freedom made possible through love. It is important to remember, however, that Zora Neale Hurston is not immune to the attitudes of society and suffers still because of who she is. This is to say that self-determination and love—intracommunal or from the self—did not shield Hurston and will not shield anyone else from the tyranny of a global racist society. Thus arises the everlasting tension between justice and reality that Du Bois, Walker, and the original author of the prayer-curse give lesson to: it is at this intersection that the temptation to submit becomes more prevalent. Why resist when the outcome is inevitable?

"Bloodchild" by Octavia Butler is a tale set in an alien world where a race of beings implants their eggs into the bodies of humans in order to reproduce. The Tlic, T'Gatoi, has chosen Gan, a human, to house her eggs when he comes of age. As a child, Gan is naive to the depths of this dynamic in his society, believing ultimately that he—the humans, egg carriers—have a choice and are loved by their egg-laying partners. Over the course of the story, the reader journeys with Gan as he recalls his "last night of childhood"—the night T'Gatoi plans to implant her eggs in him, when he discovers the truth about his position in the world (Butler, np). Gan first witnesses another human man giving birth to a Tlic's eggs. It is a painful and dangerous experience as the larvae eat their way through their host. The Tlic must slice open the human and remove the worms for fear of the larvae devouring or poisoning their host's body. Afterwards, Gan's brother describes seeing another birth gone wrong, and a human begging his Tlic to kill him to escape the pain of being eaten alive by the Tlic's hatchlings:

> The Tlic wouldn't open the man because she had nothing to feed the grubs. The man couldn't go any further and there were no houses around. He was in so much pain, he told her to kill him. He begged her to kill him. Finally, she did. She cut his throat. One swipe of one claw. I saw the grubs eat their way out, then burrow in again, still eating. (Butler, np)

In this scene, the reader witnesses the Tlic trading a human life for preservation of her eggs, her race. Gan is traumatized. He toys with the idea of murder—of himself or perhaps T'Gatoi—or sacrificing one of his siblings to take his place so he can avoid the fate that awaits him. At the end, he chooses to accept his role. That night, T'Gatoi will be implanting her eggs into *someone*: if he refuses, she will go to his sister.

After their argument, and Gan's threat of refusal, the two are depicted in a moment of vulnerability: "I leaned my forehead against her. She was cool velvet, deceptively soft. 'And to keep you for myself,' I said. It was so. I didn't understand it, but it was so" (Butler, np). Gan is revealed, perhaps against his better judgement, to have a certain affection for T'Gatoi despite their relationship dynamic. He shares that he has chosen to accept her eggs because he would have rather had T'Gatoi for himself.

This, like the theory offerings from W. E. B. Du Bois, Alice Walker, and Zora Neale Hurston, analyzes freedom within insurmountable situations—whether they be oppressive societies or exploitative relationships begotten by oppressive societies. Gan relies on his love for his family, the need to protect his siblings from suffering the fate he's just witnessed, and his love for T'Gatoi to accept the reality of receiving her eggs. Like Easter in Kai Ashante Wilson's "The Devil in America," he is a child interfacing with a being who has far more control and knowledge of the situation, and who uses that advantage as leverage to manipulate the vulnerable. Gan and his siblings each battle the tension and temptation that comes with the unknown, known, and not fully understood within their society. Ultimately, love becomes the foundation on which Gan's self-sacrificing decision is made.

Kai Ashante Wilson explores a similar issue in his "The Devil in America" (2014), a short story following a family of shapeshifting farmers just years after the Civil War. The main character, Easter, has the gift—or curse—of shapeshifting, received matrilineally from her African ancestors. Unfortunately, the Trans-Atlantic Human Trade and subsequent enslavement disconnected her family from their "old Africa Magic" (Wilson, np). They no longer have access to knowledge of how to navigate their powers in a safe, sure, or reversible way. The story follows Easter as she comes of age but has a terribly tragic end involving the banker, a spirit with whom Easter made a deal at the age of six. In recompense for the help he provides, Easter's entire church is brutally murdered at the hands of a mad horde of racist townspeople at the spirit—the banker's—behest. Though she has been instructed not to, Easter has dabbled with magic and everyone she knows has paid the price.

The evil spirits of the land take advantage of her trust, friendship, confidence, and naïveté to bring about destruction of the vulnerable. What could have been a coming-of-age tale of young queer love becomes a caution against American magic. Even though she has been warned, the lure of connection and the love she holds for her family are too much temptation for Easter to resist. She reasons, "The angels were nice, anyway, and it felt good keeping them to herself, having a secret. No need to tell anybody" (Wilson, np). Easter feels as if she can trust the angels she has been communicating with, that they look out for her. It is for this reason that Easter disobeys her mother's warning and adjusts the rig on her father's tobacco farm, thinking it will provide him with enough help for his crop:

> And this whirligig thing'um, right here, was exactly what kept all the angels hereabouts leashed, year after year, to chase away pests, bring up water from deep underground when too little rain fell, or dry the extra drops in thin air when it rained too much. (Wilson, np)

This rig, which keeps the angels working on the family's behalf, holds the keys to the family's fortune and thus, their ability to survive.

In six-year-old Easter's mind, repairing that rig will save her father from a burdensome workload:

> Pa and Señor did work *awful* hard every May shoveling dirt to make those hills, and now in August they had to come every day to cut whichever leaves had grown big enough. Seemed like the angels could just do *everything* [....] She could *help* if she just knocked this rickety old thing down, and put it back together better. (Wilson, np)

This action unlocks a fury of "angels" who wreak havoc over the tobacco field and would have consumed it in its entirety if Easter had not made a blood pact with the banker.

Hazel Mae, Easter's mother, has warned her daughter against dealing with magic of any kind. Over the years, the reader learns Hazel Mae has lost all her children to her family's blessing-turned-curse. Like Gan's mother, Hazel Mae must wrestle with the fate that she has borne her beloved children into. At the end, she sacrifices herself for the life of her daughter in a powerful act of motherlove, hoping for literal freedom and salvation for her remaining child. The magic in their veins has tempted Easter and all the rest of her siblings to their respective downfalls; however, Easter's mother has also been tempted. Hazel Mae struggles with the temptation to withhold or disclose to her children information about the danger of their powers, learning that whether she tells them or not, they all suffer the same fate. Wilson's text is steeped in temptation and love as both proponents of and detractors from freedom. This story, using fiction to make sense of the horrific crimes against African American communities at the hands of European immigrants and colonists provides yet another example of the quest for freedom and self-determination presented by the previous authors. Hazel Mae, instead of choosing to refrain from having children or lie down and die, has lived. She has lived and has loved child after child, siblings, her husband, her community, and herself. She does not let her position in society, or her generational curse, rob her of her humanity—which is her very right to live. Even with a crazed mob at her door, she protects her love—her last child—as best she can. This act of sacrifice is the ultimate symbol of love for freedom, for survival, in action.

Each of the tales grapples with existence in a society that does not care whether those who are othered and oppressed live or die. In fact, they will be exploited in both life and death, regardless. Love is shown to be the driving force by which freedom is achieved, whether that be freedom to speak the truth, freedom to own and express one's feelings, freedom to love oneself, the freedom to live, or the freedom to choose. Throughout each piece, the writers also contend with temptation. Though the temptation may lead to unsavory ends, I argue that the temptation further humanizes each of the authors and characters studied. It is a grossly human thing to contemplate and go against better judgement. It is human to prioritize family or love or comfort over what should be common sense—what someone "knows better." As such, love may be the driving force behind revolution. At the same time, temptation is the mantle on which that love is leveraged. Temptation is but another example of the expanses of one's humanity.

[Works Cited]

Butler, Octavia E. "Bloodchild." *Isaac Asimov's Science Fiction Magazine* vol. 8, no. 6, 1984, pp. 34–54. http://english.ncu.edu.tw/Stewart/Library/ReadingPri/Bloodchild .pdf. Accessed 2022.

Du Bois, W.E. B. "The Souls of White Folk." *The Independent*, August 18, 1910. Revised in *Darkwater: Voices from Within the Veil*. Harcourt, Brace & Co., 1920. https://www.gutenberg.org/files/15210/15210-h/15210-h.htm#Chapter_II. Accessed 2022.

Hurston, Zora Neale. "How it Feels to Be Colored Me." *The World Tomorrow* vol. 11, no. 5, 1928. https://www.wheelersburg.net/Downloads/Hurston.pdf. Accessed 2022.

Walker, Alice. "Only Justice Can Stop a Curse." *In Search of Our Mothers' Gardens: Womanist Prose*. Harcourt Brace Jovanovich, 1982, pp. 338–342. https://thedewdrop.org/2020/07/17/only-justice-can-stop-a-curse/. Accessed 2022.

Wilson, Kai Ashante. "The Devil in America." *Tor.com*, 2014, https://www.tor.com/2014/04/02/the-devil-in-america-kai-ashante-wilson/. Accessed 2022.

♦

End

The Weird Sisters of Onapatu Bog

"SO, THEY'RE JUST OUT THERE IN THE BOG? Anyone can go find 'em?" Coker asked the older man sitting across the table from us. Shortly after we'd arrived in town and checked in at a relatively reputable-looking inn, Coker and Stills had decided to go out and search for clues as to how to locate our quarry. I tagged along, hoping to get some leads on the story and a good start to my narrative. Maybe even a few interviews. We stopped in a tavern and Coker quickly found a promising contact in the Reverend Belliveau, a native of the area who had lived in the small town of Onapatu for more than forty years, or so he claimed.

Reverend Belliveau was a retired preacher who spoke of Onapatu's small community with a sense of meaning that struck me as old-fashioned—if not outdated—and downright charming. I guessed that he was in his sixties. He had clearly been around long enough to have seen a lot, but not so long that he'd started getting slow or feeble. With his graying long beard and mustache and wise-sounding country-folk demeanor, he would make a perfect interview subject for the documentary, I thought as I sat down and introduced myself.

Belliveau seemed more willing to talk than most of the other locals we came across, who were reasonably polite but reserved, so Coker ordered him another beer and started inquiring about the strange, fabled denizens of the bog we had come to find.

"Yeah, they're just out there. But no one in his right mind would wanna look for 'em," Belliveau answered.

"Why not?" Coker asked, his tone polite but firm.

"Fear o' death, I reckon," Belliveau answered, looking into his mug as he took a swig. "Or worse."

"Are they that dangerous?" Coker pressed.

The Reverend cocked his head to the side and looked at Coker out of the corner of his eye before turning back to his food. "If y'all are comin' out here lookin' for the sisters, then you know the numbers. Over five hundred declared dead to date, since they started countin', and that's just the people who they know went into the bog in the first place."

"That's a pretty high body count," Stills said.

"Ain't only ever been but one body found, son. That's the *death* count. The official one, not the actual one, mind you."

"What's the actual count?" Coker asked.

"Damned if I know," Belliveau said, staring out the window.

"Wait," Stills interjected. "How do they even know what the death toll is if there aren't any bodies? You mean people have just gone missing and the local police decide they're dead?"

Belliveau gave Stills a hard stare, and then answered, "Yes, people just go missin'. And then their families come lookin' for 'em. And sometimes family members go missin'. Sometimes they hire private investigators, wilderness experts—professional swamp men, you've seen 'em on TV—heck, even bounty hunters to go find the ones gone missin'. And then sometimes the people who they hire to go out lookin' go missin', too. The smart ones come back after steppin' foot in the bog and say no, thank you to the money they were offered. Ain't no prize worth throwin' your life away to try to find a dead body that likely ain't there nohow. Once, there was even a team of federal agents went out in the bog. Someone important done come out here on vacation, thought he'd do a little sight-seein'—like it was some damn tourist attraction."

Belliveau turned his head, cleared his throat and snorted angrily before resuming his story, his voice more solemn than before. "They made sure to go out on a clear day. Musta been the last time there was ever sunshine 'round here. Some of the local young'ns followed along to see how far they'd make it. The kids came back sayin' the agents had made it out to the main cave entrance, but they were too scared to go in after 'em."

The Reverend nodded. "I'm glad those kids didn't go into the cave. It's one thing for a grown man to decide to risk his life; it's another for a child to go out to a place like that. I know all of those kids, and you can bet I gave each one of 'em a stern talkin'-to after we were sure they were safe. They've gone on to live their lives, have families. Who knows what could'a happened to 'em if they had gone in, or if the sisters had been out in the bog that day..."

Belliveau's voice trailed off, wavering slightly. Coker nodded, and his sympathy struck me as sincere. I realized that I had never really talked with Coker about things like family or children. I wondered what he was thinking.

"What happened to the feds?" Coker asked softly.

"Never came back. Not long after, some more agents came around askin' about the first lot. Didn't go out in the bog. Never went any closer to it than the edge of town. They asked some questions, they took some notes, and they left, and that was that. Like everybody else who loses someone down here, at some point they decided that enough was enough and it just wasn't worth it to lose someone else. I hate to sound harsh, but here, you have to pray for the dead and move on."

"Wait a minute," I said. "Reverend, you said there was one body found. What's the story there?"

Belliveau looked at me and nodded. "That wasn't so long ago. Some damn fool showed up talkin' about how he'd gone to the caves. Braggin' about bein' the only one ever to come back alive. May be true, but he didn't make it through the night. They found his body the next mornin' in the motel room where he was stayin'."

"What happened to it?" Stills asked.

"It was all over the room," Belliveau replied.

There was a long pause.

Stills eventually spoke again. "These ladies only go after men?" he asked.

"I ain't never met a woman who was stupid enough to go out into the bog," Belliveau replied.

He took a drink and fixed his gaze on Coker. "What do you plan to do once you find 'em? What makes you think you'll fare any better?"

"We can handle ourselves, Reverend," Coker said. "I was a cop in a past life. After that came the Marines, and multiple tours in Afghanistan and Iraq. I've been in dangerous places before. I know how to come out alive. Part of it is having a team you can count on. Stills here earned two Purple Hearts as a field medic in Iraq. He can shoot, too. We have a few more veterans coming with us. Good men. Good fighters."

"That's all well and good, son, and I thank you for your service," Belliveau replied. "But you don't know what all y'all are fixin' to go up against."

"Why do you say that?" Coker asked.

"Because you think that bullets can kill 'em. Why do you want to look for the sisters anyway? Who hears that the Devil has appeared on Earth and rushes to meet 'im?"

240

"I don't mean to be rude, Reverend," Coker responded, "but I'd rather not talk about my reasons for coming to Onapatu. Let's just say we have a good reason to be here."

Belliveau harrumphed and turned to me. "And what's your motive for gettin' involved in this idiocy? You clearly ain't never been no soldier. Pardon me for sayin' so."

I shrank a bit into my drink. "I'm a journalist," I shrugged.

Belliveau gave a noncommittal "huh" and tilted his head back, looking down his nose at me. "So you wanna write about 'em?"

"Well... sort of," I stammered. "I'm more of a photojournalist—I do video, too—"

"So you wanna get 'em on videotape, is what you're sayin'," Belliveau cut in.

"Well...yes," I concurred. "I think visual media is the best way to share what's out there with the rest of the—"

"And why in God's name would you want to share what's in that godforsaken bog with anyone?" Belliveau stared at me incredulously.

"I—well, bringing problems to the light is the best way to solve them, right?" I offered uncertainly.

"You think you can solve this problem, son?"

I struggled for a moment to come up with a response. "I think that I can be part of the solution. I can at least shed some light on what's going on out here. Someone has to start the process."

"And what process is that? Your heart's in the right place, son, but you're in way over your head on this one."

I pursed my lips. "What do you think it would take to get whoever's in there out of the bog? To get them to stop killing people?"

Belliveau shifted back in his chair and exhaled loudly through his mouth. "Come back with an army of exorcists and

241

you might stand a fighting chance," he offered.

I couldn't help snickering.

"You don't believe that the sisters are out there, do you, son?" Belliveau asked calmly, his eyes locked steadily on mine.

I gulped. My throat felt dry. "I... don't believe that there's something supernatural in the bog, no."

Belliveau shrugged. "Call 'em natural, unnatural, supernatural, contaminated natural, nature's vengeance natural—whatever you want, son, but the sisters are out there in that filthy water, and they'll take you if you make it as far as the caves. I hope you come to your senses before you make it that far."

"Look, Reverend Belliveau," I said, "I believe you when you say there's a dangerous family out in the bog. I believe that they've been killing people for a long time. Not the same people, though. They must have had kids and grandkids and raised them to do the same horrible things to people who enter the bog. But that's all the more reason to go out there. If we stay here where it's safe, they'll just keep doing what they're doing for generations to come. Somebody has to go out there and show the world that these people—real people, flesh and blood—are killing people right here in Onapatu, and it has to stop. If we don't expose these people, then more curious visitors will come in thinking that this is some sort of ghost town that they can explore—or worse yet, people with no idea of the history of this place—and more people will die."

Belliveau looked at me mournfully. "Like I said, son, your heart's in the right place. You just don't understand what you're trying to confront, and I'm afraid that's going to cost you."

I stared down into my drink.

"So have you ever seen 'em?" Coker asked.

Belliveau stared coolly at Coker for several seconds before responding. "Yeah, I seen 'em."

242

"I thought you said people couldn't go to the caves and survive," quipped Stills.

"I didn't go to the caves, son. I figure that's why I'm alive today. I was a damn fool to go into the bog at all, but even then, at that age, I wasn't as much of a fool as you insist on bein'."

"So, what did you see?" Coker asked Belliveau before Stills could respond. "And may we ask how you did make it out alive?"

The Reverend nodded. "I went with a group. Like y'all are doin'. An even bigger group, mind you, although we may have had less sophisticated equipment."

He stopped to take a drink, then resumed his tale. "For some reason, we decided to split up in pairs and fan out to cover as much of the bog as we could at once. Thought we had strength in numbers. Thought our guns would protect us. Thought we'd stay near enough to each other that we could call for help and the rest would come runnin' at a moment's notice."

He shook his head. "Damn fools...the bog is enough to trap you on its own. Poisons you. Disorients you. You can't tell direction in there. Even if there were no sisters, it'd be too dangerous to risk goin' in. You can get lost right quick just tryin' to walk in a straight line. In any case, the sisters *are* there. I don't know exactly how it happened, but someone got spooked—maybe by the bog, or maybe surprised by one of the sisters—or maybe someone saw what I saw and panicked. Whatever it was, people started runnin' and hollerin' and goin' every which way. I reckon some thought we'd found the sisters and rushed off to fight 'em, and some got scared and tried to run away.

"I got separated from my buddy. Soon enough, I was separated from the whole group. I don't know how long I was runnin', then wanderin' by myself. God, I was scared. All alone in that bog, didn't know where on God's green Earth I was. Thought I might not make it home ever again. Almost didn't."

The Reverend stopped to take another drink. He looked at

each of us, then continued. "I came across a small clearin'. I can't tell you where, 'cause I don't rightfully know. But I saw 'em there. All three sisters. They seemed to be performin' some kind of ceremony."

"A ceremony?" Coker asked, his brow furrowed.

Belliveau nodded. "They were gathered around somethin'. Someone. There was a pole in the middle of the clearin', like a big stake. Like if they wanted to burn a witch in the old days. There was a man on it. I can see him clear as day. Just as if he was sittin' here by y'all right now. Couldn't tell who he was, though. He might'a been one o' ours, or he might'a been there already. His face was all covered in blood. He was nailed to it."

"To the stake?" Stills asked.

Belliveau nodded. "I saw each of the sisters, too. They ain't human. I saw 'em, and I saw what they are, and they ain't human. They couldn't see me, though. I stayed hidden. I hid, and I watched until I realized what was goin' on, then I couldn't bear to look no more."

He paused. "They was pullin' parts off him."

Stills frowned. "Parts of what?"

"Parts of his body," Belliveau responded. "He was still alive; at least halfway."

We all sat in silence for a while. I don't think any of us knew how to respond. Eventually, Coker broke the silence.

"Why have you stayed here, Reverend? If you saw that out there, why didn't you leave Onapatu?"

"That's a fair question," Belliveau said. "I suppose I see this as my duty. I think the only reason God kept me alive and helped me find my way out of that bog was so that I could keep other people from goin' in."

He looked at me and Stills, then addressed all of us earnestly. "I'm gonna tell y'all one more time. Don't go into the bog. And if I have somehow failed to convince y'all to stay the Hell out, then

244

for the love of God, at least don't try to go to the caves. Please."

Coker licked his lips and took a deep breath. "I appreciate you taking the time to talk with us, but we came here for a reason."

We finished the rest of our meal in silence.

"I'm gonna pray for you fellas," Belliveau finally said with a sigh of resignation.

"Do you think that'll protect us?" Stills asked with a smirk.

"Only your souls," Belliveau answered sadly.

Stills's smirk faded a little.

♦

"What's up with the perma-cloud, anyway?" Bennie said to no one in particular.

"I mean, it was bad in town," he continued, "but this is even worse. At least the clouds were gray there. They look brown out here."

"It must be the bog," Coker said.

"Or smog," said one of the other men. Even though I had seen everyone in our group by now, I had only actually talked with Coker, who was one of the first contacts I made when researching Onapatu; Stills, who I'd met only after arriving in town and joining Coker to set out for leads; and Bennie, still in his twenties, with whom I chatted while the others were still getting ready for the expedition. I felt awkward about introducing myself to the other two.

"This ain't L.A., buddy," Bennie said.

"Yes, I'm sure the Deep South has much higher environmental standards," Stills chimed in.

"All right, let's move, ladies," Coker interrupted. "Stay sharp. In and out. Remember, we're not trying to take 'em all out ourselves. No Rambo today."

The other men laughed, and we waded into the bog. I

realized then that I didn't actually know what Coker and the ex-soldiers had planned for this excursion. I was excited, but anticipation was starting to make me nervous. The danger of the situation, in particular, was beginning to truly sink in. I had been conceptually aware of it all along, of course—that's why I came to Onapatu, after all—but I now felt my skin begin to tingle with the sense that something dangerous and foreign to me was somewhere just in front of me, somewhere I couldn't see—but soon would.

"So, Tipton," Coker called out from ahead. "Why Onapatu, of all places? You wanted to see some action. Why not one of the wars? You want a conflict, people killing each other, you got it there. You definitely could have made a name for yourself if you found a story out there."

I scratched the back of my head and grimaced a bit. "I just finished school," I said, feeling silly about the response.

All of the ex-soldiers laughed, and I felt my face flush. "Fair enough," Coker chuckled, his eyes still scanning the swamp in front of us. "Well, you picked a hell of a place to start your journalistic career. Just stay behind us and you'll be fine, kid. These people may be crazy, but they ain't no guerrillas. My intel says they don't use booby traps either, so you just sit tight and leave the fighting to us."

Coker turned around and winked at me. "Make sure I look pretty in your pictures, okay, Tipton?"

"I'm sure that'll come naturally for you," I said, making a lame attempt to keep up with Coker's humor. He laughed and turned his face back to the murky bog ahead.

"Hey, Coke," Stills called from my right. "I just realized we never gave Tipton here a name."

"He wasn't a soldier. They'd'a given him a name," Bennie said from my left.

"Hey, now," Stills retorted, "Tipton's a part of the team. He helped us gather intel. Ain't that right, Tip?"

"Doing what I can," I said. The men laughed again.

"Well, how about 'Tip?'" Coker called back. "I think you already decided for us, Stills."

More laughter. "Tip!" Stills shouted. "Going once! Going twice! All right, sold!"

"All right, keep it down, tiger," Coker said, his voice warm but serious.

"I just got so excited," Stills said, to more chuckles.

"'Tip' ain't very creative. You just chopped off the end of his name," Bennie said.

"Worked for Coke," Stills replied.

"Yeah, but it wasn't creative then, either," Coker said.

"Stills is your real name, isn't it?" I asked Stills.

"Yes, but don't tell anybody," he said, glaring at me. My eyes widened a bit.

"Nah, I'm just playing," he added, laughing. "It is my name, though. The guys I came up with just got a kick out of the last name 'Stills' for some reason."

He shrugged.

"This gentleman on my right is called Taco," Coker called back to me. "Real name's Klinger."

"Why do they call you Taco?" I asked Klinger.

"'Cause I freakin' love tacos, man," Klinger said, turning to me with a wry smile.

"Staple product of his granddaddy's native Germany," Coker added. "It's in his blood."

The men shared another laugh. I joined them this time.

"They called me Popeye," said the man on Coker's left. "Drill sergeant didn't like the way I squint when I aim. Real name's Cory. I hate Popeye."

"Last name Cory?" I asked.

"Jeez, do I have to tell you everything?" he groaned, then

laughed. "Cory Maes. Pleased to meet you. Is this all going in your documentary?"

"I thought it was a news report," Klinger said.

"Wait, we're being recorded?" Stills asked.

"My fifteen minutes are coming!" Bennie said gleefully. More laughter.

Klinger's laughter stopped abruptly, and he quickly dropped down and moved to his right, staying low, gun in front of him.

"Whatchu got, Taco?" Coker asked, scanning the area to Klinger's left through the sight of his rifle. Stills scanned the area to Klinger's right. I moved toward the middle of the group. I could hear my heartbeat in my ears.

"It's dead," Klinger responded. I followed the barrel of his gun with my eyes and saw the dark mass it was pointing at. He moved closer. "Think it was a pig."

"A pig?" Bennie said, wiping sweat from his brow.

"Wild hog. Boar. Whatever you call 'em. Razorback. Do I look like a farmer to you?"

"I don't think they grow razorbacks on farms," Bennie answered with a chuckle.

Klinger flipped Bennie off and moved closer to the corpse, lowering his gun and putting his arm over his nose and mouth.

"Still smells pretty fresh," he said, "but it's getting there."

He straightened up. "Damn."

"What is it?" Coker asked.

"Thing's been torn up. Eyes are gone. Guts, too. Whatever did this left all the meat, though."

"Sick," Stills said.

Klinger looked at Stills—or rather, past him—a look of consternation on his face.

"What?" Coker asked.

"Have you noticed there are no animals around here? This is the first living thing I've seen in this swamp, other than the trees.

Formerly living, anyway. We're walking through this swamp in the heat, and I haven't even been bitten by a mosquito or a leech."

The other men looked around as if to confirm Klinger's observation.

"There aren't even any bugs on the body," Klinger continued. "No flies or maggots. Nothing. That's not natural."

"Weird," Bennie offered.

Does radiation clear out insect life? I wondered.

"Well, we're not looking for wildlife," Coker said. "Let's keep moving. Stay low, and let's keep it down, boys."

We moved on in silence, the other men keeping their guns ready. I clutched my video camera with sweaty hands. I wondered if we would see our targets in the bog, or if they were all hidden in the caves. Questions raced through my mind. Would we surprise them? Would they—Heaven forbid—ambush us? Could they know we were coming? What was Coker's plan, anyway? Were we going to take a prisoner for information? For leverage? *Am I going to see someone die today?* I cringed at the thought. The bog was still, however, and in what seemed to be no time at all, we found ourselves in front of a large cave entrance. It didn't look anywhere near as dark as I thought it should have.

"Gentlemen, this is it," Coker said. "Entry. You know the drill. Maes, shotgun. Bennie and Taco, cover Maes. Stills and I cover the flanks. Tip, make sure I look pretty."

We entered the cave, and gazed around at a space that looked almost like a grand entry hall. The ceiling was high above our heads, the walls clean and bright, and a strange light permeated the space. I looked for its source but was unable to spot anything that could have been emitting light. There were no electric lights to be seen, no lamps, no torches, not even something that might glow. There was simply a cold, gray light throughout. I shuddered.

We walked further into the surprisingly spacious, bright space, and Maes pointed at something in the middle of the floor that looked like a small table or even a podium. We drew nearer, and I saw that there was an oddly-shaped bowl on top. The bowl had a strange stem for its base, which had apparently been driven into the table, or whatever it was. The thing on which the bowl rested looked like a mix of materials. Something like a resin held together bits of what might have been wood or stone, fashioned together in a shape like a tree trunk.

"Some kind of altar?" Klinger asked, reaching out a hand.

"Don't," Coker said abruptly. Klinger looked at him. Coker pointed at the base of the structure. I looked down and felt my breath leave my body quickly as I saw what he was looking at. Two large bones stuck out of the base, resting on the floor, and joined together to form a triangle—like a leg, knee sticking out, picked clean. The bones were much larger than the dead boar's.

"Look at the shape," Coker said, pointing to the bowl. We all looked, and I realized that it was not a bowl. The shape was that of a human skull, but only the back half—as if someone had neatly chopped off the front of the head and cleaned out the contents. The protruding skull and spine, and what I now realized must be withered flesh and skin clinging to them, were the same color as what I had thought was a table, as if mummified by the substance encasing the bones.

"Stay sharp," Coker said. "These people aren't playing around."

The other men shook their heads and started to walk past the morbid display. Stills hesitated.

Coker turned to him. "Are you getting cold feet?"

Stills looked up at Coker. "The precision of this cut... this is better than a surgeon. And no fracturing of the bone. You don't just lift half of a person's head off."

"We knew who we were dealing with when we signed up for

this," Coker responded solemnly.

"I'm not sure now that we really do understand who or what we're dealing with," Stills said.

"Come on," Coker said, firmly but not insistently. "We didn't come all this way for nothing."

Stills nodded slowly and rejoined the group. We moved forward, toward the back of the entryway, where the gray light started to fade. Several dark openings in the rock wall led into the depths. Coker nodded toward the leftmost opening, and we moved toward it. The men turned on flashlights strapped to their jackets. I felt a knot in the pit of my stomach. Were we really going in there? What I had envisioned was a cave made livable, with signs of human habitation—rustic lights, perhaps doors and artificial pathways to facilitate traversing the caves for the people who lived here. Instead, our foray into the earth had started with eerie, seemingly source-less gray light and a macabre altar, and now a descent into what, as far as I could tell, was a randomly chosen pitch-black tunnel.

I hadn't asked for many details when I arranged to come with Coker's group. I'd been excited about the opportunity I saw to make my mark and did not want to lose it, but this was a far cry from what I'd had in mind at the time. We were wandering into unfamiliar territory, with no clear idea exactly how many people lay in wait for us. The local legends said three, but if their kill total was as prolific as Belliveau had said, then there must have been many more. What sort of place was this, really, and what sort of family? We moved down the tunnel, through the darkness, but although I was scared out of my wits, I suddenly felt an unprecedented surge of excitement. Maybe it was adrenaline, I mused. Genuine fear spurring a fight-or-flight response—and it was strangely thrilling. I had never done anything like this before.

After several more moments trudging forward through the

dark tunnel, the men stopped, as if waiting for something. I stopped and listened. I could hear it, too. A faint voice could be heard from up ahead, around a bend. Coker nodded at Klinger, Maes and Bennie.

"Maes," he said quietly. Maes nodded and moved forward. Bennie and Klinger followed on Maes's flanks.

Coker gave Stills a look and Stills nodded, and the two turned toward the darkness behind us to make sure we weren't being followed. I didn't know which way to turn. The camera shook in my hand. I tried to concentrate on keeping it steady and focusing on the action in front of me, hoping that Coker and Stills would take care of anything that might happen behind me. I also hoped that I wouldn't miss any footage of them in action if someone did try to ambush us. I was terrified, but thrilled. As we drew closer to the bend, the voice became clearer. It was a woman, not too young but not old. She wasn't saying anything; only crying. Our group kept moving forward, guns ready, and I kept filming. We rounded the corner and my heart skipped a beat.

The woman sat on the floor of the cave, in the middle of an otherwise empty space the size of a small room. Her back was turned to us. She was nude, and her whole body was covered in what seemed to be blood. Her hands clutched the sides of her head, her fingertips buried in her hair. Her body shook visibly as she sobbed. As we drew closer, I saw that her back was covered in lacerations. The gashes were open and glistening. I started to feel queasy. I hadn't expected to see something quite like this.

"Clear," Bennie said. Klinger confirmed.

Maes stepped closer to the woman on the floor. "Miss, it's okay. We're here to help."

The woman didn't answer. She rocked back and forth, clenching and unclenching her fingers and crying loudly.

Maes lowered his shotgun and slowly reached out a hand as he drew within a few steps of the woman. "Miss—"

With a bloodcurdling shriek and inhuman speed, the woman turned and leapt on Maes, shoving her hands into his eyes and clamping onto his face with her teeth. Everything else was a blur to me. The other men shouted, and Bennie and Klinger opened fire on the woman. The bullets riddled her body and she fell back for a split second, just long enough for me to glimpse her face. Blood clots filled the cavities where her eyes should have been. Her front teeth and gums were completely exposed, the flesh around her mouth covered in jagged tears. Lacerations covered the front of her torso and her face as well, creating holes in her cheeks. Something wet and pink was clenched between her teeth, and something white and red fell from her open hands. She screamed and again leapt on Maes, who was lying on his back on the floor of the cave, screaming in agony.

My voice caught in my throat. My body felt numb, my feet stuck in place. Maes's red eye sockets and the oozing red gash where his lip and cheek had been made him look strangely like the thing attacking him. She clawed furiously at his abdomen and face with fleshless fingertips, unfazed by the steady stream of gunfire the ex-soldiers unleashed on her. I felt a strong body shove me away from the monster, and another one dragging me further away, out of the small cave and into another passageway, while the soldiers fell back. The thing leapt toward Klinger with another howl that chilled me to the bone with the sound of despair and rage, hooking her fingers into his leg and knocking him down. There was more shouting and more gunfire, and someone again pulled me away. I came to my senses enough to propel myself, and I lurched up the dark tunnel. I stumbled and hit rock walls as I ran, scraping myself on the jagged surfaces of the cave, but I didn't care. I just wanted to get as far away from that horrible scene as I could.

I came to an abrupt stop as something grabbed me, and I shouted and flailed until I felt a steely hand clamp over my

253

mouth. I stared, wide-eyed, at my attacker, until my eyes adjusted to the darkness and I realized that it was Stills. He had turned off his light, and we were in a more open space faintly illuminated by gray light emanating from a far corner. Stills pinned me against a large stalagmite with his hand over my mouth until he was sure I had recognized him, then put a finger over his lips and let go. I sank to the cavern floor, shuddering. Faintly, in the distance, I could hear the repeated rhythmic clang of metal against stone.

Coker emerged from the passageway shortly after. He had also turned off his light. He crouched down beside me and Stills behind the small bank of stalagmites where we were hiding.

"Where's Bennie?" Stills asked after a moment.

Coker looked around and swore. "He was in front of me. He didn't come out here?"

Stills shook his head. "Just you and Tip."

There was a pause. "He must have taken another passage," Stills said.

"I thought I was right behind him the whole way up," Coker said, and swore again.

The sound of metal hitting stone stopped, and a strange popping sound took its place. Stills looked at Coker and tersely shook his head. "We need to get out of here."

Coker nodded and took a deep breath. He looked at me. "You okay, kid?"

I nodded, although I clearly wasn't.

"We're gonna get out of here alive," Coker said, eyes locked on mine. He pursed his lips in what appeared to be an attempt at a smile. I was too shaken to manage anything further.

Our exchange was interrupted by a loud, hollow croaking sound that filled the cavern and made me flinch. Coker and Stills looked up, hands on their guns, but they stayed on the ground behind the cover of the stalagmites. The sound had not come from the passageway with the bloody creature on the other side, and it had not come from the corner far to our right where the gray light hinted at freedom and safety. Somewhere to our left, deeper within the cavern, the croaking sound emerged again, closer this time, along with the scrape of metal against stone. I cringed. The scraping sound drew closer, and as it did, the sound of something large and dull being dragged across the stone floor came with it. Stills put a hand on my shoulder and motioned again for me to stay quiet.

A small figure emerged from the darkness. I stared through a narrow gap between two stalagmites, and as the figure moved toward the light, I could see it. I could no longer deny the existence of the three sisters. We had been attacked by the first one we came across, and here was the second. Her whole body appeared to have burned to a crisp. Her skin was charred, gray and black ash that blended with the cave around her and the gray light streaming softly into the cavern. Her eye sockets were empty and black, cavernous like the abyss from which she had emerged. The soft parts of her face and her breasts had almost completely melted or burned away, leaving her well-preserved teeth bared in two long rows extending along the length of her jaw. Scattered strands of wispy, dry hair floated around her head like the tendrils of a jellyfish suspended in water.

She moved slowly and deliberately with a stiff gait, pushing forward laboriously on one leg at a time, each step an abrupt lurch. In one hand, she held a long machete, rusty and charred, which scraped against the cavern floor as she walked. Her other hand gripped a filthy canvas bag, larger than her body, whose lumpy contents stuck out at odd angles as she dragged it along behind her. A steady, dark smear marked the bag's path. I shrank away from the gap and pressed my hands over my mouth. Tears welled in my eyes and I drew my legs up to my chest. The burnt sister stopped, raised her head, and opened her mouth as if to howl, and the croaking sound filled my ears. I wanted to scream. I felt as if I would either burst or collapse, but I put every ounce of strength I had into staying silent. Coker and Stills remained motionless, not making a single sound. The sister lowered her head and resumed her steady march toward the light, and after what felt like an eternity, vanished around an outcropping of rock.

After several minutes of complete silence, Coker and Stills exhaled audibly and looked at each other and me.

"We have to go that way," Coker whispered, motioning toward the gray light.

"That's where she just went," Stills objected.

"We don't have much of a choice," Coker responded. "We can't wait here, and we're sure as hell not going in the direction she came from. That's sunlight. We need to follow it."

Stills nodded, and for the first time, I saw trepidation in his face. "We'd better move, then. Don't know how long our window will be open."

Coker turned to me. "I'm going first, in case our friend isn't as far ahead of us as we hope she is. You stay between me and Stills, got that?"

I nodded, unable to speak. We left our safe haven and moved into the wide cavern. As strange as it seemed, I found myself immediately longing for the relative security of our hiding place behind the stalagmites, but equally eager to reach the light shining dimly through the large crevice ahead of us. Coker and Stills moved quickly and quietly, staying low and keeping their guns ready. I felt clumsy and loud as I tried to keep pace, but neither man said anything. I didn't have any faith left in the ability of the guns to protect us in this place, and I doubted that my guardians did, either, but the ex-soldiers' show of readiness, even if only a façade, was reassuring to me.

We passed through the crevice and into another open space

with an eerie glow similar to the passage where we entered the caves, albeit not as bright. At the far end, the bog beckoned. It was still a foreboding sight, but it looked like a sanctuary next to what I had just seen. We quickened our pace. There was no sign of the burnt sister, and the bloody sister seemed to have stayed in the bowels of the cave. My pulse quickened, and I smiled, despite myself. *We can make it,* I thought. *We can get out.* We were almost at the entrance.

Then we heard another voice. We stopped. Coker and Stills raised their weapons to eye level and scanned the space in front of us and behind us. Nothing. I clutched my camera uselessly. The voice came again, from a niche in the cave wall ahead of us and to the left, near the entrance. It was a whimper. Stills moved toward the sound, Coker covering him. I hung back, a knot growing in my stomach, but then I moved forward behind Coker, afraid to be left behind. We came around the edge of the niche. It extended about ten feet away from the direction of the entrance. Sitting in the corner was a ghostly pale, unclothed figure.

I felt a sinking feeling. Her body was intact, but she sat as if crumpled in on herself, wringing her hands together incessantly. Her face was malformed and twisted, as if the right side of the lower half had been sucked down her throat. Despite the grotesque appearance of her face, I was mesmerized by her eyes. The sclera were black, the pupils white, her irises a brilliant blue. Her eyes terrified me, but I could not stop looking. I felt myself sinking into the deep pools of black, then startled by the gleaming blue, and absolutely undone by the impenetrable stillness of the white pupils. No sooner had the hostile white points jarred me to my senses, however, than I felt myself pulled back into the numbing blackness surrounding them.

"Stills, no," Coker said softly. "We need to get out of here. Now."

Stills did not take his eye off the sight on his rifle. The pale sister leaned away from Stills, looking up like a beaten dog, her terrifying, beautiful eyes shifting from him to me and back.

"We won't... leave... empty-handed," Stills said slowly. "She's... in..."

"Stills!" Coker whispered stridently.

The speed of the pale figure's attack was even more startling than that of the bloody fiend in the dark. In an instant, with seemingly no effort, she was upon Stills, past the barrel of his gun, and her mouth unfurled from within and expanded, formless and gaping, to clamp onto Stills' face. The only sound was her face, wretched and surreal, unfolding itself and expanding. Coker raised his gun and slammed the butt of it into her side twice, but it simply sank into her flesh as harmlessly as it would a pillow. Her arms flailed, and her body writhed as if there were no skeleton inside, and she remained latched to Stills's face.

Coker's face showed his disbelief and horror. There was the sound of something solid turning to mulch, followed by a gulping sound, and Stills's body fell away from the pale sister. The front half of his head had separated from the back in a clean, straight line and vanished, the cavities in the back of his skull empty and dry like the half-skull in the grand entryway.

"Run!" Coker shouted, and this time I was able to move of my own accord, but as we turned to run, Coker came face to face with the burnt sister. With a raspy howl, she swung her machete and hit his shoulder. Coker lost his balance, spinning as he fell and landing with a thud on his back. His rifle clattered away on the cave floor.

"Run!" Coker wheezed again, fumbling for his handgun.

I wanted to help him, but terror now spurred my legs, and I obeyed his command. I ran headlong out of the cave and through the bog, too terrified to stop or look back. Gunshots rang out behind me.

Please live, I thought, my mind frantic, my vision blurring. *Please don't leave me alone out here.*

I ran until my lungs burned and I couldn't see through my tears. I didn't know which way I was going. Nothing in the bog looked familiar, and the sky was quickly darkening. I kept running until I tripped over something rigid and fell into the noxious water. A sharp pain shot up my leg, and my back and arm ached where I had landed on them. I looked up and saw the root that had tripped me. I wanted to get up again and run, to find my way to the town of Onapatu, to find Reverend Belliveau or anyone else who might help me, to get as far away from this place as I could. But I couldn't get up. My body ached, and I felt a deep chill.

I panted for breath and managed to sit up, soaking wet and partially submerged in the swamp, my back against a large tree. And heard footsteps.

I froze. The footsteps drew closer. Hot tears dripped slowly down my face, mixing with the filthy water. *Please, Coker. It has to be you.* The footsteps came closer, splashing softly. I couldn't see anyone. *Coker. Belliveau. Someone...please don't leave me here. Please help me*, I thought. I began to sob, and I prayed for the comfort of a familiar face—or any human face—to appear. The footsteps came closer still. And then I saw her.

The pale sister came into view around a nearby tree. She turned and spotted me. She began to walk toward me, doubled over as if cringing, weaving side to side, hands wringing together. I tried to move, to get up and run, but my body went numb as I once again stared into her awful eyes.

◆

End

HOW DID IT GET TO THIS, YOU ASK? Well, it started about 100 years ago when we had an unlikely encounter.

The aliens?

Yes, the aliens or Aquabeggans, as they are now popularly known.

They hated that name, yes?

Of course, it was a slur because they did tell us what they were to be called.

When the Aquabeggans arrived on our blue, dreamy planet, as they called it, they had done extensive research on us, sending tiny, undetectable quantum nanoprobes.

How did that work?

Well, I cannot explain to you how their technology worked. Shockingly, we never bothered with that. They had scoured endless hours of videos, news, articles, and records about humans. They knew the planet was split into countries, divided by races and other seemingly ridiculous concepts.

Well how great for the Aquabeggians: they all looked the same so obviously they had no reason to not be united.

When they finally arrived in their flying saucer.

A flying saucer?

Yes, it is said that they flew in a saucer-like ship; we do not know if we inspired them or if it was a coincidence, but that probably doesn't matter. They decided to land in the country most likely to ensure a successful expedition. They landed in our very own country!

Why were they sure?

Well, after all the years and years of studying humanity's greatest stories, films and theories on alien arrivals, they noticed a trope: landing in a global superpower was likely to lead to failure. These were willing to nuke themselves if it became necessary.

Doesn't it matter that any species advanced enough to reach Earth would possess technology beyond reckoning, nuke or not?

Well, it probably does and they probably did, but they decided to take their chances; to them, every life was as sacred as water and they had to avoid any death as much as they possibly could.

Well, their technology couldn't be all that advanced if they could not manufacture water out of thin air.

As the saucer spun comically overhead, its eerie roar was unlike anything anyone had ever heard; the security personnel at the President's Villa had stood frozen, pointing their puny outdated guns at it, not exactly sure of what to do.

No one had noticed the 400-meter-wide silver behemoth looming in the sky until it was already too late. How had they not?

How, you ask? Because Honorable Jaloki, the head of the NAA at the time, had deemed it more important to ensure that the organization's executives had bulletproof cars. After all, securing the airspace might make them targets. So, instead of using the $100 million budget for air defence radars and satellites, the money had gone toward shiny, armoured luxury cars.

No one said anything?

When he was asked about this on a government-owned TV station, he had famously responded angrily with, "If we finish protecting the air, won't we come back to the ground? Who will save the protectors on the ground then?" Of course, that made sense and the interviewer could not respond. They had tried though; they had shipped in the old tech from the United States instead.

Wasn't this tech that those countries deemed inaccurate and outdated?

Yes, yes, but you are missing the point: we were third world and as such we can use what the first world countries don't necessarily need. Not only had substandard technology been purchased but Hon. Jaloki also secured his position through his father-in-law, who had a favour owed to him by the President. He had been crucial during an election in a densely populated area where the President needed votes. Naturally, the father-in-law couldn't sway the entire electorate on his own, so he had the election rigged and delivered his constituency, as they called it.

Ah, and as such, the favors trickled down?

Of course.

Now, Hon. Jaloki, if he had any intention of being useful, could have hired a tech genius, an expert, or anyone with the know-how to properly manage the second-hand equipment. But his father-in-law had suggested Kerele, his grandson, who had just graduated with a degree in Agriculture. Kerele had helped his grandfather a few times with minor issues on his iPad and laptop, and as such he was tech-savvy enough. As a result, Kerele was appointed head of technology with some mild backlash in the media. Kerele, using his technological savvy, later tweeted, "The only cronyism happening here is you people that are just crying for nothing; you will cry.

That wasn't enough to get him removed?

It wasn't, but he trended online for days and the people were really mad.

Of course, bullets flew through the air, spraying mercilessly at the descending object. The SSD had joined in with the police, and the heavy firing continued as the noise almost deafened all who were in the vicinity. The bullets did nothing, simply bouncing off what appeared to be a malleable, soft gel-like substance that shielded the ship. Soon enough the bullets and refill ammo were exhausted. No one dared to ask why they were so woefully under-supplied. This was because everyone already knew. Somewhere, someone had pocketed the defence budget, trading national security for luxury estates and offshore accounts. Undisturbed, the ship opened up, and out came the Aliens.

The emerging humanoid dry-skinned aliens were friendly, hovering down from the ship in a showcase of their superior technology. They explained via their language device that they simply wanted to meet with the President. They meant no harm, and that was convincing enough, as it was pretty obvious that if they wanted to, they could have levelled the villa in seconds. The President was on a trip to the Bahamas for a medical check-up and had to rush back to meet the Aliens; the drama was already trending online.

The meeting with the President of the country went smoother than the Alien envoys anticipated. They simply introduced themselves with calm precision and as little information as possible.

We really did not ask for their technology. I find that ridiculous.

What part of this story does not seem ridiculous to you, at this point? This was the reality of how we were.

The Aliens told us who they were— "Klueunans," travelers from a distant desert exomoon orbiting a gas giant about 42 light years away. Their world sat dangerously close to their carbon-rich star, teetering on the edge of habitability, and as such they had extreme temperatures of over 2,000°C. Water was a sacred rarity; in fact, their image of a creator was one made entirely of water.

To survive, they had evolved a silicon-based physiology, engineered over millennia to minimize the loss of water. In their homeworld, water was more than a resource: it was life itself, almost a currency, strictly governed, rationed and now vanishing entirely.

So, couldn't they manage?

They could not; stellar radiation had stolen what little they had left, putting them on the brink of extinction, despite their best efforts. They had sent probes across the cosmos for salvation and finally found us: the blessed blue planet filled with water, wasted and taken for granted.

I mean we still had droughts in certain places from time to time, right?

Yes, but what you call drought was abundance to them. They were here to mine water to take back and supply their home planet. They understood human nature, though, and they had not come to beg. They had come to trade. They had another planet in their solar system which orbited closer to their star and was rich in diamonds. They had brought enough to elevate our country with unprecedented wealth, tipping the balance of global power in our favour. All they asked in return was water.

Sure enough, that would not be much of a reasonable trade.

Oh, apparently not.

The President jumped on this immediately; it is said that the alien envoys could be seen exchanging glances that we now know as shock and disappointment. This was simply their first offer, and our great shortsighted leader had jumped on it.

What did they need more money for? I thought they already embezzled and siphoned the country's wealth on a ridiculous scale?

I don't have an answer to why our bad leaders did what they did. Greed is probably too simple an explanation. Perhaps it runs deeper, something far worse, a deep-rooted primal need for self-preservation and accumulation, to the detriment of others. It rears its head in the very worst of our people when they are given unchecked power, and oh, we gave it to them all the time.

How did he explain to the country what the aliens came for?

The incident at the villa was reported as a quelled terrorist attack, a convenient cover for the chaos that had unfolded. Behind the scenes, the President issued a direct order to the Aquabeggans. They were to hide themselves completely, never to be seen by the public. They complied. Any whispers of extraterrestrial involvement were dismissed as outrageous conspiracy theories and buried under layers of disinformation. And, as expected, the people moved on because who would believe such a thing without seeing it with their own eyes?

Were the machines not enough evidence of something suspicious?

It was, but by then, it was far too late.

The Drought Machine, as we came to call it, was placed in our major cities. The nano-powered structures were erected in days to everyone's surprise. It stretched some meters skyward and was holographically manipulated to seem as nonthreatening as possible. Somehow it siphoned groundwater, rivers, streams, and even moisture from the air.

Were questions asked? Did no one protest?

People did; the younger generation came out in droves questioning the erection of something largely unexplained and seemingly ominous. They were dispatched off, quelled mercilessly. Human rights lawyers and advocacy groups fought relentlessly to prove that the protesters had been harmed, but opposing parties dismissed their claims as mere propaganda. The narrative quickly shifted when it was pointed out that the President hailed from the Thoro ethnic group, a group that had never held power since independence.

How did that have any effect? Again, did people not see the giant machines erected everywhere?

They did, but his supporters framed the backlash, the protests, the debates, and the concerns as nothing but orchestrated attempts by other tribes and the opposing parties to undermine his administration. They hated the progress unfolding before their eyes. For a time, this strategy worked and what should have been a matter of human rights and plain transparency was reduced to a tribal conflict, then a political party conflict, then a religious conflict, all the while diverting attention from the machines that whirred on, undisturbed.

The media was later told that they were diamond-extracting machines, despite certain news reports that this was a lie. Information was diluted, distorted and buried under a flood of contradictory narratives to the point where no one knew what was true. The President declared on national television: "This wealth is for our people. We will build new roads, new schools, better churches, better mosques! We will build our very own nuclear plants and stand alongside the U.S., Russia, and China as rivals!"

Lakunle Whesu

Did anyone question how a country with virtually no history of large-scale diamond mining had become a global supplier overnight?

No one that mattered, and if you pay attention to the pattern of our people, it should be obvious. Most of them cheered for the coming progress, while the other reasonable voices were drowned out.

There had to be some effect that people noticed soon enough, right?

Of course, within months the signs were undeniable. It became obvious that something was wrong. Our air grew dry and suffocating, our aquifers depleted, rivers drained, streams transformed into brittle cracked earth, and extreme drought gripped the land. Naturally, the government tried to distract the masses, parading the new institutions they were building from the diamond money. They even handed out bags of imported food, a feeble attempt to pacify the growing unrest. But hunger was not the real issue; it was thirst. And soon, no amount of rations could mask the truth. Our rivers were gone. Our wells empty. Our plants dead.

The people finally woke up?

Sadly, not then.

Ultimately, it wasn't the yachts, the private aeroplanes, the tiny islands, or the limited-edition luxury cars bought by every politician in the President's cabinet that angered the people. That kind of corruption had long been expected and tolerated. It was the importation of freshwater by the government that did it: we exported diamonds and imported water. The irony was maddening.

Even then, all was not lost until a video surfaced online of the politicians keeping huge reserves of water tanks in their lavish mansions while people were dying of thirst. The outrage was instant. No one continued their activism online as half of the population took to the streets in violent protests, but the government managed to control it, hoping to break the people as they typically did. Then came the final revelation: undeniable proof of alien involvement, with their evil machines that drained the land dry.

All hell broke loose. The machines were torn apart, burned and destroyed. Government officials and politicians met their end at the hands of jungle justice. Millions of lives were lost. *The aliens? Were they attacked too?*

They would have been too powerful, and they vanished as swiftly as they had arrived, disappearing into the vast emptiness of space, leaving behind a shriveled, uninhabitable wasteland.

But in a way, wasn't this a good thing? Our people finally woke up.

Good? They woke up after death. When there was nothing left to save. No country, no future, no hope: just a wasteland where a country once stood.

So, you ask: how did it come to this? How did an entire land crumble into dust? It happened because our people waited. They waited until their very last breaths were stolen, before they fought back.

And now, a hundred years later, we still haven't recovered. We are still trying to get our water back and we have no water for tears.

◆

End

A Dry Death

[A Dry Death]
[Vuyokazi Ngemntu]

THE PARCHED EARTH
Ravaged by drought
Fracked and impaired
The land has forgotten to sing
Does not remember
How to hold our roots
To nurture and cultivate
The barren seed
Of a bleak tomorrow
Poisoned by greed
Replete with inequity
Reeking of hypocrisy
Its emaciated trees
Fodder for this rot
Remain barren
Despite the manure
Of corporations' corruption
Suffocating the air.

◆

End

[Biographies]

Desireé Y. Amboree is a writer, full circle doula, and energy worker who blends the magical and the mundane. As a mixed methods researcher, her work focuses on reproductive justice, mass incarceration, and the intersections of state sanctioned violence and Black motherhood. She synergizes activism, advocacy, scholarship, and energetic healing as the owner of Divinely Aligned Holistic Health and Healing, a birth work business, and founder of the Gulf Coast Doula Coalition, a community doula non-profit based in the greater Houston, Texas area. In her spare time, she enjoys ramen and reality television.

Ceschino, Domer, Harvard JD, Longhorn MBA. Wordsmith. Works in product/content marketing, UX/design, and strategy with multiple tech companies based in the Bay Area and central Texas. He creates games and art through BlackFireTiger, has publications in several anthologies including "The Bringer of Light becomes the Fallen Angel: Sephiroth, Lucifer, and Frankenstein's Creature" in *The World of Final Fantasy VII: Essays on the Game and Its Legacy (Studies in Gaming),* "The Argument" in *Love and Darker Passions,* "Tailed" in *Tales in Firelight and Shadow,* and has published a brain-teasing mobile game in Apple's App Store and a speculative fiction podcast available through Apple Podcasts, Spotify, and more streaming platforms. Avid gamer, reader, thinker, and consumer of hot peppers.

Joyce Chng lives in Singapore. Their speculative fiction has appeared in *The Apex Book of World SF II, We See A Different Frontier, Cranky Ladies of History,* and *Accessing the Future.* Joyce also co-edited *THE SEA IS OURS: Tales of Steampunk Southeast Asia* with Jaymee Goh. Their novels span across wolf clans (*Starfang: Rise of the Clan*), vineyards (*Water into Wine*) and swordmaking forges (*Fire Heart*) respectively. Joyce wrangles article editing at Strange Horizons and is diversity coordinator for IGDN (Independent Game Designer Network). Alter-ego J. Damask writes about werewolves in Singapore. *Star Pattern Traveller*, a novella about first contact, is published in February 2024.You can find Joyce at http://awolfstale.wordpress.com and @jolantru.bsky.social on Bluesky. (Pronouns: she/her, they/their)

F. Brett Cox is the author of *The End of All Our Exploring: Stories* (Fairwood, 2018) and *Roger Zelazny* (U of Illinois, 2021). With Andy Duncan, he co-edited the anthology *Crossroads: Tales of the Southern Literary Fantastic* (Tor, 2004). His fiction, poetry, plays, articles, and reviews have appeared in numerous magazines and anthologies. A native of North Carolina, Brett is Dana Professor of English at Norwich University and lives in Vermont with his wife, playwright Jeanne Beckwith.

Mame Bougouma Diene is a French-Senegalese American humanitarian currently based in Senegal, an African migration and drug policy expert (with a preference for refugee and emergency work, criminal/social justice reform and women's rights), a speculative fiction (science fiction, horror and fantasy) author, a regular columnist at *Strange Horizons* magazine, the francophone spokesperson for the African Speculative Fiction Society, and the francophone editor at *Omenana Magazine*. He and his wife, attorney, educator and activist Woppa Diallo, won the Caine Prize for their short story, "A Soul of Small Places," published in *Africa Risen*, and were jointly awarded Distinguished Scholars at the International Conference on the

Fantastic in the Arts, themed "Whimsy," in March 2024.

Oghenechovwe Donald Ekpeki is a Nigerian writer, editor and publisher. He has won the Nebula, Otherwise, Locus, British, and World Fantasy awards, and has been a finalist for the Hugo, Sturgeon, British Science Fiction, and NAACP Image Awards. His works have appeared in *Asimov's, Fantasy & Science Fiction, Uncanny Magazine, Tordotcom*, and other publications. He was a CanCon and ICFA 44 Guest of Honour for the theme "Afrofuturism," where he coined the term *Afropantheology. Between Dystopias: The Road to Afropantheology*, co-authored by Joshua Uchenna Omenga, earned a Publishers Weekly starred review: https://www.publishersweekly.com/9781647100841

He is the Virtual International Conference for the Fantastic in the Arts Coordinator, and a member of the IAFA Executive Board: https://ekpeki.wordpress.com/2023/11/09/my-2023-award-eligibility-list/
Intro to Afropantheology:
https://www.publicbooks.org/introduction-to-afropantheology/
OD Ekpeki Presents/The Pantheology project:
https://odekpeki.com/od-ekpeki-presents-the-pantheologist/

Virgília Leonilde Tembo Ferrão was born on October 3, 1986. Her first novel is titled *O Romeu é Xingondo e Julieta Machangane*, published by the University Press of UEM, in Maputo, followed by the novel *O Inspector de Xindzimila*, published in 2016 by Brazilian publishing house Selo Jovem. Her third novel, *Sina de Aruanda*, was published in 2021 by Fundação Fernando Leite Couto. She currently works for TotalEnergies in Mozambique, as a legal consultant. She was awarded the Literary Prize 10 of November, 2019, by the Maputo City Council, being the first woman to win this prize. She is

272

editor of the anthology *Quantum Spirits: a journey through stories from Africa in Speculative Fiction* Vol. I and Vol. II, published by Diário de Uma Qawwi, in April 2022 and June 2024, respectively, and author of the novel *Os Nossos Feitiços*, published in June 2022, by the Brazilian publisher Katuka Edições, for which she was awarded the Bunkyo Literature Award Literature 2023, in second place.

A.E. Fonsworth is a Poetry Fellow and Recovery Instructor at Sam Houston State University in Huntsville, Texas. The San Francisco native and Texas Southern University Alum is a literary analyst and multi-modal performance artist with work published in *The Maroon Journal, The SFRA Review, The Taj Mahal Review*, and in the international anthology *Yemoja's Tears*. Her most recent research into counter narrative linguistic praxis has been presented at SAMLA via Georgia State University and at the Form & Transformation Conference at CUNY University in New York City.

James H. Ford, Jr. is the multi-awarded author of poetry, tall tales, scholarly research, and biographies of African American men, including the psychological and literary study of *Rational Blindness* published by Edwin Mellen Press, *The Peddler's Son* about the historically awarded African American university debate coach Dr. Thomas Freeman, who inspired Denzel Washington's portrayal of his character in *The Great Debaters*, and "Stay out of the Street," published in *Forty Years of Texas Storytelling* by Parkhurst Brothers Publishers.

Eileen Gunn's stories are known for their wry intelligence and sharp imagination. She is a short-story writer, essayist, and editor, and author of three story collections: *Stable Strategies and Others* (Tachyon Publications, 2004), *Questionable*

Practices (Small Beer Press, 2014), and *Night Shift* (PM Press, 2022). Her fiction has received the Nebula Award in the US and the Sense of Gender Award in Japan, has been nominated for the Hugo, Philip K. Dick, and World Fantasy awards, and was short-listed for the James Tiptree, Jr. award. Gunn was the editor/publisher of the *Infinite Matrix*, an influential online SF magazine, from 2001–2008. She serves on the board of directors of the Locus Foundation and served for 22 years on the board of directors of the Clarion West Writers Workshop.

Regina M. Hansen is the author of *The Coming Storm* (Atheneum/Simon and Schuster), nominated for the Mythopoeic and Red Maple Awards. Her nonfiction work on fantasy, horror, and mythological subjects has appeared in *The Boston Globe, Enchanted Living, The Wall Street Journal Review, The Conversation*, the children's magazines *Calliope* and *Dig Into History*, and various journals. Her most recent scholarly collection, *Giving the Devil His Due: Satan and Cinema* with Jeffrey Weinstock, was nominated for a Bram Stoker Award. She teaches at Boston University and lives in Cambridge, Massachusetts.

Joshua Keghnen Ichor is a visionary Geoscientist, hydrogeologist, water expert, and climate innovator hailing from Nigeria. Born with a fervent passion for environmental sustainability and social impact, he has dedicated his life to addressing the pressing challenges of water scarcity and climate change in sub-Saharan Africa. His journey into the science of water development and climate resilience began at a young age, fueled by a deep-rooted desire to make a meaningful difference in his community and beyond. Growing up in a village in Northern Nigeria, Joshua suffered from water scarcity, and his own experience with a life-threatening illness led him to vow to become a geoscientist and develop technologies to address this issue. Over the years, he has specialized in innovative groundwater exploration and management, utilizing cutting-edge technologies to address water resource challenges and promote sustainability in Africa. He has developed a smart IoT-enabled system called GeoTek Monitor to monitor water wells and report their downtime for quick repairs as well as water quality. He is a 776 Fellow, Young Climate Prize winner and winner of the Swarovski Creatives prize. His mission is to enhance water management and accessibility, ensuring that even the most underserved communities have reliable access to clean water.

The technological solutions he has developed include:

1. **GeoTek -Water Monitoring system**: It is a water utility monitoring system that provides real-time data on water usage and maintenance needs, enabling proactive management and reducing downtime.
2. **Water Kiosk**: Designed to deliver safe, filtered drinking water to communities, his Water Kiosk utilizes advanced filtration technologies to ensure the highest standards of water quality.

His work and technology were captured in a BBC documentary in partnership with the Swarovski foundation as part of the climate and Us series, available through this link: https://www.youtube.com/watch?v=RmqrTZ-xEsQ&t=239s.

Alex Jennings is a writer/editor/teacher/poet living in New Orleans. He was born in Wiesbaden (Germany) and raised in Gaborone (Botswana), Tunis (Tunisia), Paramaribo (Surinam) and the United States. He constantly devours pop culture and writes mostly jokes on Twitter (@magicknegro). He loves music, film, comix, and even some TV. He's going a little nuts shut up in his Central City apartment, but thankfully he has two of the best roommates on earth, one of whom is a beautiful dog named Karate Valentino. His debut novel, *The Ballad of Perilous Graves*, was published by Redhook in 2022. Find him goofing around on Instagram: (@magicknegro).

Wuraola Kayode writes on issues related to the SDGs, Music, Movies and everything in between.

Annette Meserve is the writer/artist/poet author of *Life at the Far End: Poems considering the unusual,* poetry that captures one random aspect each day, examining one little thing closely in a spontaneous poem; these poems together describe a broader experience in a mosaic describing choices that were made differently from most, in a life lived on the fringes of society.

Mingle Moore, Jr. teaches English and coaches competitive gaming for college students. He has published a chapter on African literature titled "Living Black Skin, Wearing White Masks: Frantz Fanon and Wole Soyinka on Dependency and Inadequacy in Colonised African Communities" in *The Cultural and Historical Heritage of Colonialism*, poetry, and articles of literary analysis in *Inspiring Pedagogical Connections* and *The Griot: The Journal of African American Studies*. He is an active member in Lambda Iota Tau Literary Honor Society and Alpha Kappa Delta Sociological Honor Society, won the 2015 Lone Star College at University Park's Adjunct Faculty Excellence Award and 2017's San Jacinto College-South's "You Make a Difference" Award. He is completing a dissertation in Literature and Criticism, tentatively titled *Exploratory Analysis of Francophone Texts in the African Diaspora through a Mythological Lens.*

A native of Roslyn, Pennsylvania, a Philadelphia suburb, **James Morrow** spent his adolescence in the local cemetery. While such a preoccupation might bespeak a morbid state of mind, in Jim's case the explanation lay in his passion for 8mm moviemaking. Before heading off to college, he and his friends employed their favorite graveyard in a series of genre films, including adaptations of "The Rime of the Ancient Mariner" and "The Tell-Tale Heart." Upon receiving an MAT from Harvard, Morrow channeled his storytelling urge into satiric speculative fiction. The BBC praised his third such offering, *This Is the Way the World Ends*, as the best SF novel of 1986. Next came *Only Begotten Daughter*, winner of the World Fantasy Award. Throughout the 1990's Morrow devoted his literary energies to killing the Supreme Being. The inaugural volume of the Godhead Trilogy, *Towing Jehovah*, received a World Fantasy Award. He followed it with *Blameless in Abaddon*, a New York Times Notable Book, and *The Eternal Footman*. Having grown sick of his Creator, and vice-versa, the author then attempted to dramatize the coming of the 18th-century Enlightenment. *The Last Witchfinder* was called "literary magic" by Washington Post critic Ron Charles. A follow-up phantasmagoria, *The Philosopher's Apprentice*, struck NPR's Maureen Corrigan as "an ingenious riff on Frankenstein." The French translation of Morrow's most recent novel, *Galápagos Regained*, a faux-Victorian epic about the birth of Darwin's natural-selection theory, won the Grand Prix de l'Imaginaire. In the short-fiction realm, Morrow's efforts include the Nebula Award-winning "Bible Stories for Adults, No. 17: The Deluge" and such novellas as *City of Truth*, a Nebula winner, *Shambling Towards Hiroshima*, which received the Sturgeon Memorial Award, and, most recently, *Behold the Ape*. A full-time writer, Jim lives in central Pennsylvania with his wife, Kathy, and three professional dogs.

MultiMind resides in her hometown, Baltimore City, Maryland. She writes books that are fairly Black, usually queer, and very much embedded in the world of Sci-Fi, Fantasy and Horror. Her short fiction "Null(Void)" has previously appeared in the award-winning Nightlight Podcast. Her works include *Dreamer*, *In Search of Amika*, *Kinetics*, and *The Glassman*.

Isaac Nesla is a photographer and student based in Jos, Nigeria.

Vuyokazi Ngemntu [She/Them] is a writer-performer situated in Cape Town, South Africa, whose praxis uses poetry, song, physical theatre, storytelling and ritual to navigate epigenetic trauma and centre Indigenous Knowledge Systems in the creation of new Black imaginaries. Her short story, "Binnegoed," was selected as the overall winner of *Ibua Journal*'s 2022 "Bold: Food" regional. More recently, "Blood and Ballots" made *The Year's Best African Speculative Fiction* Vol. 3. A 2024 Mamandla Fellow, she is an alumnus of the Voodoonauts 2024 Fellowship as well as the 2023 SFWA Mentorship Program. Her work has appeared in *World Literature Today*, *African Voices*, *Kalahari Review*, *Herri*, *Short.Sharp.Stories*, *Ake Review*, *Ibua Journal*, and in other venues.

Uchechukwu Nwaka is an Igbo medical student at University of Ibadan, Nigeria. His works have appeared in *PodCastle*, *Escape Pod*, *Fusion Fragment*, and *Omenana*, among others. When he's not writing, he can be found reading manga, streaming TV shows, playing amateur volleyball, or trying to catch up with his endless schoolwork.

Dr. Gillian Polack is an award-winning Australian speculative fiction writer. Her novels include the time-travelling *Langue[dot]doc 1305*, drawing on her background as a Medieval historian, the first ever Australian Jewish fantasy novel (*The Wizardry of Jewish Women*), the Ditmar-winning *The Year of the Fruit Cake* (where aliens and perimenopausal women are not so far apart) and *The Green Children Help Out* (with French superheroes). She was the 2020 recipient of the A. Bertram Chandler (lifetime achievement in science fiction) award and has been an Ambassador for Australia Reads. When not writing fiction, she is an ethnohistorian with a special interest in how story transmits culture, both Medieval and modern. Her most recent non-fiction book is *Story Matrices: Cultural Encoding and Cultural Baggage in Science Fiction and Fantasy*. She can be found at her own website (https://gillianpolack.com/), The History Girls (https://the-history-girls.blogspot.com/) and in the Treehouse (https://treehousewriters.com/wp53/) as well as on social media.

Cyrielle Prückner aka Jenekacy is a French/Malian painter and illustrator born in 1988 in Tremblay-en-France, France. Her passion for art was passed on to her very early by her parents, former sailors eager for culture who traveled to the four corners of the world.

After a few stints in different graphic design schools in Tours and Paris, and having put artistic creation aside for a few years, she gradually took up brushes again. She paints mainly with acrylics, on paper and sometimes on canvas. From the Bambara divinity Faro to the Yoruba orisha Oshun, via historical figures such as Marie Laveau, it's close to her heart to highlight the richness of African mysticism and the currents of thought that arise from it throughout the world, often overlooked or sometimes forgotten. Painting is something therapeutic for her; working with textures and paying particular attention to color and details allows her to escape from reality for a few moments. Her ancestors and her roots are her source of inspiration and creating is for her a way of thanking them and being grateful for what they have given to her.

Alfonso Arteaga Rodríguez: Compositor, poeta, y escritor contemporáneo nacido en Rioverde, San Luis Potosí, México el 31 de octubre de 1959. Desde muy joven fue dando muestras de su amor por las letras. Destacándose por sus prosas y por sus rima constantes perfectas. Es un escritor que da vida a los escritos en todos los géneros. Ha escrito un sin número de poesías. Escribe sobre la naturaleza, al hombre, y al amor. Sus obras literarias han sido escuchadas desde las aulas de una escuela rural, hasta el Aula Magna del Centro Nacional de las Artes de la ciudad de México. Recibió el doctorado Honoris Causa precisamente por sus escritos, en los cuales manifiesta siempre su pesar por lo paulatino en que el ser humano está terminando ambiciosamente con los ecosistemas de nuestro planeta.

Alfonso Arteaga Rodríguez: Composer, poet, and contemporary writer born in Rioverde, San Luis Potosí, Mexico on October 31 in 1959. From a very young age, he demonstrated his love of literature, distinguishing himself by his prose and always perfect rhyme. He is writer who gives life to his writings in all genres. He has written innumerable poems. He writes about nature, (hu)mankind, and love. His literary works have been heard in lecture halls and rural schools, all the way to the Aula Magna del Centro Nacional de las Artes in Mexico City. He received an Honorary Doctorate specifically for his writings in which he manifests the gravity of the gradual destruction by human ambition of our planet's ecosystems.

Candice Thornton's M.A. thesis, which examines archetypal and mythatypical patterns in the novels of Toni Morrison and Alice Walker, won the Most Outstanding Thesis Award from the Graduate School of Texas Southern University, an historically African American university established when Thurgood Marshall won *Sweatt vs. Painter,* a landmark lawsuit protesting the inherent inequality of resources and educational opportunities allocated racially segregated U.S. colleges and universities. They are currently enrolled in the Humanities doctoral program while teaching College Composition as an adjunct professor at Clark Atlanta University. Their research continues to center the literary traditions of women and gender expansive people of the African Diaspora. They have presented their scholarship nationally and internationally and been inducted into the International English Honor Society, Sigma Tau Delta. They have presented their research at the CoFutures Science Fiction Research Association Conference, the National Association of African American Studies, the International Conference on the Fantastic in the Arts, and in a peer-reviewed journal for the Science Fiction Research Association Review. Their article "Born-to-Die: Abiku/Ogbanje in *Beloved* and *Kindred,*" is featured in a Black Horror special edition of *Studies in The Fantastic* by University of Tampa Press, as well a chapter in an anthology for Oxford University Press titled "For the Culture: Pathways in Linguistics for Black and HBCU Scholars," and a forthcoming chapter for *Reading Between the Lines: A Genealogy of Racial Discourse in American Literature* by Edwin Mellen Press titled "Myth and Memory in *Twelve Years a Slave, Kindred, Beloved,* and *The Good Lord Bird.*" Ultimately, they intend to continue writing and serving as a cultural preservationist.

Dr. Albert Uriah Turner, Jr. is a poet and essayist who is influenced by the sounds of community—be they the rhythms and existential arguments of jazz, R& B, and reggae or the people and stories to which he was exposed growing up in the Mattapan of the 1970s. His poetry is also influenced by 19th century Romantic poets such as Wordsworth and Whitman, writers of the "beat generation," post-World War II American "confessional" poets, and Black Arts Movement writers such as the late Amiri Baraka. His work is featured in venues such as the *Journal of Pedagogy, Pluralism, and Practice's* special edition, titled *Spectacle, Identity, and Otherness: Nine Poets Speak*, among other publications.

Mary A. Turzillo, an International Conference on the Fantastic in the Arts Guest of Honor for the theme "Whimsy" (March 2024) won a Nebula award ("Mars Is No Place for Children" 1999) and two Elgin awards (*Sweet Poison*, with Marge Simon, 2014, and *Lovers & Killers*, 2012, solo). She has been a British SF Association, Pushcart, Stoker, Dwarf Stars, and Rhysling finalist. Her novel *Mars Girls* (Apex) features two young Martian women rescuing themselves from Face-on-Mars crazies. *Victims*, again with Marge Simon, was a Stoker finalist. Her purrfectly delicious story collection *Cosmic Cats & Fantastic Furballs* appeared March 2022 from WordFire. It contains her Nebula-nominated story "Pride." A high rated woman épée fencer in the U.S. in her age class, she lives with scientist-author-fencer Geoffrey Landis.

Solomon Uhiara is a Speculative fiction writer, conceptual photographer, and Fire Fighter from Nigeria who resides in Port Harcourt. He studied Bio-Resources Engineering. His works are published in several issues of *Dark Matter Magazine, Omenana, The World's Revolution, African Writer, Starline, Polutexni*, and other venues. His story, "The Extermination Device of the Blacksmith," was performed by Ato Essandoh in 2021, and he is a Nommo Awards Finalist. He likes machines and music.

Lakunle Whesu is a Lagos-based speculative fiction writer, playwright and lawyer whose work interrogates the realities of the human condition. When he isn't writing stories inspired by his environment he curates art. His art exhibition *The Mis-predilections of Aboya*, based on his play of the same name, was hailed by Channels TV as "one of the most inspiring art projects of the year." When not drafting stories about water-siphoning aliens or curating theatre-inspired artworks, he battles Lekki's infamous undrinkable tap water, a daily reminder of the urgent need for clean water access for all.

♦